I0563837

THE ROM COM MOVIE CLUB - BOOK THREE

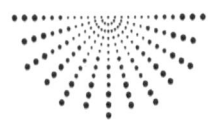

BERNADETTE MARIE

5 PRINCE PUBLISHING

Copyright © 2022 by Bernadette Marie, ROM COM MOVIE CLUB No.3

All rights reserved.

This is a fictional work. The names, characters, incidents, and locations are solely the concepts and products of the author's imagination, or are used to create a fictitious story and should not be construed as real. No part of this book may be reproduced in any form or by any electronic or mechanical means, including information storage and retrieval systems, without written permission from the author, except for the use of brief quotations in a book review.

Published by 5 PRINCE PUBLISHING & BOOKS, LLC

PO Box 865, Arvada, CO 80001

www.5PrinceBooks.com

ISBN digital: 978-1-63112-305-4

ISBN print: 978-1-63112-306-1

Cover Credit: Bernadette Soehner / Marianne Nowicki

To Stan,
You may always borrow envelopes and stamps.
I will always take you shopping to impress.
I will always wonder why you turned away from the classroom to
walk with me in the other direction.
I will always think of you in a snowstorm.

"I came here tonight because when you realize you want to spend
the rest of your life with somebody, you want the rest of your life to
start as soon as possible." -When Harry Met Sally

ACKNOWLEDGMENTS

T, N, G, S, J – To me, you're the whole package! I love you, all. *"I want the fairy tale." Pretty Woman*

Mama and Sissy – And so he did. I love you both. *"What do you want? You want the moon? Just say the world and I'll throw a lasso around it and pull it down. Hey that's a pretty good idea. I'll give you the moon." It's a Wonderful Life*

Cate – What a team! I couldn't ask for a better person to work with. *"It was a million tiny little things, that, when you added them all up, they meant we were supposed to be together, and I knew it." Sleepless in Seattle*

Sophie, Cayla, Grace, Marianne Nowicki, and Whitney Dykhouse – Thank you for your time and expertise in all matters. *"People do fall in love. People do belong to each other, because that's the only chance that anyone's got for true happiness." Breakfast at Tiffany's*

My Loyal Readers – Thank you, always! *"I've come here with no expectations, only to profess, now that I am at liberty to do so, that my heart is, and always will be, yours." Sense and Sensibility*

OTHER TITLES BY

THE ROM COM MOVIE CLUB

The Rom Com Movie Club - Book One

The Rom Com Movie Club - Book Two

The Rom Com Movie Club - Book Three

FUNERALS AND WEDDINGS SERIES

Something Lost

Something Discovered

Something Found

Something Forbidden

Something New

THE DEVEREAUX FAMILY SERIES

Kennedy Devereaux

Chase Devereaux

Max Devereaux

Paige Devereaux

STAND ALONE TITLES

The Happily Ever After Bookstore

THE MATCHMAKER SERIES

Matchmakers

Encore

Finding Hope

THE THREE MRS. MONROES TRILOGY

Amelia

Penelope

Vivian

THE ASPEN CREEK SERIES

THE ROM COM MOVIE CLUB - BOOK THREE

CHAPTER ONE

CHERRY RED NAIL POLISH, CHERRY WINE, AND PINK CHAMPAGNE facial masks. Rom Com Movie Club was in full swing. Ruby couldn't have been more disappointed that they didn't have cherry facials to go with her theme, but when did anything ever work out for her in that way? Not that it was a deal breaker for having a great time, but just for once, Ruby would like to have that perfect moment.

Sitting with her friends in her living room, *Mamma Mia!* paused on the TV, the four women, laughed at the expense of Tina's tales of pregnancy, childbirth, and motherhood as she nursed her daughter.

"I have a list for all of you," Tina said. "Things no one mentioned to me—at all."

Mindy, newly engaged to her next-door neighbor, stared at Tina with wide eyes. "Never, in my entire life, have I heard someone say you might poop when you give birth."

"That's what I'm telling you," Tina confirmed through gritted teeth in a hushed tone, as to not stir her daughter who suckled at her breast. "There are these little things that people keep secret. They want you to think this is glorious, and it is not."

Lisa wiggled her cherry red polished toes. "You're making me think that if Ryan and I want to have babies, maybe I should adopt."

Ruby nodded in agreement. "Thank God I'm single."

Tina blew out an annoyed breath. "First of all," she directed the comment toward Lisa, "you'd better be thinking about a baby, and soon. I'm not carrying this alone. Their mother wants a house full of grandkids and that's up to you and me now."

Lisa wrinkled her nose, her mask cracking. "I reconsider my marriage to your brother-in-law," she said and that warranted a laugh.

"You'll be a good mom," Ruby said, playing with the ruby slipper charm on her wine glass.

"You think so?" Lisa asked.

"You'll take your childhood as the example of what not to do. You'll be attentive and loving. I mean, you're already ahead of the game. You're married to an amazing man who understands love and commitment. You'll be okay."

Lisa batted her eyes, as if tears had begun to sting them. "Thank you," she said, and Ruby knew it would be true.

Lisa had been brought up in foster care. The first family to really take her in and love her hadn't happened until she was twelve, and they moved to England when she was sixteen, having to leave her behind before they could officially adopt her. But the impact they had on Lisa in those few short years changed her life. Ruby knew that Lisa would take those lessons to heart, and create a wonderful life for her own children.

Just as Lisa started in on some story about the foster family that had loved her so dearly, the front door opened, and her foster brother, who was also Ruby's roommate, Jason, walked through.

Dressed in scrubs, his hospital ID clipped to his pocket, he stopped and looked around the room. His face was unshaven, eyes dark with lack of sleep, but he smiled when he saw them all.

He'd moved in with Ruby shortly after he'd returned to America to work in a local hospital. So far, he'd only been there a few months, and already he'd lasted longer than some of her other roommates had.

She still wasn't sure what made all the others just up and leave, but Jason seemed to be stable enough to stick around.

Since he was a doctor, and worked crazy shifts, Ruby didn't see much of Jason at all, and she thought it was a shame he wasn't around more. With all of her friends being otherwise in committed relationships, these days she spent more nights alone than she'd have liked. Her mother would argue that it meant she should spend more time with her, but Ruby needed her space, too. When Jason was around, though, they cooked dinner together, took walks around the lake not far from their place, and watched her beloved rom coms together.

To his credit, coming home to four women with pink masks on their face, and Tina with her boob out, he didn't look all that surprised.

"Movie night," he said matter-of-factly. "I forgot that was tonight."

Ruby stood, walking on her heels to keep her toes from touching. "I thought you were working a twenty-four."

Jason scanned a look over her, smiled, then nodded. "I got lucky. Someone wanted the second half of the shift, and I'll cover for them next week. By the way, nice T-shirt." He tugged on the sleeve of the Oxford University T-shirt which was his.

"It was in the laundry," Ruby said quickly in defense of her T-shirt choice.

Jason winked, then moved toward the couch and kissed Lisa on the top of the head. "I won't bother you all," he said before lifting his head and sniffing deeply. "Is that a Lisa pizza in the oven?"

Lisa stood, also walking on heels, she moved to Jason. "I made two pizzas just so you'd have left-overs. Would you like some, fresh from the oven?"

Ruby watched as he licked his lips and nodded, as if the offer had made his mouth water and rendered him unable to talk.

Of course she understood the reaction. Lisa was a food blogger and an amazing cook. They were all lucky when she wanted to cook for them—even pizza.

Lisa linked her arm with her brother's. "C'mon. Mama Rose would want me to take care of you."

Ruby watched until they disappeared into the kitchen before she plopped back down on the couch next to Mindy.

"I'm going to go change her," Tina said, lifting her daughter onto her shoulder and righting herself back into her T-shirt.

They both watched Tina walk toward Ruby's bedroom, and when she was out of sight, Mindy pulled back and slapped Ruby on the arm.

"What the hell was that for?" Ruby gritted her teeth.

"What's going on with you?" Mindy whispered loudly.

"I have no idea what the hell you're talking about."

Mindy sat there staring at her from behind the cracked pink champagne mask. Her eyes were wide, and the smile on her lips cracked the sides of the mask even further.

"You and Jason. What's going on between you?" she asked again in a whisper.

Ruby stared at her, and then turned her eyes toward the

kitchen where she could hear the muffled sounds of Lisa and Jason talking.

"Nothing is going on between us. Why did you hit me?"

"What's going on?" she asked again.

"Nothing."

Pieces of Mindy's mask were falling off into her lap. "There will be," she said. "Did you see how he looked at you?"

"Like his roommate in a facial mask?"

"Like his roommate in his T-shirt. That's a sexy thing, you know. Wearing the roommate's T-shirt."

Ruby shook her head. "It's only sexy if you're wearing it in lieu of clothing."

"So when we leave…"

"I'll put the T-shirt in the hamper and wash it. Then it'll go back with his laundry."

Mindy shook her head. "I'm not one to say don't get involved with the guy *next door*," she laughed since that was exactly what Mindy had done, and now she and Vic were engaged. "I have to take this mask off."

Mindy stood and started toward the bathroom, before she turned and looked at Ruby. "You could do worse." She winked, and disappeared as she closed the bathroom door behind her.

Ruby sat back, and let out a breath.

She ran a hand over the T-shirt and thought of Jason in it. He'd worn it when he'd moved in, and again just the other day when he'd worked out.

It hadn't appeared that he was upset that she had it on, but admittedly, Ruby, in her pathetic state of singlehood, found it comforting to wear his T-shirts—should one end up left in the dryer.

Lisa and Jason walked back through the living room. He carried a plate in his hand and a bottle of water.

"Thanks for letting me crash your party," he said.

"You live here. It's not crashing," Ruby said. "Unless you stay for the movie."

Jason looked at the screen. "*Mamma Mia!?*"

Ruby nodded. "I figure it's the story of my life."

A line formed between Jason's brows as if he didn't understand her comment. "It's a good one. Maybe one of these days when we're both off, we can watch it. For now, I'm taking my coveted pizza to my room. I'm going to take a shower, and go to bed for a day."

He kissed Lisa on the cheek. "Love you, sis."

"I love you, too."

As he passed by the back of the couch, Jason leaned down and kissed the top of Ruby's head, much the same as he had to Lisa when he'd walked in.

"Night, roomie in my T-shirt," he whispered in her ear.

Everything inside of Ruby went liquid at his breath against her skin.

Why had that seemed like such an intimate gesture? It was the norm where they were concerned, but that was the first time it swelled into heat in her belly.

She really needed to think about dating again. If she didn't, she was going to cost herself another roommate.

CHAPTER TWO

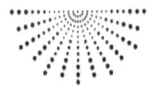

His body was exhausted. Jason hadn't realized just how exhausted until he'd awoken sitting up in bed, his TV still on, and his plate of pizza crust still on his lap.

It was just past midnight, and he wondered if the party in the living room was over.

Aiming his remote toward the TV, he turned it off, and listened. He couldn't hear any voices, and those girls were anything but quiet. Chances were good that he could freely move about the condo.

He turned off his bedroom light, pulled open the bedroom door slightly, and looked down the hallway. The living room was dark.

There was an extra Gatorade in the refrigerator, and he could use some hydration after his shift.

In only his boxers, he moved through the dark toward the kitchen. As he cleared the entry, the refrigerator opened, and the light fully exposed Ruby standing there in only his T-shirt.

The thought that he should just turn around crossed his

mind, but not before Ruby turned around and screamed when she saw him standing there.

"Shit!" She pressed her hand to her chest, holding a spoonful of something in her other hand. "Why are you lurking in the dark?"

Jason grinned. "Why are you?"

"I'm not lurking. I'm," she looked at the spoon, "snacking."

"In the dark?"

"Well, yeah. I'm headed to bed."

"In my shirt," he teased, but noticed that his voice was full of gravel, because when she'd jumped, and pressed her hand to her chest, the shirt had risen just enough to expose bright pink panties.

Ruby let out a groan. "Do you want me to take the shirt off?"

Heat moved through him with her just mentioning taking off the shirt. What would she do if he said yes?

"No," he said with just a hint of regret.

Reaching out, he took hold of her wrist, and studied the spoon in the refrigerator light.

"Are you eating frosting right out of the container?" he asked.

"Don't judge me," Ruby bit back.

"Who said I was judging you? I've lived here for months and have never seen you make cupcakes, so I've wondered why we always have frosting."

"Can't help it. I love frosting," she admitted as Jason kept hold of her hand.

Lifting his other hand, he took his finger and ran it through the frosting on the spoon, and then licked it off. "I can see where that could be addictive," he said and watched as Ruby's lips parted.

He wasn't sure why he was licking frosting off of her

spoon and still standing in the coolness of the refrigerator, except that it was forcing his body to behave. He should have just grabbed his Gatorade and gone back to bed. But seeing Ruby earlier tonight in his shirt, with that pink mask on, had stirred him up. And now, standing in the kitchen with her in only the T-shirt and pink panties, his boxers weren't going to contain him much longer.

This wasn't a new sensation. It wasn't just this T-shirt and the moment. Hell, she'd always stirred him up. She was fresh and honest, curvy and soft, funny and crass. There was a lot to like about his roommate and he'd lost more than a few nights' sleep over it.

But there were lines not to be crossed, he knew.

Dragging his finger through the icing again, he dabbed it on the end of Ruby's nose before licking the rest of it off his finger.

"Enjoy your snack, and sweet dreams," he said, reaching past her for his Gatorade, and then turning to hightail it out of the kitchen before he lost his composure and did something he'd regret.

RUBY STOOD IN THE KITCHEN AND WATCHED JASON walk away. When she heard his bedroom door close, she pressed her head to the metal of the refrigerator, and let the air from the open door cool her, because her body temperature had risen at least a hundred degrees.

He was Lisa's brother—off limits. But oh, she'd like to test those limits.

Swiping her fingers over the tip of her nose, she wiped away the frosting Jason had placed there.

He'd been awful playful lately. Had he said he wanted her to take off the shirt, she would have done it. Squeezing her thighs together, she tried to ward off the heat that pooled there, too.

She would have been completely broken if she'd taken off the shirt and he'd headed back to the bedroom without her. But what if that's not what he did?

Reaching back into the refrigerator, Ruby pulled out the container of frosting, opened the lid, and replenished the scoop on her spoon.

She might as well go to bed with a sugar high.

Closing the door to the refrigerator, she giggled to herself. She'd have to make a plan to make cupcakes now.

When Ruby reached her bedroom, she turned on the lamp on her night stand, and picked up her phone and texted Mindy.

Do you have time for coffee later today? She had to talk to someone about what had just happened, and the feelings that had been stirring inside of her since Jason had moved in. She certainly couldn't talk to Lisa about it.

Mindy texted back, *Why are you still up? And yes, I can meet for coffee. Is everything okay?*

Ruby put the spoon in her mouth and held it there with the frosting against her tongue.

Everything is fine, she typed. *Ten o'clock?*

Those annoying bubbles popped up, then disappeared. A moment later, Mindy sent a thumbs up emoji, and plans were confirmed.

She plugged her charger into her phone, and laid back with the spoon still in her mouth. With itchy fingers, she opened her Instagram account and searched for Jason Hughes.

Scrolling through his pictures, Mindy licked the frosting off of the spoon. Oxford rowing team, top in his class, military, and a doctor to boot. Not to mention that he was the epitome of tall, dark, and handsome.

Tanned skin, dark dreamy eyes, and luscious, dark, wavy hair. She could get lost in tangling her fingers in that hair for sure.

This wasn't healthy, she thought, scrolling through family photos, vacation photos, and of course photos with leggy girls in short dresses.

Well, that wasn't her. Ruby was anything but fashion magazine perfect.

She enjoyed having him live with her. After all, once he'd moved back to Colorado, he'd become a brother to them all.

They'd cooked, cleaned, watched her favorite rom coms and a couple British comedy shows he enjoyed.

She still didn't understand why roommates came and went as frequently as they had for her, but in this case it seemed to be working out just fine with Jason.

When there was a knock on her bedroom door, Ruby nearly choked on the spoon.

"What?" she shouted, mostly because her heart was thudding in her chest.

Jason opened the door and stepped in. He was still in his boxers, and this time, Ruby took a moment to appreciate him in the lamp light.

"Sorry," she said. "I didn't mean to holler. You just scared me."

She watched him stand there for a moment, then he closed the door behind him, which had the hammering in her chest kicking up a notch.

Running his fingers over the stubble on his chin, he sent a look over her that started a sizzle beneath her skin.

"What's wrong?" she asked, kicking her feet off the side of the bed, realizing that the shirt moved and exposed her in her panties.

Jason licked his lips and took another step toward the bed.

"I was just thinking," he paused and she watched his throat work. "I would like my shirt back."

CHAPTER THREE

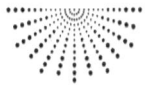

RUBY STARED UP AT JASON, EYES WIDE, JAW SLACK. WELL, HE thought, it had surprised him too.

She finally blinked.

Jason didn't move, but he was committed. Not making a move in the kitchen was the hardest thing he'd ever done, but he couldn't go to bed, knowing what had surged through them tonight.

Surely, Ruby could do the sensible thing and say something like, *"You're kidding, right?"* or roll her eyes and say, *"Go to bed,"* and leave it at that. But she wasn't saying anything at all.

Jason kept his eyes laser-focused on hers. If he dropped his gaze and looked at her thighs again, or those pink panties, the fabric of the boxers absolutely wouldn't hold.

Ruby set the empty spoon on the nightstand, and then her phone as well. She swallowed hard and drew in a breath.

This was where she'd make him come to his senses. This was where she'd laugh it off and tell him she was his sister's best friend and wasn't interested in him like that. This was where she mended his misguided thoughts.

Instead, Ruby stood and took the three steps to meet him by the door. The red cherry color of her toenails was a stark contrast to the soft pink of her skin in the dim light.

He licked his lips as those green eyes looked up at him—burned right into him.

Toe to toe, his boxers stretched now, and for one brief moment, Ruby lowered her eyes, then raised them back to his face, where they scanned over his lips before rising to lock with his again.

Grabbing hold of the hem of the shirt, Ruby lifted it up. Her bare, ample breasts fully exposed to him. Her long red hair fell over her shoulders once the T-shirt had been lifted up and over her head.

Pulling her bottom lip through her teeth, she held the T-shirt behind her back. "You want this back?" she asked as her cheeks grew red with heat. "Come and get it."

Jason had started this, but now was paralyzed in her presence. He took one more scan over the mostly naked woman in front of him, appreciating every soft curve of her, before he leapt.

RUBY HUFFED OUT ALL THE BREATH IN HER LUNGS WHEN JASON gripped her hips and pulled her to him. Flesh to flesh. His erection pressed into her belly, and her taut nipples brushed against the soft hair on his chest.

She dropped the shirt to the floor.

One of his hands went directly to the small of her back, pulling her closer. The other up into her hair, where his fingers wound into strands, taking hold.

Ruby wrapped her arms around the firm body of her best friend's younger brother, and accepted his mouth when it took hers.

Heat, that was all she could taste. It burned between them

when tongues met, as hands wandered, and that heat turned her insides into molten lava.

Jason's fingers slid under the waistband of her panties, and his hand cupped her ass, causing her to moan into his open mouth.

They stumbled back until the backs of her knees hit the bed, but he held her upright.

"You're more beautiful than I could have imagined," Jason said before diving back into the kiss.

His hands skimmed her sides upward, then his fingers brushed softly over her breasts. The pads of his thumbs traveled over her sensitive nipples, as his mouth trailed over her jaw, and down her throat.

Ruby gripped his shoulders, her knees weak under his touch.

What were they doing?

Fuck that, she countered in her own head. She'd spent years wanting these kinds of details from her friends, and now here she was, about to have unexpected sex with her roommate, her best friend's brother—shit!

As the thoughts stirred in her, Jason eased her back on the bed. He brushed kisses over her soft belly.

"Jesus, Ruby, you're incredible," he said.

No man had ever done that to her. How could they have? This was the first time she'd ever been with a man where the lights were even on. She was too conscious of the fact that she wasn't fit and firm. No man wanted that—well, except apparently this one.

Jason lowered himself, and her knees parted to make room for him. His erection pressed against that heat between her legs, through the fabric, and threatened to undo her right there.

His mouth was on hers again, and her fingers moved up and down the defined muscles in his back.

"I've dreamed about this since I met you," he whispered in her ear.

"You have?" She was breathless beneath him.

Jason eased up on his elbows and looked down at her, the slightest grin on his swollen lips. "You're so beautiful, and kind, and funny, and honest, and—"

"You really think all of that?"

"I really do," he said before kissing her in the crevice of her neck, right above her collarbone and making her arch up into him. "Do you want this, Ruby? Do you want me?"

The answer screamed through her head—YES! But a warning rang through her too.

Fuck it! As a thirty-year-old woman she deserved to have sex with a man who seemed to find her irresistible. A good man. A man raised with decent morals, though questionable at the moment as he ground atop his sister's best friend. Fuck that too. Lisa would be happy for them.

Just as Ruby inhaled to answer her consent, ready to find pleasure in this man whom she was completely attracted to, had forged a friendship with, whose erection pulsed against her sensitive spots, the loud ringing echoed down the hallway.

"Fuck!" Jason growled out the word as his head lowered to her chest.

"What is that?"

"It's my work phone." He rose to his knees. "I have to go answer it."

Jason rolled off the bed and hurried out of the room, leaving Ruby exposed and alone.

She pressed her hand to her belly, and draped the other over her heated forehead.

When he returned only a few moments later, he already had pants on. "I have to go," he said and Ruby sat up, not bothering to cover herself.

"Why?"

"The E.R. is flooded with people. Huge crash on I-70 and they're bringing people in. There was also some concert at Red Rocks and someone passed around something tainted."

Ruby's stomach twisted. This was normal. It was his normal, she decided.

She'd watched him run out of the condo numerous times, just like this. This was what he was faced with each time?

Jason picked up the T-shirt Ruby had dropped on the ground and pulled it on. He moved to her, easing her to her feet.

"I'm going to wear this and think of you all night," he said as he pressed his forehead to hers. "I'm so sorry about this."

"It's okay. It's probably—"

"It's not for the best," he finished her thought. "I want this, Ruby. I want you," his voice trailed off as he pressed a hard kiss to her lips. "Get another one of my shirts from my room. Wear it. I want to know when I get home you're here in one of my shirts."

Again, her knees went weak.

"Okay."

Jason kissed her one more time before stepping back.

His phone rang again, and he groaned. "I'll be back. We'll finish this."

Ruby watched as he hurried out of the room, and only a few moments later, she heard the front door open and close.

She sat back down on her bed and drew in a breath.

Well, shit, she thought. How in the hell was this going to work out now? She might as well put an ad on the internet for a new roommate, because after this, she was going to misread the situation, fall in love with Jason Hughes, and ruin what had been a great roommate experience.

CHAPTER FOUR

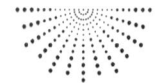

RUBY'S LEG BOUNCED. IT MIGHT HAVE BEEN THE SECOND CUP of coffee she'd had while waiting for Mindy. Or it might be left over anxiety from what had happened earlier that morning.

"You're already here," Mindy said walking up to the table. But Ruby jumped, sloshing her coffee out of the drinking hole of her cup lid. "Whoa, what's up?"

Ruby sopped up the mess with her napkin. "Sorry."

"How many of those have you had?" Mindy asked looking at the extra mess Ruby was making.

"Two."

Mindy pressed her hand on top of Ruby's to stop her. She picked up the wet napkins, threw them in the trash can behind her, and grabbed another handful of napkins from the dispenser.

Ruby watched as Mindy cleaned up the mess and then sat down.

"Don't you want to get something?" Ruby asked.

Mindy took Ruby's coffee and pulled it to her. She looked

at the label and then sipped. "I'll drink this. You've had enough."

Nodding, Ruby reached for one of the dry napkins and began to twist it.

"I don't know what happened to you after we left last night, but you're a mess," Mindy said sipping the coffee. "Did you even brush your hair? And where did you get that T-shirt?"

Looking down at the T-shirt, Ruby realized she didn't even know what was on it. Manchester Football was printed on the shirt, and in the center, there was a soccer ball. Perhaps that was a dead giveaway as to where she'd gotten the shirt. Did the man own any T-shirts from America? Then again why would he? He'd lived in England most of his life.

"It's Jason's," Ruby said.

Mindy nodded, the coffee cupped between her hands. "I guessed that."

"Then why did you ask?"

"Because you wore his T-shirt yesterday too, and you said nothing was going on."

"There wasn't anything going on."

"You said you got the shirt from the dryer."

"I did."

"Where'd you get this one?"

"Out of his drawer."

"Why?"

"Because he told me to."

"Why?"

"Because he took the other one back."

"When?"

"This morning."

"Where was it?"

"On the floor."

"Why?"

"Because I took it off," Ruby said, growing light-headed with the rapid questions.

Mindy's smile widened behind the rim of the cup. "Why did you take it off, Ruby?"

"He asked me to."

"When did he ask you to do that?"

"When he came into my room."

The apples of Mindy's cheeks were bright red because the smile she wore was so wide. "You had sex with your roommate!" She nearly shouted it, but Ruby noticed that she'd muted it enough no one seemed to have heard her.

"I didn't."

"Well, you certainly didn't get any sleep. You look like shit."

Ruby scrubbed her hands over her face. "We almost had sex."

Mindy leaned in closer. "Almost, huh? Fill me in."

Ruby deserved this. Not only was she always begging for details when it came to her friends and their love lives, but she'd been the one to text Mindy to talk. Of course that was before she had anything to talk about.

"Listen, I'm just confused by all of this and I need you to help me decide what to do."

Mindy blinked hard. "I think you'd better get home and actually have sex. I don't know what *almost had sex* really is."

Ruby gripped her fingers into her wild hair, which she should have pulled back.

"This is Lisa's brother. Jason is Lisa's brother."

"Yeah, I know who he is," Mindy giggled. "You're a mess."

"God, Mind, he's amazing," Ruby admitted pulling the coffee back and taking a sip. "I've never been kissed like that."

Mindy did a little jiggle dance in her seat. "I want to hear it all."

Wrinkling up her nose, Ruby pushed the coffee back

toward Mindy. "This is what I sound like, isn't it? I mean, I do this to all of you."

"You do. You always want sexy details, and now I want them."

"We've been roommates for months, and nothing like this happened before."

"You had to get to know each other. I saw how he looked at you last night. Rube, he's interested. I mean very interested."

Pressing her lips together, Ruby thought about what Mindy was saying. "Okay, I know that now. He's interested. God, what do I do?"

Mindy reached for her hands. "Honey, enjoy this."

"Lisa's going to kill me."

"No she's not. She loves you."

"Tina was going to kill her when Lisa started dating her brother-in-law."

"Tina was in bridezilla mode. Besides, you're already living with the man. You're already friends. He's sexy as hell —yes, I said it. And you are one very sexy woman."

Ruby snorted a laugh. "It sounds stupid when you say it."

"You're the one that always says she knows when a man appreciates the curves. Jason is that man."

And hadn't he said she was incredible as he feathered kisses over her stomach?

"So why are you wearing the shirt?" Mindy asked before sipping the coffee.

"He asked me to. He said he wanted to know I was home in another one of his shirts."

Nodding, Mindy pushed the coffee back to her.

"That's hella sexy, Rube."

"Mindy!"

"A new romance is exciting, isn't it?"

"What if he only wants sex?"

Mindy shrugged. "Well, then have sex with him. Live a little. It's what you've always wanted to do. You know, to be a little reckless. And hell, if you're just going to have some torrid affair with a man, have it with a sexy doctor that comes from a good home."

That caused them both to laugh.

"And what if he decides it was the wrong thing to have started?" Ruby sipped the coffee.

"Then you have one hell of a story to tell at parties," she said smiling. "But he's not going to change his mind. He's interested in you. I saw how he looked at you. I don't think it's for just the sex."

Ruby finished the coffee and felt it surge through her with the other coffees she'd already had, and the fully energized set of nerves. Her hands shook and her stomach threatened to betray her.

All she could think about was getting home and waiting for Jason in his T-shirt.

CHAPTER FIVE

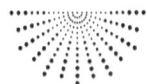

IT WAS NEARLY NOON WHEN RUBY WALKED THROUGH THE DOOR of her condo. It was dark. The blinds had been closed, which she knew Jason often did if he were sleeping during the day.

Setting her purse on the table, Ruby listened for him. It was silent. Walking down the hallway, she noticed his bedroom door was closed, which meant he was certainly home. She hadn't closed it after taking his T-shirt out of his drawer.

She pressed her hand to his door, as if it somehow made him seem closer to her. She wouldn't wake him. He'd need his sleep, that was for sure. And it was just one more sign that whatever had happened last night wasn't meant to be.

Ruby walked to her bedroom and closed the door. She'd shower, then spend the rest of the day on the couch watching her beloved rom coms. She, too, was exhausted.

When Jason woke, they could talk about what happened.

HER AFTERNOON OF ROM COMS STARTED WITH *WHAT'S YOUR Number?*. Mindy stretched out on the couch and watched

Anna Faris try and find all of the men she'd slept with. The premise was enjoyably stupid, but really, it was a winner because Chris Evans was the sexy next-door neighbor who gets the girl in the end.

But the stupid movie always had her thinking. She only needed a few fingers to count the number of lovers she'd had, and to her credit, they'd all been relationships. But what about the Oxford grad whose Instagram was filled with sexy women clinging to him?

When that movie was over, she scrolled through her list of movies she'd saved. *Friends with Benefits* seemed appropriate. Who wouldn't want to wallow in the what-ifs and watch Justin Timberlake sneeze every time he had an orgasm?

But the movie hit home harder than she'd expected it to. Was that what she was starting with Jason? A 'friends with benefits' relationship?

Was she just in close proximity, and that would make her an easy and handy conquest?

She squeezed her eyes closed. No, he wasn't that kind of man—was he? If he was, was she woman enough to go through with a relationship like that?

The thought intrigued her. Did she have it in her?

Ruby was the friend who always wanted the details. She wanted to hear about the sex. She wanted to absorb the feelings second hand.

There wasn't a time one of her friends had met a sexy man that she hadn't encouraged them to take a chance, even if it meant a one-night stand. But could she be just sex to someone she adored as a friend?

Draping her arm over her eyes, she lay there listening to the movie, having committed it to memory, and thinking about what she wanted from a man.

All of her friends were in committed relationships now.

Tina and Aaron were married with a baby. Lisa and Ryan were married and living in Mindy's grandmother's house. And Mindy and Vic were engaged and living next door to Lisa and Ryan in Vic's grandmother's house.

And then there was her.

She expelled a long breath. In her life she'd never had a man around growing up. Relationships weren't something she was privy to until she'd fallen into one. *Mamma Mia!* was like her theme movie, the girl who didn't even know her father's name. Love was always out of reach.

She was destined to just be the funny, fat friend.

She winced. That wasn't the case anymore, and she knew it. Her friends cherished her as much as she cherished them. They were the first solid relationship she'd ever been in, and her relationship status with a man didn't define her.

Ruby jumped when a hand touched her knee, and she realized she'd nearly kneed Jason in the groin.

"Shhh," he said, running his hand up her thigh, and lowering himself down on top of her. "You were sleeping."

"I was not."

He chuckled. "But you were."

Mindy turned her head toward the TV to see that the menu to the movie was playing annoying music, and the movie was, in fact, over.

"Oh, I guess I was."

Jason's hand slid under the hem of the T-shirt and rested against her stomach. "I see you borrowed another shirt."

"You told me to."

He smiled down at her. "I did. And all I could think about today was coming home to see you in it. I was surprised you weren't here."

"I had a coffee date with Mindy."

"How is she?"

"Fine," Ruby said, feeling him move against her leg. "You saw her yesterday."

"Right. I didn't notice." His hand wandered to her breast, and her eyes closed again.

"Jason—"

"Yeah?"

Ruby opened her eyes. "What are we doing?"

"Talking."

She reached for his wrist. "I mean, this?"

He didn't move his hand away, and she didn't want him to, but he stilled it.

His eyes were dark and smoldering as he licked his lips and watched her. "You're not interested in this?"

She actually winced. "I didn't say that."

"So are you interested in this?"

God, what was she supposed to say? Of course she was interested. Could he not feel the heat of her against his knee as he ground it against her? But could she do this knowing there was nothing on the other side? Or was there something more than easy sex?

"Yes," she said on an airy breath.

"Good, because I can't stop thinking about it." He lifted her shirt and lowered his mouth to her breast, teasing her nipple with his tongue through the lace of her bra.

"Wait," she said, and he eased back. "Why do you want this?"

His gaze narrowed. "Who wouldn't want this?"

"I mean, why do you want this with me?"

His lips tightened. "What's wrong with you?"

"C'mon, look at me."

"I've been looking since I met you. I like you. It's been a long few months, and last night everything just played out —sort of."

She let out a tiny laugh. "You like me for me?"

"I do."

"This isn't just sex because I live in the next room?"

Jason eased back a bit more, his hand moving from under her shirt to balance himself against the couch.

"I wouldn't do that—unless that's what you want."

Okay, now what should she say? Blow this off as casual sex so that she wouldn't get hurt, or tell him she wanted the whole package?

"I—"

This time it wasn't his phone that rang, it was his computer. There was a FaceTime call coming in.

He winced. "That's my mother," he laughed and eased back off the couch. "Don't think we're done with this conversation. I'm not done with you."

He walked to his bedroom and she heard the door close.

Scrubbing her hands over her face, she needed to quickly decide how she wanted to handle this. There had to be a reason things kept getting interrupted.

To hell with it. Wasn't she a modern woman? Hadn't she had relationships that didn't last, and a short affair that was just for fun, which she'd thought was going to be a long romance, but she'd enjoyed it equally as much? No matter where this thing with Jason ended up, they could still be friends. Lisa was forever going to be in both their lives, so they would never be rid of one another. If a relationship wasn't going to work with the sexy doctor, then she might as well enjoy what he had to offer at home.

Yes, she could do this.

CHAPTER SIX

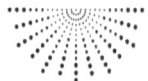

"Ruby, come here," Jason shouted from his bedroom.

Then a bit of clarity hit him. He'd left Ruby on the couch, in his T-shirt, and turned on. If he was yelling at her to come to his bedroom, he wasn't sure which state he was going to get her in. He stood and hurried to the door, just as she pushed it open.

She stood before him with only the T-shirt on, and this time a pair of purple panties. She had knotted the shirt under her breasts, and his fingers itched to touch her, but he quickly pushed her out further into the hall.

"Sorry," he started. "My mom has the baby, my brother's baby. I thought you'd like to see him. I didn't think."

Her eyes went wide in the dark hallway. "Did she see me?"

"I don't think so."

"Shit! What if I'd waltzed in there naked?"

"That's why I ran out here." He scanned a quick look over her. "God, you're beautiful."

Ruby unknotted the top. "Stop it. She can probably hear you."

"Go put on another shirt, that's not mine, and some pants, then come back in here."

She kept a cool eye on him and backed herself to her room.

Jason let out a long and steady breath. It had to have been the longest day of his life. He'd never been so pent up over a woman, and fate seemed to be keeping them apart.

Collected, he walked back to his computer and sat down in front of it.

"Everything okay?" his mother asked.

"Yeah. She just wanted to look presentable," he said, not lying, but sure he had some facial tic that told his mother everything. "She was on the couch watching rom coms."

That made his mother laugh. "Do she and the girls still get together each month and watch a movie?"

He nodded. "She hosted last night, in fact. They watched *Mamma Mia!*"

"That's a good one."

Jason felt her before he saw her. Ruby moved into his room and right in next to him. She'd changed into a sundress and pulled her hair back into a ponytail. Now she appeared more sun-kissed than passion-filled.

"Hello, Mama Rose," Ruby said, calling his mother by the name Lisa called her.

"Ruby, it's so nice to see you. I'm babysitting," she boasted. "This is Ken's newest. Isn't he a doll?"

His mother held the baby up, just slightly. Ruby leaned in next to Jason, her hand steadied on the back of his chair, and he fisted his hands in his lap so he wouldn't touch her.

"He's precious," Ruby cooed.

"He is." Jason's mother kissed her grandson on the forehead and settled him back in her arms. "Tina had a little girl?"

"She did. We figure she'll be watching rom coms and painting her nails in no time."

"Perhaps if I get out there this year, I could get in on one of those nights."

Ruby nodded. "We'll plan one for whenever you're here. I'm sure Lisa would enjoy that immensely."

"I'm counting on her to be the next one to give me a grandbaby. Then I'll have reason to visit more often."

Jason let out a hurt groan. "I'm not reason enough?"

"Oh, honey, you are. But a baby..." his mother said, unapologetically. "You're much too busy to give me a grand-baby, or to entertain me."

He shook his head. "We can discuss that when I'm there in a few weeks."

He felt Ruby ease from him.

"Lisa said she was sending Daddy some cookies. Don't forget to bring them with you."

"Sure, you'll visit for babies, and I'll tote cookies across the ocean for you, but I'm too busy for you to visit me," he teased.

His mother grinned back at him. "I'm so proud of you," she said, and it shone in her eyes. "I think you made the right choice going back to Colorado, even if I miss you like crazy."

Ruby eased further away, and he shifted a glance up at her to see that perhaps she felt as if she were now intruding. Reaching for her, out of the view of the camera, he managed to hook a hand around her thigh.

"I'll send you my itinerary," he said and his mother smiled.

"I'll watch for it. It would be amazing if you could convince Lisa to come with you."

He chuckled. "I'll mention it."

"I know she's busy and all, but—"

"It wouldn't hurt to ask. Maybe I can convince her to do a British cooking segment for her YouTube channel," he said.

"I'd love to see her," she told him. "Ruby, darling," his mother said, and Ruby moved back into view of the camera. "It was very nice to talk to you. I hope Jason is behaving."

He couldn't help but give the back of her thigh a squeeze and he saw her lips flatten, fighting off any other noise that might have wanted to escape.

"He's been a perfect roommate. He even does dishes, and that's a first for me," she admitted.

"Then I taught him well," his mother boasted. "I'll talk to you both later. I love you, my son."

"I love you, too, Mom."

A moment later the screen went dark and the light signaling that the camera was on had disappeared.

Ruby eased back a step. "Well, that wasn't uncomfortable at all," she said.

"It shouldn't have been. My mother loves you."

"Yes. She loves me because I'm her *daughter's* best friend," she said using air quotes around the word daughter.

"You don't have to do that."

"Do what?"

"Use air quotes. Lisa is my sister, as far as we've always been concerned. The only reason we left her here was because they couldn't get the adoption to go through before we had to leave. My mother thinks of her as her daughter and nothing less."

Hurt flashed in Ruby's eyes. "I didn't mean anything by it."

He nodded. "I know. I just think everyone needs to know where we, as a family, stand on that. And you of all people should be grateful that it didn't work out."

"Me?" She pressed her hand to her chest. "Why would I be grateful for that?"

"Because then she was here to meet you."

Ruby's shoulders dropped. "You're right." Her gaze moved over his desk, and she picked up a squishy stress ball in the shape of a soccer ball. "So you're going home soon?"

"Just for a visit."

"I hadn't heard you mention it."

"Yeah, hadn't thought it too important to mention yet," he admitted.

"How long will you be gone?"

"Three weeks."

Ruby tightened the grip on the ball. "That'll be nice for you."

"It will be. I miss my family," he admitted.

Ruby set the ball back on the desk, and Jason took the opportunity to grab hold of her waist and move her in front of him, then urged her to straddle him.

Her arms draped over his shoulders and her forehead pressed to his.

"You could go with me," he said.

Ruby shook her head. "I can't. I don't have vacation time like that."

"You could come for a week."

She shook her head again. "I have a huge project that's only in the early stages. I can't—"

"I know." He let out a breath. "Someday."

"Sure."

Jason slid his hands up her back, keeping her close. "I just thought it would be nice to have you there since Mom is going to figure out what's happening."

Ruby eased back, her lips tight, and brows drawn in. "I beg your pardon?"

"What's confusing?"

"What's happening? Nothing has happened—yet. And we're roommates."

Jason studied her. He wasn't sure she understood how he felt about her. How could she? He'd potentially made an ass out of himself when he asked for his shirt back. But, the electricity that stirred between them told him they both were feeling out the attraction. Their friendship was the catalyst to that attraction. The fact that there was only four feet between their bedroom doors, well that made it interesting.

He trailed a finger down her arm. "Do you think I only made a move on you to have sex with you?"

"Yes," she answered much too quickly, he thought.

"That's not my intent. Though, I find you irresistible, and I'm not sure how I've made it this long without touching you."

She worried her bottom lip. "Really?"

Jason chuckled. "Is that so hard to believe?"

"Yes." Again, the answer came too quickly.

"Maybe I'm going about this all wrong." He brushed his hand over her hair. "Can I take you to dinner?"

"You want to take me out to dinner?"

"I do. I should have started with something like asking you out on a date. Then kissing you."

Ruby licked her lips. "You want to date me?"

"I do. Consider me swiping right. Or is it left?"

"You're asking the wrong person," she said. "I'd love to go to dinner with you."

"Then, it's a date."

CHAPTER SEVEN

RUBY RETREATED TO HER ROOM TO GET READY. SHE SORTED through her closet no less than four times trying to find something to wear. It wasn't as if he hadn't seen her at her worst, she wasn't one to doll up around the house. But she wanted to look nice for him.

She pulled a different sundress from the closet and sat back down on the bed with it.

What were they doing? Oh, she'd been attracted to the man from the moment she'd met him. But really—Lisa's brother?

This had disaster written all over it. Honestly, it had been one thing when he'd walked into her room and told her he wanted his shirt back.

Sex. They could just have been having sex. Only now he'd admitted that he was interested and that took it to a whole new level.

When was the last time someone was interested in her?

Okay, she wasn't some reject, but men didn't usually make moves on her like that.

A smile twitched at the corner of her mouth. Dr. Hughes was interested in her, and not just for sex.

They were going on a date, she humored herself. They were dating—well, okay, not officially or anything.

Ruby wrinkled up her nose. She wouldn't have considered them a couple just because he'd walked into her room and she'd taken off her shirt—his shirt.

Had he built this up in his head for that long? Was she going to disappoint him as a girlfriend—as a lover?

She shook her head and stood, walking to the bathroom and plugging in her curling iron.

Overthinking the situation was classic Ruby, and she needed to stop. Jason Hughes was interested in her and found her irresistible. It was about time someone did.

Screw the negative thinking. Tonight, she was going to dinner with the man she was dating—not just her roommate.

She laughed to herself. They'd gone out to dinner many times. Why on earth did this seem so odd?

Because, she reminded herself, at the end of the night, there was no doubt, they were going to end up in one bed.

Jason was standing in the kitchen, his hip propped up against the counter, looking at his phone when Ruby walked through the door. He lifted his eyes, scanned an appreciative look over her, and smiled.

"You changed," he said.

"I did."

"You are stunning," he said and she could feel the heat in her cheeks.

"You've seen me in this dress a dozen times."

"And each time I've thought you were stunning."

She couldn't ward off the smile, even if she'd tried. "Where are we going for dinner?"

Jason lifted a brow and turned his phone toward her. "According to my sister, we're going to dinner with her and Ryan."

"Why?" The question came out dripping with annoyance, which she hadn't meant. There were no other two people she'd rather have dinner with.

Jason puckered his lips. "I forgot I had plans to go out with them tonight."

"Oh," Ruby swallowed down the disappointment. "We can go to dinner another night."

"We can go tonight," he said moving to her and pulling her in close to him, his arms circling her. "We'll just go with them. They won't mind if I bring a plus one."

Ruby licked her lips, letting her arms wrap around him. "You're going to tell her about us?"

Jason, bit down on his bottom lip. "Should we?"

Ruby shrugged. "What's to tell, right?"

He searched her eyes. "She's going to know the minute we get there."

"We haven't done anything for her to know."

"We've done enough," he said. "I mean, I *did* ask you for my shirt back, and you *did* take it off."

Ruby let out a hum. "We need to decide how to play it."

"I'd like to know what you think first," he said.

"What do you mean?"

Jason looped his finger into one of her curls, and then ran it down the side of her throat. "I came at you out of nowhere. I know that. I should have thought it through more."

"That would have taken all the spontaneity out of it."

"I surprised us both, didn't I?"

"You did."

"Maybe we should know exactly what we're doing before we let her in on it."

Ruby nodded. "Agreed." Though she agreed with him, Lisa was going to see right through them. "Maybe you should tell them I'm joining you."

"We'll let that be the surprise."

Ruby agreed, and moved to turn out of his embrace, but he held her there.

"You're beautiful," he said.

"And you're full of compliments."

"I mean them."

She took a moment to appreciate that. "Thank you."

"I want to finish what we started today," he said, lifting his hand to cup her cheek.

"Luck hasn't been much on our side today."

"Luck changes," he said, brushing his thumb over her lips.

"I guess we'll see how this pans out."

THEY DROVE JASON'S CAR TO DINNER. NOT MUCH WAS SAID between them, only the sound of the radio filled the silence. But when he'd reached for her hand and interlaced their fingers, Ruby felt something surge through her that had never been there before.

There was a warmth and a comfort that came from this connection to him. His thumb brushed over her knuckles and her knees went weak with the energy that it created.

She was in deep with him. It was going to hurt like hell when she found out he was like every other man and sex wrote the rules. But even in *Friends with Benefits*, they had a happily ever after. Ruby wanted her happily ever after.

Turning toward the window, she squeezed her eyes closed. What if they did share a bed tonight and there was no magic in it? What if the build-up only led to disappointment? It could happen.

Or worse, what if it was great, and they couldn't keep themselves from one another, and then he went home and realized he didn't want to return to Colorado?

"You're a million miles away," he said giving her hand a squeeze.

Ruby opened her eyes and turned toward him. "I'm nervous."

"About having dinner with my sister?"

"I'm nervous about what she'll think about it."

"I thought we weren't going to say anything."

Ruby let out a little laugh. "Ten bucks says she calls me out before we leave the restaurant."

"I say she won't say anything at all."

"I think I know her better," Ruby challenged.

"Ouch."

"I've been around her for the last decade. I don't mean anything by it, but…"

"I get it." He pulled into the parking lot and parked the car. He turned to her. "I'll take your bet. My goal tonight is to convince her to go back home with me for a week. I don't think she'll notice anything between us."

"I think you're wrong."

"Ten bucks to you if she says anything about something going on between us. Ten bucks to me, if we get home without anything said."

Ruby held out her hand. "Deal."

"Deal."

"Now we decide. It benefits me to go in there holding hands. It benefits you if we don't."

Jason's smile grew wide. "I'll give you your money, if you want to expose yourself right up front. I'm all in, Ruby. I want to be that someone special to you."

She swallowed down the lump that had formed in her throat. "I'm not ready for her opinion."

"Then we go in as friends—which we are," he added.

"Right. Friends."

He took her hand again and gave it a squeeze. "And, Ruby, if you change your mind on all of this, that's okay. But, we'll always be friends."

CHAPTER EIGHT

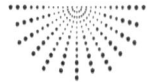

Lisa waved from the booth where she and Ryan sat. As Ruby and Jason neared, Lisa moved from the booth and hugged Ruby.

"What are you doing here?" she asked.

"I happened to be around and scored me an invite. I hope you don't mind."

Lisa's eyes went wide at the accusation that Ruby had put out there.

"Why would I mind?"

Ruby shrugged. "Maybe you had business with your brother."

Lisa let out a snort. "You're as much my sister as he is my brother. In my situation, I get to pick my family," she said, and Ruby felt an uncomfortable stirring in her belly when she thought of herself as Lisa's sister, and Jason as her brother.

Jason waited for Ruby to scoot into the booth before he sat down next to her. Just to keep it as platonic as possible, she set her purse between them on the seat.

"I've had the garlic shrimp here," Lisa said. "It's delicious.

I'm going to try to recreate it."

Ryan grinned over the top of his menu. "I've only gained six pounds since we've been married. I think I'm doing okay," he teased and Lisa nudged him with her elbow before he leaned into her and kissed her softly.

Ruby watched the exchange. She'd never been so happy to have seen someone fall in love as she had been when Lisa and Ryan had. No one deserved love more than Lisa.

Under the table, Jason's foot snaked around the back of Ruby's leg. In order to not gasp, or make any kind of sound at all, Ruby held her breath for a moment. She watched from the corner of her eye as he looked over the menu, his body still, except for the foot that was now brushing against hers.

She did what she could to concentrate on the menu, all the while delighting herself with Jason's secret touches as their ankles brushed.

"I talked to Mom today," Jason said as he set down his menu. "She wants me to ask if you'd go home with me."

Lisa lowered her menu and studied her brother. "She wants me to go home with you?"

He nodded. "I'll be there for three weeks. But you wouldn't have to go that long. You could go for a week, or stay for them all."

"Oh, I don't—"

Ryan wrapped his hand around Lisa's which rested on the top of the table. "Why don't you go?"

"Because, I—we..." she blew out a breath. "I've never been able to afford to go, or I would have gone."

"You can afford it now, sweetheart," Ryan said taking her hand and interlocking their fingers. "I can afford to send you, if you're worried about your own savings."

Her mouth opened and then pursed. "You think I should go?"

"Of course I think you should go," he said. "They're your

family. You've created a life for yourself so that you can drop anything and travel the world."

"That's not why I do what I do," she countered.

"It's a perk then," he lifted her fingers to his lips and brushed them with a kiss. "Mama Rose wants to see you. You haven't seen her since our wedding, and you have an empty passport in the lock box."

Lisa let out a laugh. "It's not empty. We all have a stamp from Mexico," she said, and moved her gaze to Ruby. "Remember when you all surprised me and bought me the trip?"

"Most drunken weekend I've ever had," Ruby chimed in, and she could feel Jason's stare on her.

Ryan laughed. "So go. I won't be lonely. I have my brother and Tina. My mother would be thrilled to feed me every night. The girls won't have a Rom Com Movie Club night without you. Right, Ruby?" he asked looking in her direction.

"Right," she added, wishing desperately that she could just pack up and head to England too. "She'd really like to see you."

Lisa let out another breath. "Okay. I guess I'm going home with you." She held up her hand. "I'm shaking. Why am I shaking?"

"You hate airplanes," Jason said.

"I do. And this one will be flying over water."

"I'll hold your hand the entire way if I have to. I can get you something to calm you, too," he offered.

Lisa shook her head. "I'll be fine. Wow, I'm going to see my family." She leaned into Ryan, who draped an arm over her shoulder.

"Just the first of many trips," Ryan promised.

Jason pulled his phone from his pocket and began to text. "I'll let her know you'll deliver the cookies to Dad personally."

Lisa reached across the table and covered his phone with her hand. "Don't tell her. Do you think we can make it a surprise? Or will she not have room for me if we don't tell her?"

Jason took his sister's hand and held it in his. "We can make it a surprise. But know one thing, she'd always have room for you no matter what. She loves you."

Lisa batted away tears, and Ruby thought about the conversation they'd had about Lisa being part of the family—about her being Rose and John's daughter. Ryan had flown them out for Lisa and Ryan's wedding and surprised Lisa. They'd given her away and stayed for the few days before Ryan and Lisa left for their honeymoon.

Lisa belonged to the Hughes family as much as she belonged to her family of friends.

Ruby eased back against the booth. For as long as she'd known Lisa, Ruby had hoped and prayed that Lisa would find a family and a man to love her. Ruby had never considered that Lisa had a family that longed to have her near, as the Hughes family did. Ruby knew they'd loved Lisa and regretted leaving. But their pain ran deep.

They all should have dragged Lisa's ass to England years ago, she thought, as Jason explained his travel plans to his sister. Why had it never occurred to them?

Maybe they were all afraid Lisa would want to stay and not return with them. And what would Ruby, Mindy, and Tina do without Lisa?

Then again, Ruby knew she'd take it in stride. Her father had never come for her—if he even knew about her. Roommates moved out in the middle of the night without a word. At least if Lisa had gone, she'd have kept in touch.

The server arrived and took orders, and the conversation continued to circle around their pending trip. As Jason talked about the new baby and his brother's family, he eased back and draped his arm over the back of the booth in a simple move. Ruby could feel the heat resonate off of him, but there was nothing that flashed in Lisa or Ryan's eyes to say that they knew she'd been naked in front of the man and kissing him madly as he ground on top of her only a few hours ago.

As Jason talked about booking Lisa's flight, Ruby wondered how she was going to make it through those three weeks he was gone. Everything was different now.

"Mom told Ruby that she'd like to partake in one of your rom com nights," Jason said, his hand falling to Ruby's shoulder before he retracted his arm and leaned in on the table.

"Wouldn't that be fun?" Lisa's eyes widened as she grinned.

Ruby nodded. "I told her we'd plan a special one just for her if she were able to visit and we didn't have one planned."

"So while we're there, maybe we can plan their trip out here," Jason said. "She says she'd come if you had a baby. I'm not that important, but..."

Lisa's cheeks went fiery red. "She said that?"

"Yep."

Ruby laughed. "It appears you're the next hope for both sides of your family," she said recalling Tina's conversation about adding more grandchildren to the mix.

Ryan wrapped his arm around his wife's shoulders. "I keep telling her that practice makes perfect. We're just going to have to keep at it," he teased and Lisa slapped his arm.

Jason's ankle brushed against Ruby's again. Her stomach tightened and heat sizzled over her skin. They had plans after dinner, she thought. She was going to have to drink in all of him before he left for weeks and she'd be without him.

CHAPTER NINE

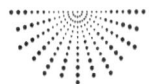

THE DRIVE HOME WAS QUIET, BUT JASON TOOK COMFORT IN the fact that the moment they'd climbed into his car, she'd taken his hand. With their fingers intertwined on the center console, he swore he could feel her pulse against his wrist. Then again, maybe that was his pulse that rapidly beat with the anticipation for what was to come.

"Are you sure you can't get away and come with us?" he asked as they slowed at a stop light.

"I'm sure. I wish I could."

He nodded. "I understand. Mom will flip when I show up with Lisa."

"I know she used to save and save to go out to see you all. But something would always come up. A broken-down car. A medical bill. She'd lose her job..."

"I didn't know that."

Ruby smiled. "She wanted to be with her family."

Jason let out a breath. "I wish we could have afforded to take her with us, once she'd emancipated." He brushed his thumb over Ruby's knuckles. "But she created a family of her own here." He smiled. "I will never forget the phone call the day after she met you girls."

Ruby turned her head toward him. Those green eyes sparkled in the dimly lit car. "What did she say?"

Jason turned down the street toward their place. "She was like some little girl who had just met her favorite celebrity. You could hear her squeal on the other end of the phone," he laughed. "On that day, the names Tina, Mindy, and Ruby became synonymous with her happiness."

Ruby's other hand pressed to her chest. "That means a lot," she choked out the words and he was quite sure tears might follow. "She was like a lost puppy. But, that night we met her at the coffee shop, we just knew she had to come back and hang out with us. Since then, I don't think there has ever been a day where I haven't talked to at least one of them."

"Your sisterhood is something enviable."

"I know. I talk to people at work and they don't even have friends. Or the ones they talk about, they never see. I know what I have is a gift. It wasn't until tonight that I realized it never occurred to us to help her get to England."

"What do you mean?"

"I mean, we took her to Mexico. We always planned big, elaborate things for her birthday, but not once did we think of sending her to you or going with her."

"It would have been expensive."

"And now that I know Mama Rose and John, they would have let all of us sleep on your living room floor."

Jason laughed. "They would have."

"I think deep down, we were afraid of her not coming home with us. At least, that's what I figured out tonight."

He gave her hand a squeeze. He understood that.

Jason pulled into the designated parking space and put

the car in park. When he turned off the engine, there was silence again.

He could hear her breathe. He was damn sure he could hear her heartbeat. Then again, that still might be his own.

He chuckled and she turned.

"What's funny?" she asked.

"I'm trying to relate this moment to one of your rom coms."

"What moment?"

"That awkward moment before we get out of the safety of the car and walk into the house. The moment before we commit to what we started or—"

"There won't be any or," she promised.

Jason nodded. "I just want to emphasize again, it's not about the sex. I really do like you. I can wait. I—"

His words were cut off when Ruby moved from her seat, crawled over the console, and straddled his lap. When her backside hit the horn, they both laughed, and Jason slid the seat back.

"I'm not made for sex in cars," she said. Both humor and irritation flashed in her eyes simultaneously.

"Cars are not made for sex. That's what makes it so exciting."

Her eyes were focused on his face, and her hands firmly on his shoulders. "If it were all about sex, I wouldn't have let you take me to dinner and introduce me to your family," she teased.

"Yeah, that big sister thing…"

"Exactly," she agreed before she lowered her mouth to his and took them into the kiss that would start it all.

The windows quickly began to fog up with the breath they expelled. He could feel the heat of her on his lap, and he knew his own body temperature had risen to the point he was sure that the blood that pumped through his veins was now boiling.

A moment later Ruby popped her head up and grinned down at him.

"Parenthood!" she shouted, then covered her mouth as if she'd realized just how loud she'd been.

Jason laughed, steadying his wandering hands on her hips. "What the hell is that about?"

"The movie. Sex in the car."

Jason shook his head. "I don't think I've ever seen it."

"Are you kidding me?" she asked, still perched on top of him, her head lowered to accommodate her height on his lap.

"Tell me about it," he said, pushing back the hair from her face.

"It wasn't really sex," she mused. "Steve Martin's character was stressed, and Mary Steenburgen's character thought she'd help. But, they were driving in the minivan when she ducked into his lap," she said with raised brows.

"Oh," seemed to be all he could muster with her still on his lap.

"Anyway, they crash."

"That's not sex in the car."

"I know," she laughed. And then her eyes lit again. "Oh, and she did the same thing to Craig T. Nelson in *Book Club*."

"Same thing?"

"Same thing," she emphasized the words.

"I've never seen that one either."

She grinned down at him. "I'm going to make a list of movies you have to watch with me."

"It's a date."

Her eyes grew wide again. "Wait! *Book Club* had car sex too."

Jason smiled up at her, amused by her excitement over the movies she spoke of.

"Tell me about it."

"Candice Bergen and Richard Dreyfuss."

He was sure his face contorted in confusion when she laughed. "How old is that movie?"

She gave it some thought. "Only a few years old."

"And Candice Bergen and Richard Dreyfuss' characters have sex in a car?"

"It's a mature movie. You know, age wise."

The smile tugged at his lips. "I get it. I just can't unsee it in my head."

"You don't see anything in the movie. Just them getting out of the car disheveled."

Quiet fell between them again and Jason opened the door. "Let's take this inside. Car sex doesn't sound as appealing as it might have once."

Ruby nodded, then climbed from him, and they both exited the car through the driver's side.

Jason reached into the car and retrieved her purse. She thanked him as he handed it to her, and they stood in the parking lot for another silent moment.

He took her hand, and they made the long walk to their front door.

Jason deeply inhaled as he took his key from his pocket and slid it into the lock. This was where it changed. This was where he crossed the line and ended his friendship with Ruby and started something else. This was where he crossed the line with his sister's best friend.

"Are you going to open the door?" Ruby asked.

He turned to look at her under the porch light.

He could walk away now and save their friendship.

Her tongue darted between parted lips and licked her bottom lip.

Screw friendship.

Jason scooped Ruby up in his arms and kicked open the

door.

CHAPTER TEN

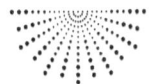

RUBY SQUEALED AS JASON CARRIED HER INTO THEIR HOME, HER arms wrapped tightly around his neck

She'd never been literally swept off her feet. She had to be much too heavy for him to carry her—but he was doing it.

Jason kicked the door closed and continued carrying her through the condo.

"You can put me down," Ruby argued.

"Why would I do that?" he asked as they moved through the living room.

"I'm heavy."

"You're perfect," he said, walking down the hall to her room. "Your room is nicer than mine. Your bed is bigger. Is it okay to go in there?"

"Yes," she said as he walked into her bedroom.

"It's dark," he laughed.

"Alexa, turn on bedroom lights," Ruby said and the lights turned on brightly. Ruby winced. "Alexa, set lights to soft."

The lighting in the room muted to a soft hue.

Jason grinned down at her. "Use that skill a lot when men carry you into your room?"

Her body stiffened. "No."

"I was kidding, Ruby," he said as he walked to her bed and lay her on it.

Ruby leaned back on her elbows and looked up at the man who had carried her through the condo without even breathing hard. Her heart hammered in her chest, and already it was hard to breathe.

"You're beautiful," he said, gazing down at her.

"You could be with any woman you want," she began her usual monologue against herself. "Why are you here with me? Convenience?"

She saw the flash in his eyes, the hint of anger when she said it, but it fizzled out as he moved in closer to her, his body between her thighs. Her skirt pushed up to her hips as Jason lowered himself, propping a hand on the bed on each side of her.

"If convenience were the case, I'd have made this move to get the room down the hall." He rubbed his nose against hers. "If convenience were the case, I would have made a move on you the first night." He nipped her lips with a quick kiss. "If convenience were the case, I wouldn't want to take you home to my mother."

Ruby inhaled sharply as he lowered his body to hers, taking her flat to the mattress.

"I'm scared," she said with her hands on his shoulders and his weight on her.

"I am too," he admitted. "We can just make out and keep our clothes on," he offered, pressing another kiss to her mouth.

"I don't think that's what I want."

The corner of his mouth turned up in a sexy grin. "Then you have to understand, if I didn't want to be here, and be here with you, I wouldn't be. I hope you can say the same thing."

"I want you here," Ruby said lifting her fingers to the buttons on his shirt and releasing them one by one. "And I want to be right here with you."

"Okay then," he said rolling to his back on the bed and taking her with him so that she straddled him.

The skirt of Ruby's dress skimmed up her thighs and Jason's hands pressed against her skin just under the fabric.

She continued to unbutton his shirt until it fell open, and his chest, that glorious chest was exposed.

Ruby took a moment to admire him beneath her. He was taut, but not muscular. Trim, but not skinny. And firm—though she couldn't see that part, she could just feel it beneath her and she was growing hotter by the moment.

His hands moved further up her skirt, sliding round to her butt and cupping her supple flesh.

Now wasn't the time to get self-conscious, she thought. She had no problem flashing her body on a normal basis, so now was a time to find comfort in herself—with a man who found her to be worthy of admiration.

Ruby reached for the skirt of her dress and pulled it up and over her head, leaving her exposed in just her bra and panties—which didn't even match.

The smile on Jason's face widened, but his eyes were on hers. That kicked the heart rate up even higher.

"You're so lovely, Ruby," he said lifting his finger to her lips, then letting it slide down her throat, over her collarbone, and down to the well between her breasts where the clasp to her bra was.

Easily, perhaps a bit too easily, he unfastened her bra with one hand. The garment opened and she spilled out from it.

He'd already seen her topless, and just like before, his eyes stayed on hers, and his face smiled in appreciation.

Jason's hands fanned out on her soft belly, and she found the urge to suck in. Then he raised his hands to her breasts.

"You're so beautiful," he said.

"You really—"

"Shh," he said before rolling her to her back beneath him now. "I really think so. Let me love you, Ruby. Let me show you just how much I appreciate every single part of you."

His mouth began to work against her skin and Ruby's eyes closed as she welcomed every new and fascinating sensation he brought to life.

No man's touch had ever resonated through her as Jason's did. Why was this man so different? Was it the secret they were now sharing between them? Was it how he talked to her? His skillful hands, she wondered as he eased her panties from her body?

Jason pleased her with his tongue, his fingers, the feel and weight of his body on hers. He took his time and cared for her as no man ever had.

Ruby's back pressed into the mattress and her hands twisted in the sheets. When she already thought she couldn't take any more soft and careful pleasure offered by him, he moved himself between her legs again.

"I have condoms in my room. I'll be—"

"In my drawer," she managed on a breath, which she fought for.

Again, that mouth of his turned up into a sexy smile. "Thank God," he said as he rolled from her and reached for the drawer.

Handing her the small package, he stepped out of his shorts while Ruby opened the foil, then handed him the condom. When he'd sheathed himself, he returned atop her. Her thighs easing open for him.

He brushed gentle kisses over her jaw and leaned in close to her ear.

"I'm so grateful to be the man loving you," he said.

Before she could even contemplate what it was he was really saying, he took her under again, and Ruby's mind went blank as pleasure shot straight through her.

CHAPTER ELEVEN

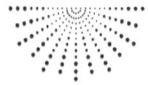

S<small>TEPPING OUT INTO THE HALLWAY AFTER HER SHOWER</small>, <small>SHE</small> could smell coffee brewing, and something in the toaster.

Deciding to investigate, she walked to the kitchen.

Jason stood at the stove in a pair of boxers cooking something in a pan.

"Do you eat eggs?" he asked without ever looking behind him.

"I do."

"Good. I thought after last night you could use a decent breakfast." He looked over his shoulder and smiled as he scanned a look over her. "You could have used your own shower."

"I didn't want to wake you."

"I'll catch a nap later. I'm on three twelves this week, all nights."

Her stomach clenched. "Oh."

"Yeah, we'll be playing that game at the front door again where you walk out as I walk in."

She nodded, thinking about how often they did just that.

Jason plated the eggs he'd been cooking and carried it to

the table. "I thought we could share a plate," he said grinning at her.

"That's fine."

He finished their breakfast by pulling the toast from the toaster and slathering it in butter.

Ruby took a seat, and Jason joined her at the table, sitting so their knees brushed.

"If the towel isn't comfortable, you could lose it," he offered, but Ruby only picked up her fork and stabbed at the eggs.

Her mind was somewhere else. Instead of being focused on the man in front of her, she was thinking about the next three nights where she'd be alone.

As a roommate, Jason's absence was normal. But as her lover, she wasn't sure what to think about it.

"You can eat them. You don't have to just push them around," Jason said, lifting his fork to his mouth.

"Sorry." Ruby took a fork full of eggs and ate them.

"You seem to have a lot on your mind," Jason said, setting his fork down and picking up a piece of toast. "Please don't tell me you're having second thoughts about what we did last night."

"No. Oh, gosh no." She set down her fork and pressed her hand to her chest. "I'm disappointed that I have to leave for work and that I won't see you for days."

"You could call in sick. I could write you a doctor's note," he teased with his sexy grin in place.

"No." Ruby picked up Jason's mug of coffee and sipped from it. "I'll miss you."

Jason moved his chair closer, hooking his finger into the knot of her towel. "You'll miss me?"

"Yes."

"I gave you a memorable experience?"

Ruby licked her lips. "You could say that."

"If you have time, I could—"

Ruby silenced him with her finger to his lips. "I have to go."

"I guess I'll just have to borrow this towel for my shower," he said, giving the fabric a tug. "It'll help me miss you less."

"Oh, yeah? You're making it hard for me to get out the door."

"If you're already going to be late," he began by tugging the towel off of her, "you might as well have a good reason."

RUBY'S BODY FELT HEAVY AS SHE SAT BEHIND HER DESK AND closed her eyes for just a moment. She hadn't gotten but a few hours sleep, and then she was late, but it was so worth it.

Jason had done things to her that no man ever had. And the things she had done before, well they were given new promise with Jason.

Her breath hitched when she thought of what he'd sighed when he was poised to enter her for the first time. *I'm so grateful to be the man loving you.*

God, he was even poetic.

"Ruby?"

She jumped in her chair, her eyes flying open at the calling of her name.

The young intern stood at her door, a grin being tamed as he looked at her. "The meeting starts in five."

"Right. Right. I'll be right there. I was just going over my notes."

The young man nodded slowly then made his way down the hall.

Shit! She wasn't as prepared as she'd wanted to be.

Three months she'd been working on this presentation,

and here she was, the day of, and she'd spent all night rolling around in bed with some man.

Oh, who was she fooling? Jason wasn't just some man.

Heat rose through her. He was a doctor. He was a god in bed. He was considerate and sweet. He was Lisa's brother.

Ruby squeezed her eyes shut one more time, before opening them and gathering her notes. Standing, her laptop and notebook held against her chest, she checked herself in the mirror by her door. Somehow she'd managed to make her hair look decent, and she'd done a fair job of covering up the dark circles under her eyes.

But wait! Oh, shit, shit, shit!

Ruby lifted her chin and moved her hair slightly. *Damn it!* There on her neck, just above that sensitive spot on her collarbone that made her knees go weak when Jason kissed it, was a fucking hickey!

* * *

JASON CLEANED THE KITCHEN, GRINNING TO HIMSELF THE entire time. He'd lived in the condo for months. He'd cooked many meals, and he'd even shared them with Ruby. But that morning's eggs and toast was the best meal he'd ever eaten.

It was stupid to be as worked up over her as he was. But he couldn't help himself. Ruby had been on his radar from the very first moment he'd ever laid eyes on her. And now, he let out a slow breath, he knew he'd fallen head over heels in love with the woman.

Oh, it was much too early to tell her that. In his head, he'd been in this relationship months longer than she had. But since he'd agreed to move in, his eyes had been set on Ruby.

He poured himself another cup of coffee and walked out to the living room. Setting the cup on the coffee table, he plopped down on the couch and kicked his feet up. He took the remote and aimed it toward the TV. When he turned it on, he realized Ruby had paused one of her beloved rom coms.

He pressed play.

Ashton Kutcher and Natalie Portman were rolling around in bed, and he found himself grinning at the scene. Not because it was supposed to be sexy, but because he was thinking of himself and Ruby doing the same thing.

He hit the information button. He wasn't sure he'd ever seen the movie he was now intrigued with. *No Strings Attached.* Well, surely a movie that Ruby would have been watching wouldn't just end with two friends having sex only, would it? Wasn't the purpose of all her movies to have a happily ever after?

Curious now, Jason fast forwarded, stopping long enough when he saw Natalie Portman in a white coat in a hospital.

There was a sharp pain in his chest when he saw that. She was a doctor? Okay, so why was Ruby watching a friends with benefits movie with a doctor? Was this what she wanted? She didn't want the whole package? Was this research?

When there was a knock on the door, Jason jumped. He managed to pause the movie and hurry to the door. Pulling it open, he noticed his sister's startled look.

"Good morning, sunshine," she said laughing, keeping her eyes averted above his head.

It was then he remembered he was only in boxers. "Come in. I'll be right back," he said hurrying down the hallway to change.

When Jason returned, Lisa was loading his refrigerator with food.

"What's the ten dollars under the magnet?" she asked.

Jason moved in to see the note that read, *you win,* on it covering most of a ten dollar bill.

He chewed the inside of his cheek to keep from letting the smile spread. "We had a bet. I won. She paid up."

Lisa nodded, and kept moving. "I made a take and bake pizza and a lasagna," she said, closing the refrigerator.

"Instructions are written on the top," they both said at the same time, and Lisa laughed.

"I guess you know my process," she said smiling at him. "Having yourself a relaxing day?" She raised her brows, taking in the disheveled look of him now in a pair of basketball shorts and a T-shirt—the one Ruby had worn for him.

"I have three twelves starting tonight. Just taking it easy."

"And you're watching rom coms."

Jason shrugged. "I turned on the TV and that was what Ruby had cued up."

Lisa nodded as she turned toward the coffee pot, took a mug from the cupboard, and filled it. Leaning against the counter, she lifted the mug to her lips. "Ruby's a romantic, that's for sure. Her favorites are friends with benefits movies, or those that have a lack of commitment."

Well he wasn't finding that comforting.

"She chose *Mamma Mia!* for movie night," he reminded her.

"The tropes are all happily ever after, but seriously, *Mamma Mia!* is full of quick affairs that went askew. It also mimics her life a little. It was always just her and her mother, and much like the movie she doesn't know who her father is."

"Seriously?"

"Seriously. She wants, and believes, in happily ever after for everyone else. She just doesn't believe in it for herself."

Jason considered that. "You don't think she wants a relationship?"

Lisa raised a brow. "No, I don't think that. I think she's

just drawn to those kinds of stories of friends with benefits or happily-for-now. Why would you ask that?"

Running his fingers through his hair, he did everything he could to keep his face neutral. "She's just a great gal. She deserves to have what you all have."

"She does. She just has to stop projecting her mother's romantic failures on herself and then stop hating herself."

"I don't think she hates herself," he said.

"She's hard on herself. She thinks she's undesirable."

Well Jason had a different opinion on that for sure.

Lisa sipped her coffee. "She's always been hard on herself about her body, the unruliness of her red hair, and her spontaneous cursing."

"There's nothing wrong with her body, her hair, or her language. It's refreshing," he said, thinking about her using a certain word over and over last night.

He hoped his body wasn't flushing with the heat that ran through it as he thought about it.

"She's perfect, and when the right guy comes around, she'll realize that," Lisa offered taking one last sip from her mug, then turning to dump the rest into the sink. "I wonder what she's got going on tonight. Maybe the girls and I should take her out. Maybe we could be her wingmen and hook her up with someone. If she's cued up friends with benefits movies, she must be needing some release," she said on a laugh.

"I think it was just coincidence," he countered, not wanting to even think of Ruby going out to hook up with someone.

"Ruby's the kind of girl who likes sexy details. I think it's time she had some sexy details to share with us. I'll call her. If we eat somewhere awesome, we'll bring home leftovers," she said moving to him and kissing him on the cheek. Then she sniffed deeply. "You should go buy new soap," she said.

"What does that mean?"

"It means you have Ruby's scent. She's rather particular about people using her body wash."

Jason felt the weight of what he and Ruby had done sink to the pit of his stomach. "Yeah. I'll have to do that."

His sister smiled at him and let herself out the front door.

Jason leaned up against the doorway to the kitchen. He didn't want a short-term thing with Ruby. They were friends, but he didn't just want the benefits. He wanted the whole package.

God he hoped his sister's plan didn't pan out. It was going to be a long three nights without Ruby wrapped in his arms.

CHAPTER TWELVE

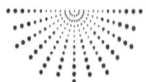

THANK GOD FOR HER TEAM, RUBY THOUGHT AS SHE FELL INTO her chair behind her desk. If they hadn't been as prepared as they were, the whole project might have gone off the rails. Luckily, her hair had stayed in place and no one seemed to notice the hickey—or at least they had the good grace not to say anything.

She covered her face with her hands and rested her elbows on her desk.

She should feel like a queen, so why was she so miserable? Okay, it wasn't misery, it was being tired, anxious, well loved, and guilt-ridden.

When her phone rang, she jumped, knocking her pencil cup over the side of the desk and onto the floor. Shuffling around on her desk, she found her phone.

"Hello?" she answered quickly.

"You doing okay?" Lisa asked on the other end.

"Fine. Fine."

"Uh-huh. Well, I just talked to my brother and he's working three twelves starting tonight, not that you care what your roommate is up to. But I told him the girls and I were going to take you out."

Ruby blinked hard, and then folded herself in half to pick the pencils up off the floor.

"Why am I going out?" she grunted, as the air in her lungs was cut off by her body being folded as it was.

"I think it's time we start looking for a man for you to hook up with."

Ruby sat back up in her chair, only to have the hydraulics give and plummet her down. "Fuck!"

"Is that good or bad?" Lisa asked, laughing into the phone.

"My chair just broke, or something." She blew out a breath. "Sorry, you're taking me out to hook me up with someone?"

Lisa laughed. "We all need to get out. The girls are on board. And if we find you someone, you can make all the noise you want tonight because my brother won't be around."

Ruby had to steady herself. This was a conversation she would have had with any one of those girls before they got married. She was always the wingman and all about getting everyone laid. But this was new, and what the hell?

"I don't need to hook up," Ruby said, the words sticking in her throat.

"Ha!"

"Ha what?" Her heart was racing now. What had Jason told his sister?

"Ha! It's exactly what you need. Now, I'm not forcing you to have sex with anyone, I'm just saying you could use it if it happens."

"I'm doing just fine."

"How longs it been, Rube?"

"I'm not answering that."

"Because it's been too long," Lisa countered. "We will pick you up at seven. Look sexy. We will all look sexy, even if it's just for my husband's sake when I get home. But the goal is to have you relax."

"I'm relaxed just fine."

"You don't sound fine."

She wasn't! Lisa had lost her ever-loving mind. Or had Ruby lost hers?

She'd slept with Jason, and was now having a conversation with his sister about Ruby's need to have sex? God this was a nightmare.

On any other day, Ruby would have been all in on the girls trying to set her up. She was always the one looking for the details and working the curves to her benefit—when they worked.

Now she was like some scared little virgin afraid to go out with her dearest friends. Afraid they just might hook her up with some guy.

"You know, I have this project—"

"Yeah. I know. And I know you gave your presentation today, and now you should blow off some steam. Seven o'clock. I love you."

The line went dead and Ruby rested her head back against her chair, which was so low she was looking straight across the surface of her desk.

She needed to call Jason and have him talk to his sister.

No, she reconsidered. She needed to go out with her friends, enjoy herself, and when they were ready, she and Jason would decide what to tell Lisa. But until then, she was just going to be cool about it.

Realizing she was nearly sitting on the floor, everything around her was a mess, and she was very aware of the hickey on her neck now—there was no playing it cool. Everything *was* a mess.

* * *

Jason had left her a note on her pillow.

I slept here today. I thought of you. Sleep in this.

Next to the note was another one of his T-shirts. Ruby grinned down at it. This one was a well-worn *Coca-Cola* branded shirt. She lifted it to her nose and sniffed.

The scent of him filled her nose, and she giggled to herself. Wasn't it interesting that a T-shirt could comfort both of them when they couldn't be together.

Leaving the note and the shirt on her bed, Ruby pulled a dress from the closet. She was opting for a sundress, and not her usual sexy red dress. No matter her friends' plans, Ruby didn't need to look sexier to catch a man. She smiled at herself in the mirror. Somehow, she'd already caught one, and boy, oh boy, did he appreciate her curves.

She finished her makeup and double checked the makeup on her neck about thirty times. Her hair was kept down and she made sure to keep it so it flowed forward. It would take everything she had not to pull it back when she got hot. But, she couldn't let anyone see it. Not yet. Not until she knew what she felt about what had happened.

Pressing her hand to her chest, she thought about it. What had happened was she'd had sex with her roommate—her best friend's brother. Nothing—nothing was going to fix this. This was going to crash around her so hard.

Her heart rate kicked up and her palms went damp.

There would be a time when she'd walk down the hallway and Jason's room would be empty. And just like every other roommate she'd ever had, there would be a note or a text.

Sorry. Something came up.

Ruby sat down on her bed and caught her breath.

Was this how it happened? Did she manifest these things?

She drew in a few deep breaths and steadied herself.

Okay, if that were the case, then she was going to manifest something different for herself. This time, she was going to manifest that Jason stayed—forever.

CHAPTER THIRTEEN

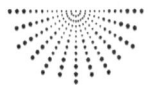

Promptly at seven o'clock, Ruby stepped out of the front door, and as promised, there were her friends.

Each of them was dressed in one of the outfits they'd have worn to the bar on any other given night. Or, a night when they'd been going out to let loose.

Tina lifted a brow when she saw Ruby walk toward them. "Bar night and you're wearing that? You look as if you're going to a summer picnic."

"What's wrong with the way I look?" Ruby asked.

"I pumped enough so I could have a drink. You're letting me down."

Ruby laughed as she pulled her friend in for a hug and kissed her noisily on the cheek. "It's Monday. None of us can afford more than one drink tonight."

"Still, don't you want to change?" Mindy asked, eyeing her coolly.

"No. Let's go."

.   .   .

LISA DROVE TO THE BAR, AND DEEMED HERSELF THE designated driver. Ruby thought the whole premise of the night was ridiculous. Drinks on a Monday night. What kind of guys were out looking to hit up a woman on a Monday night?

When they pulled up in front of a sports bar and there was a baseball game on TV, then Ruby got her answer.

As they walked into the bar, Mindy slid up next to Ruby and linked arms.

She leaned in close. "What happened?" she whispered.

"With what?"

"With what? Are you kidding me?"

"Keep your voice down. I'll tell you, but not now, not tonight."

Mindy groaned. "I'm going to assume that it didn't go well and that's why we're here."

"Assume what you like. I'm not sure what Lisa's plan is or why we're here. I do know that my presentation sucked eggs, so…"

Tina turned to look at her. "Your presentation didn't go well?"

Ruby winced, wondering what else Tina had heard. "It could have gone better," Ruby said.

Lisa lifted her hands in the air as if to rally them. "No better reason to go out for a girls' night."

Tina shook her head. "Are you celebrating?" she directed the question toward Lisa.

"I got myself an airline ticket to London today. You bet your ass I'm celebrating. In three weeks, I'll be with my family. I'll be eating Mama Rose's cooking, listening to John's stories, and kissing Ken's kids."

"You're going to London by yourself?" Mindy asked as they walked into the loud bar.

"Jason asked me to go with him and Ryan bought me the ticket. Life is so perfect right now."

Lisa headed toward a high top and Tina followed. Mindy slowed their walk, still holding on to Ruby's arm. "He's going home, already?"

"Just for a few weeks."

"Whew," Mindy blew out a breath. "I thought you'd already lost another roommate."

"Thanks for the vote of confidence. Don't think that doesn't scare the shit out of me."

Mindy gave Ruby's arm a squeeze. "He's not going anywhere." She leaned in closer. "I'm the only one that knows what's going on, aren't I?"

Ruby nodded, but Mindy didn't know shit.

"I won't say anything until you do. You have my word."

Ruby was grateful for that.

TINA ORDERED A PLATTER OF APPETIZERS, AND THEY OPTED FOR a pitcher of beer. Lisa, the designated driver, ordered a lemonade.

Tina pulled a cheese stick from the platter and tore it in half. "So why was your presentation so bad? You've been working on it for months."

Ruby shrugged her shoulder, and moved her hair so that it kept her makeup-covered hickey from showing.

"I just didn't sleep well the night before."

"Nerves, huh?" Tina bit into the cheese stick. "I don't miss having to work in an office. Lord knows I never get to sleep anymore."

Mindy plucked a cheese curd from the platter. "Doesn't Aaron help with the baby?"

"Sure, but I'm breastfeeding. I kinda have to be part of it."

They all laughed and Ruby thought of how things had changed in the past few years. Lisa and Tina were both married. Tina had a baby. Mindy was engaged and living with her fiancé, and Ruby was having an affair with her roommate.

"Oh shit!" Tina said, and Ruby realized she was zoned out.

Tina's beer had spilled and was running over the tabletop. Each girl threw their napkin on the mess.

Ruby stood. "I'll go get a rag."

She headed to the bar, standing on the foot rail, just so she was tall enough to look over the bar.

"They're a little slow tonight," the man next to her said, turning on his stool to face her.

"I just need a rag."

"Your friends already making messes?" he laughed as he reached over the bar and grabbed the rag that laid there.

"Accidents happen," she said taking the rag. "Thanks for your help."

Ruby hurried back with the rag and began to wipe up the mess.

"What in the hell is that?" Lisa's voice rose above the noise in the bar.

"What's what?" Tina looked around.

"That huge mark on Ruby's neck."

Ruby felt her eyes go wide, but she didn't look up. She continued to clean up the spilled beer.

"Let me see," Tina moved it, setting her elbows on the wet napkins. "Shit!"

"Let me clean this up," Ruby said when Lisa took the rag from her hand.

"It's cleaned up," Lisa said waving down the server who carried a tray over and gathered the napkins and the rag.

Ruby took her seat hoping that the conversation was

over, but no, Lisa took it upon herself to move Ruby's hair and expose the hickey.

"Here I'm trying to get you laid, and it looks like you already got laid," she squealed in delight.

"It's nothing."

"Nothing? Oh no. There isn't a single one of us at this table who you wouldn't be begging for explicit details about something like that. I've told you things I'd never tell anyone. So, now you have to spill."

Ruby wished she hadn't done that to all of them. Even her ally, Mindy, looked as if her interest had been piqued. Karma was certainly a bitch.

"I met a guy."

Lisa drummed on the table in giddy excitement and Ruby flinched. If it hadn't been Jason, Ruby would have shared every sexy detail. But, that wasn't the case.

"I want to know it all." Lisa beamed with delight.

"No."

Tina shook her head. "Not fair."

"I know," Ruby acknowledged the unfairness of it all. "I'm not ready to talk about it."

Lisa covered her hand with hers. "It was consensual, wasn't it?" Her voice was shrouded in concern.

"Yes. Of course. I just want to keep it to myself for now."

Tina narrowed her eyes. "Is he married. Did you fuck a married guy?" The tone was disapproving.

"No. It's just that it's nothing right now and I don't want to make anything of it."

Tina lifted her hands. "He's on her team at work and if word got out they'd both get fired." The three of them hummed and nodded in agreement.

Okay, well, they could think that, Ruby decided. Yeah, she'd let them think that.

* * *

JASON SAT IN THE BREAK ROOM AND SIPPED A CUP OF STALE, cold coffee. He was only a few hours into his shift and already he was exhausted.

He should have slept all day, but it hadn't been easy.

He should have slept in his own bed. Sleeping in Ruby's bed had only made him think of her.

When his phone buzzed in his pocket, he pulled it out and looked down at the text from his sister.

See, I know what's best for her. The text read, and was accompanied by a picture of Ruby in a sundress, leaned up against the bar in a deep conversation with a man. The man had one hand wrapped around a beer bottle, his knees pointed toward Ruby, and he was leaned in close.

Well, fuck!

"Dr. Hughes," the voice came from the doorway and he lifted his head. "The labs just came back for the patient in one."

He nodded and looked back at his phone. "I'll be right there."

Jason pinched the bridge of his nose and let out a breath. He wasn't one for just hooking up with a woman and leaving it at that, but not all women wanted what he did. That was fair.

Ruby was an older woman. Okay, a few years, but nonetheless, older. Casual sex might be all she was willing to offer.

He squeezed his eyes closed. Then again, maybe she was appeasing his sister. God, let her just be appeasing his sister.

When the pager on his hip buzzed, he knew he'd already spent too much time thinking about it. He had two more days of this shitty schedule before he could spend time with Ruby and they could figure out what last night meant.

Standing and dumping the last of the coffee into the sink, Jason threw the cup into the trash and headed back to work.

He didn't have a job that afforded him time to let his mind wander. He needed to stay focused—lives depended on it. Ruby needed to not consume his mind the way she was.

For the next three days, he would have to stay clear of her.

CHAPTER FOURTEEN

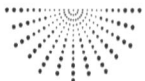

RUBY SAT ON HER BED THURSDAY MORNING WAITING FOR Jason to walk through the front door. It was already ten o'clock, and his shift had ended at eight.

There was plenty she could be doing since she'd taken a personal day. She had laundry to do. The dishwasher needed to be emptied. She'd made a meal plan for the following week to eat healthier, so she needed to go to the grocery store. There was a book she wanted at the bookstore. And, she needed to buy her mother a birthday present.

Ruby smoothed her hands over the T-shirt she'd worn to bed each night, which had gone untouched. She knew he hadn't slept in her bed either, because the note she'd left with the T-shirt was still on her pillow.

Aside from a few texts over the past three days, she hadn't heard from Jason. Nothing more than roommate banter, such as leftovers in the fridge, notice that the water bill had arrived, and one text that had Lisa's itinerary attached.

They'd made a mistake, and Ruby knew the fall was going to hurt. She just hadn't expected it to have happened so quickly.

When she heard the lock on the front door, her heart rate kicked up. She closed her eyes as she heard the door open and Jason dropped his keys in the bowl on the small table by the door.

She waited to hear him walk down the hall to his room, but he must have walked toward the kitchen.

With the shirt in her hands, she stood, and walked out to the living room.

He was moving around in the kitchen. Doors on cabinets opened and closed, and then the refrigerator opened and closed. It was loud. He was mad.

She thought she should just put the shirt down and go back to her room. But before she could turn, he walked into the living room, looking down at his phone.

He was dressed in basketball shorts. He was bare chested and his shirt was tucked into the back of his shorts. His hair was wet, and he had earbuds in. Obviously he'd gone for a run before he'd returned home, and still he hadn't seen her standing there.

It wasn't until he'd nearly ran into her that he noticed her, and he jumped back, ripping the earbuds from his ears.

"Shit, Ruby! God, what are you doing here? I didn't expect you to be standing there watching me."

She'd never heard him sound so angry, or maybe it was edgy. Maybe it was because she was edgy.

"I—I'm sorry," she stammered. "I heard you come home and—"

"Why are you home? Are you sick?" he stepped closer to her.

"No. Um, no," she repeated, wringing the shirt in her hands. "I took a personal day and I'm working from home tomorrow."

He nodded slowly. "That's nice."

"Yeah." She looked down at the shirt and then held it out. "This was still on my bed. I thought you'd like this back."

Jason stared at the shirt. "Right," he reached out to take it from her, their fingers brushing. "I need to get a shower and get some sleep."

"Right, I'm sure you're exhausted."

"It's been a long week," he said, still looking down at the shirt.

"I'll keep it quiet then," she said, and finally he raised his eyes.

"You're sure you're feeling okay?"

Ruby swallowed hard. "I'm fine."

Jason nodded and walked past her to his bedroom—no touches, no kisses. A moment later the door closed.

The first tear rolled down her cheek.

She closed her eyes and drew in a breath. At least he hadn't moved out yet.

* * *

JASON THREW HIS EARBUDS ON THE BED AND PACED A SMALL circle in his room. All he'd wanted to do was pull Ruby into his arms, but he hadn't quite worked off his attitude from Monday night.

He gripped the shirt that Ruby had handed him and lifted it to his nose. He inhaled deeply. It smelled of her. She'd slept in his shirt, just as he'd asked her to.

Dropping down on to his bed, he ran his fingers through his damp hair.

His sister's photo on his phone had soured his mood and had him staying away from Ruby in passing or even texting her or leaving her the sweet notes around the house as he'd wanted to.

He didn't want to give up on what they'd started. Yes,

they'd slept together, but they didn't say anything about being exclusive. Did they need to have that conversation?

And the picture his sister had sent was meant in good humor. Perhaps Ruby wasn't picking up men at the bar. Wouldn't it be worth a conversation?

He rubbed his tired eyes.

Standing, he took the shirt she'd given back to him, sniffed it again, and then pulled it on. He'd get a shower later, and sleep after that.

He heard Ruby's bedroom door close and he drew in a breath. Hopefully he hadn't messed everything up.

Jason opened his door and walked down the hallway. He tapped on Ruby's door, but opened it without invitation.

She sat up on her bed, wiping at her cheeks. Well, fuck! He'd made her cry by being an asshole.

"Hey," he said.

"Hey," she said back, her voice shaky.

"Can we talk?"

Ruby batted her eyes, then scanned a look over him wearing the shirt she'd slept in. "Sure."

Jason walked to the bed and knelt down in front of her, turning her so that he fit between her thighs. He ran his palms up the outsides of her legs, and he looked up at her.

"I'm sorry," he said.

"For what?" Again, the words had been choked out and it killed him that he'd done this to her.

Pulling his phone from his back pocket, he scrolled to the picture his sister had sent him. Turning his phone toward her, he shared it with her.

"Where did you get that?" she asked.

"My sister. She was showing me that you were hitting it off with men at the bar."

Her lips flattened into a line. "I was getting a rag because Tina spilled her beer."

Jason nodded and let out a breath. "I know she doesn't know, and she didn't mean anything by it, but—"

"But you've been avoiding me for three days because of it?"

"I couldn't focus. And I have a job where I need to focus."

Ruby's hands came to his shoulders and pushed him back. She stood and walked around him.

"That hurt," she spat out the words.

"I know," he admitted, standing from his position on the floor. "I'm in here to say I'm sorry."

"You should be."

"I am."

"Ten seconds after she took that stupid picture, she saw my hickey."

Jason felt the corner of his mouth lift in a grin. "What hickey?"

Ruby moved her hair. "The one you put right here," she pointed to the very faint marking.

"Oh," a smile formed on his mouth and the pain in his chest lightened. "What did you tell them?"

"On their own they decided it was someone I worked with, and if word got out, we'd both get fired. They let me off the hook. But they want details."

"Why?"

"Because I've begged for details for years. Now it's my turn. This is my karma for being the lonely best friend."

He tried to reel in his smile. "We didn't set any ground rules."

Her gaze narrowed at him. "I won't talk about us. That's a given."

He shook his head. "That's not what I mean. When we're open about us to them, you can tell them anything. I'm not embarrassed."

"Me either."

"Good. I just mean, well, I don't want casual, Ruby. I don't do casual."

She worried her lip, and he was afraid she did do casual, and he'd have to be prepared for that.

"So what do you want?" she asked.

"You," he said firmly.

"Just me? No others on the side? No girls in the doctors' sleeping quarters during shifts? No girl you left back home? No—"

He moved to her, cutting her off. "No one but you."

"Are you sure?"

"I've never been more sure."

"I wasn't picking up guys," she defended.

"I know that now," he admitted.

"I can't promise to not distract you at work. I can't control what's in your head."

"That's on me," he promised. "I can do my job and do it well, and still have a woman in my life."

Ruby let out a shaky breath. "When do we tell them?"

Okay, he thought, this was promising. "Whenever you want."

She studied him for a moment, not moving, not talking. She was considering, and he owed her that time.

Ruby moved into him, lifting the hem of the shirt he'd put on, and pulling it up over his head. "Let's drag it out a bit longer. I'm rather liking our secret, but I'm not ashamed," she reiterated.

"Someone will guess it."

"Then I guess we'll announce it then. Until then, you're all mine," she said, rising on her toes and kissing him until he almost couldn't breathe.

CHAPTER FIFTEEN

RUBY HAD SHARED JASON'S SHOWER WITH HIM. WELL, THEY'D started to take a shower, which turned into not-a-shower.

Her face heated at the thought of it.

After the past few days, when they hadn't even spoken, the need for one another had turned up between them, and they'd made use of it.

Ruby grinned when she thought about the shower, the counter, the bed, the couch, the kitchen, the closet—

Her phone chimed and she looked at the screen. *Wedding planning at my house at six?* Mindy had texted.

Ruby grimaced at the text. It was already four. She'd kept Jason up long enough, he'd finally tapped out and went to bed. She'd been watching YouTube videos on the best romance movie kisses, which hadn't helped her relax any, that was for sure. The list ranged from the kiss in the *Notebook* to Peter Parker and Mary Jane's kiss in *Spiderman*. *Lady and the Tramp* continually made the top ten, and Ruby could agree, it was one of her favorites, but maybe that was because it included spaghetti, and you could never go wrong with spaghetti.

Ruby began to text back, erased it, started it again.

Jason would be asleep for hours. He'd understand. Besides, if they weren't going to let anyone in on what was going on, right away, she couldn't turn Mindy down.

I'll be there.

Mindy sent back a meme of someone celebrating.

* * *

MINDY MET RUBY AT THE FRONT DOOR WITH A GLASS OF WINE.

"It's the newest brand I'm carrying. You have to let me know what you think," she said as Ruby took her first sip.

"I'm not wincing. It must be good."

Mindy looped her arm through Ruby's as they walked to the kitchen. "Vic went to dinner at his sister's house."

"And they didn't want you to go?"

Mindy shook her head. "I wanted to show you girls the dress I'm looking at. He can't see it."

"Oh, right." Ruby looked around the kitchen, which Mindy's fiancé had remodeled. "Where is everyone?"

"They're not coming until six-thirty. I wanted a few minutes with you."

"Why?" Ruby asked sipping her wine.

Mindy nudged her. "I know the hickey wasn't from a guy at work. I know it was from Jason. So, tell me about it."

This was Ruby's chance to have some freedom where Jason was concerned. She could tell Mindy everything. And, if she did, maybe Ruby would have some clarity on it all.

"He's amazing," Ruby sighed out, and it felt so good.

"I can tell by the look on your face. So, you did it?"

"We did it."

The pink in Mindy's cheeks was humorous. If any of Ruby's friends was the opposite of Ruby, it was Mindy. Sexy details about her and the next-door neighbor had to be pried out of Mindy. For Mindy to say a curse word, that too was rare. Yet, they seemed to mesh together nicely, she and Ruby.

"I'm happy for you," Mindy said. "What's next?"

"What's next? Are you kidding me? We're barely a week into whatever this is."

"Nah," Mindy sighed. "Whatever this is has been going on for months. It's been building. You don't even see it, do you?"

"No."

"From the minute he moved back to Colorado, he's had eyes on you—for you. You, on the other hand, looked at him as if he were your own brother."

Ruby swallowed hard. "That doesn't help."

"Seriously. You don't think of yourself as someone that can be loved or desired." Mindy held up a hand as Ruby began to take a breath in protest. "I mean it. You only find the positive in everyone else, but with yourself, you're a bit harsh. And yes, I know that's your mother's influence on you. She kept you to herself and to get you to believe you're worthy of love, even from us, was a task."

Ruby took a sip of her wine and let that sink in before Mindy continued.

"Jason is a great guy, and I can't imagine you'll find one better. I also don't imagine you'd want to try and find one better." She lifted her brows.

"When this goes south, and inevitably, it will go south, there will be more people hurt than just us," Ruby said.

"See, that's where you screw all of this up."

"Where?"

"You said when," Mindy pointed out. "Not if. You expect this to get messed up and you're deep down inside planning it."

"I am not."

"You are too. That's why all of your roommates leave. You know that, right?"

Ruby set down her wine glass, afraid she might snap the stem off of it.

"Are you accusing me of sabotaging my relationships with my roommates so they'll leave?"

"Yes."

"I never—"

"You get close to them. You forge a friendship with them. You hover. You get needy. You realize it and you step back. You shut down. You—"

"God, stop. Please," she pleaded. "Eye-opening take on how my friend feels about me," Ruby said picking up her glass and downing the wine.

"I'm just saying, accept what he has to offer and don't be too hard on yourself. This could be the most amazing thing to ever happen to you."

"Because I need a man?"

"Because you deserve to be loved by someone, and this one appears to be very fond of you."

Ruby's hands shook and she took a moment to calm. "I like him."

"I know you do."

"He's amazing in bed."

Mindy's mouth turned up into a wide grin. "I can't wait to hear about it."

"He wants to *date* me," Ruby admitted on a laugh.

"You can't go wrong with a good-looking doctor who comes from a good home."

"Yeah, I've considered that."

"And it never hurts the situation if they're amazing in bed." Mindy smiled and then rested her hand on Ruby's. "Enjoy the hell out of this. If it ends, well, that would suck. But, God, Rube, what if it doesn't?"

Ruby let out a long, slow breath. Yeah, what if it didn't end?

Mindy pulled back when the front door opened and the sound of Lisa and Tina walking in, and the squeal of a very happy baby, soared through the house.

Ruby picked up the bottle of wine and filled her glass again. The excited chatter and baby noises reminded Ruby exactly what would happen if things didn't end. She just might be in for the happiness that surrounded her.

As she sipped her wine, she thought about all the things Mindy had said to her. She could keep him, she thought. If only she didn't push him away first.

CHAPTER SIXTEEN

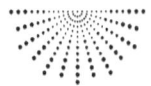

THE GLOW OF THE TV LIT THE LIVING ROOM. JASON RESTED his arm over his head and let the stillness of the night surround him. It was nearing ten o'clock and he was biding his time until Ruby came home.

He'd made the pizza his sister had brought him, and wrapped up the leftovers for lunch tomorrow. Ruby worked from home once in a while, but he stayed out of her way. But tomorrow would be different. It might kill him to stay out of her hair tomorrow.

He chuckled to himself. He couldn't be that kind of guy—the needy one that had to be with a woman all the time. But for right now, they were a secret. Only they knew what was going on. There was a kind of power in that.

The moment he heard the key in the door, he sat up. Over the back of the couch, he watched her walk into their home, put her keys in the bowl, and kick off her shoes.

"Hey," he said softly.

"Hey," she returned.

"How'd it go?"

Ruby skirted the couch, running her fingers up his bare

leg, stopping at the hem of his shorts. She knelt a knee on the couch, then let her body ease against his until they were both laying on the couch.

"Between you and me, and seriously, this goes nowhere else," she began.

"I promise," he agreed.

"Tina is still a bridezilla. Only now, she's a brides*maid*zilla."

Jason laughed. "What does that mean?"

"Mindy's pretty simple," Ruby said tracing her finger over his collarbone. "She doesn't want too fancy, but she doesn't want dull either. She wants something between Tina's wedding and Lisa's."

"So she's not *Bride Wars* material? She doesn't need June at the Plaza?"

Ruby eased herself up and grinned down at him. "Did you seriously just plot quote a movie to me?"

"I did. But it's not a rom com, so it doesn't count."

He watched as she thought it over. "I guess it's a friend comedy, isn't it?"

"Yep. They were both already in romances," he offered, smiling up at her.

"I can't believe you knew that one."

"I sorta have a thing for Anne Hathaway, so don't hold that against me."

Ruby shrugged. "How could I? She's the queen of the friend comedy."

"*The Intern*, one of my faves," Jason said, and that warranted a slap to his shoulder.

"Get out! That's one of my faves too!"

"You're a De Niro fan?"

Ruby wrinkled up her nose. "I am in *The Intern* and *Meet the Fockers*. I am not a fan of any gangster movie he's done. He's violent and vulgar."

Now he laughed. "C'mon, now those are the movies I know best."

"Your mother let you watch those?"

"Let's remember that I'm in my late twenties," he noted first. "But of course she didn't let me watch movies like that. My brother had a friend who was unsupervised. My mother would make me go with him to watch out for him. I wasn't doing much supervising. I was getting the benefits of the kid not being supervised, too."

Ruby pinched his chin. "I'm going to tell her."

"She won't believe you. Straight A's and never had a call from school. She thinks I'm a saint."

She eased back down on him so that their mouths were just a breath apart.

"Were you actually a bad boy, Jason Hughes?" Her voice was husky and he had to adjust her for his own comfort.

"I was a normal boy, thank you very much."

"I've seen what the girls look like on your Instagram. You were popular."

Jason pushed his head back into the cushion of the couch and looked up at her. "Those pictures are old."

"How old?"

"Years," he said. "Ruby, if you're digging for stuff then—"

"I'm not. I was being playful." She sat up and moved from him, posting herself at the end of the couch. "I do playful then I go too far, though."

"You didn't go too far. If you want to know about those women—"

She shook her head. "No. Maybe someday. I mean, I just realize I do this. I hound someone until I've crossed a line. Just like asking my friends for sexy details all the fucking time." She scrubbed her hands over her face. "Some of my not so stellar qualities have lovingly been pointed out to me."

Jason sat up. She'd started to take a trip inside herself, and he hadn't been prepared for that.

"You're their friend. It should be okay."

"Not the best one when I do shit like that. God, I get it now."

Jason brushed his fingers down her arm. "We can talk about it."

She shook her head. "I'd rather not. In fact, I'd rather just lose that quality all together."

Jason moved over on the couch until they were thigh to thigh. "Don't be too hard on yourself. Part of the charm of Ruby is that rawness."

"That's not charming."

"Says who?"

She pursed her lips. "It all feels ugly."

"Is this about you really? You were telling me about Mindy's wedding planning and Tina being a bridesmaidzilla," he said grinning as he ran his hand over her hair. "What's that about?"

Ruby laughed. "She just had too many opinions. She didn't like the bridesmaids' colors. She didn't like the table setting Mindy liked. She thought that the museum was a much nicer venue than the ballroom at the hotel Mindy picked."

He lifted his arm over Ruby's shoulders. "Where would you get married?"

That caused her to stand and wave her hands around. "Oh, no. I'm not diving into this conversation. We've had two nice days as a couple and three bad ones. Our record is not secure enough for me to tell you anything about wedding plans for myself."

He raised a brow. "It was an innocent question."

She kept shaking her head. "Still not going down that road."

Jason smiled up at her and held his hands out in surrender. "I promise not to bring it up again."

With what he considered was a defeated breath, Ruby dropped her hands. "I need to get to bed. I still have to work tomorrow, even if in the luxury of my pajamas."

Jason grinned and pulled off his T-shirt. "Something for you to wear to bed."

She took the shirt and studied it. "Oxford Rowing Team."

"Yep."

Pulling her bottom lip through her teeth, she dropped the shirt. "Just because I'm going to bed, didn't mean I didn't want company, or wanted to wear anything at all," she said as she pulled her own shirt off and dropped it to the floor as she walked past him and to her room.

Jason jumped up, picked up the shirts, and quickly followed.

CHAPTER SEVENTEEN

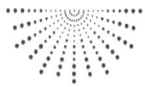

Tiny pink roses on a delicate cup with a saucer was a simple thing that brought peace and joy to Ruby. Sitting in her mother's breakfast nook looking out over the well-groomed, covenant-controlled, yard on Saturday morning made Ruby feel at home, even if she'd never lived in the home her mother purchased in her retirement.

For the past two weeks, Jason had been picking up all the shifts he'd traded to make time for his vacation. Admittedly, Ruby had needed a break from her job and wedding planning on Mindy's behalf.

When Jason was home, they spent every moment together enjoying their secret relationship. Okay, Mindy knew, but no one was getting it out of Mindy. If Ruby ever had an ally she could trust, it was Mindy.

"Scones are fresh," her mother said, setting the plate down in front of her.

Ruby watched as her mother gently lowered herself into the chair next to her. One hand steadying herself on the table and the other on the back of the chair. Her ample frame squeezing between the table and chair with arthritic knees and hips making the task harder. Of course, the piles of items that cluttered in boxes against the walls made it harder for her mother to get around at all.

Her mother was as old as her friends' grandparents, and the source of many nights of needed therapy with her friends. Not that her mother caused her constant anguish, but as she got older, she needed more of Ruby's attention. Ruby's mother never left the house, except on extreme occasions like doctor's appointments or vacations, during which she was accompanied by her sister and Ruby.

Oh, Ruby listened to her mother and aunt go on about how Ruby needed to date, get married, and have kids before they died, but inside, Ruby was quite sure her mother and aunt cherished the thought that Ruby was all theirs and they weren't having to share her with a man or kids.

Her childhood and teenage years were proof that they thought they were protecting her by keeping her close to them. When a child has no freedoms, they have no friends—therefore, no social skills. That was Ruby until she'd met Tina and Mindy, and then Lisa.

Ruby's aunt, Jose, joined them in the kitchen carrying a plain white box.

"I found these in the closet," she said, setting the box on the table. She nodded toward Ruby to lift the top.

Inside were four antique coffee cups and saucers, much like the ones that they sipped from.

"These are beautiful," Ruby said as she carefully lifted one of the cups from the box.

"I think they were Mama's," Jose said.

Ruby's mother shook her head in protest. "Gram-gram Sullivan's, I think."

Jose matched her sister's protest with a shake of her own

head. "I don't think so. You never marked any of these boxes. Why are you hoarding all of these things?"

"You live here too. You're hoarding them as well as I am."

Ruby laid the cup back in the box. "No matter where they came from, they're lovely."

Jose pushed the box toward Ruby. "Take them."

Ruby saw her mother's eyes grow wide as if her sister had just given away an heirloom that had been earmarked for her. But, Ruby knew the drill. Her aunt sent her with miscellaneous boxes and Ruby was to graciously accept them. This was the only way they could eliminate some of the items her mother collected and forgot about.

Ruby was sure the cups hadn't come from her grandmother or her great-grandmother. These were finds her mother had amassed over the years and now they took up space in the closets, or in boxes that lined the walls or piles on the counters.

"I'll cherish them. Thank you," Ruby said, and it seemed to satisfy her mother.

"So, Ruby Red," her aunt said, using the name she'd called her since birth. "Tell me what's been happening in your life."

Ruby tapped her fingers against the side of her cup and tried to decide what to tell her aunt. Jason wasn't going to make the conversation, that was for sure.

"I'm the lead on a project at work. We just got approved and now we move forward."

Her aunt's brows drew in. "What do you do again?"

Ruby's mother let out a groan. "Remember, she's smart and has a degree in building things that we don't understand. Don't make her go through that again," she argued, lifting her petite cup in meaty hands to her lips.

"Right," her aunt brushed away the comment. "Tell me about your sexy roommate."

Ruby had lifted her own cup to her lips, but was damn glad she hadn't sipped. That would have caused her to choke.

"My sexy roommate?"

Her aunt nodded enthusiastically. "Your friend Liza's brother."

"Lisa's brother," she corrected because Jose never could get her name right.

"Yeah, that one. He's hunky, right?"

Ruby's mother sighed. "Jose, do you have to—"

"It's okay, Mama." Ruby laughed, realizing that she got a lot more traits from her aunt than she did from her mother. "Jason is Lisa's foster brother from the family she was with the longest—the ones that moved when she was sixteen."

"Up and left her here," her mother scoffed.

Ruby didn't like that opinion. Not when she knew how hard Lisa tried to get to them, and now knew how hard the Hughes family struggled to get her to them.

"Things were tight all around," she offered.

"Yeah, yeah. But how do you go through med school without any money?"

Ruby hadn't considered that. Oxford. Med school. That certainly warranted money, didn't it? Why couldn't they have tried to send for Lisa?

Then she thought about what he'd said about the grades and good behavior. It was possible that he had lots of scholarships. And maybe Oxford was the equivalent of the University of Colorado, only they had castles and a rowing team, and CU had a buffalo that ran on the field at the football games.

Ruby's single mother had put her though college without loans. It was possible, wasn't it?

Then as if the thought had only popped into her head, she nearly shouted, "Military."

Jose nodded in acceptance of that answer. Still, her

mother's brows knitted together. Her mother shook her head. "I don't like you living with a boy."

Oh, Ruby thought, he wasn't a boy and her mother had reason to worry. The thought actually made her grin, so she lifted her cup to her lips to conceal it.

Jose took a scone and tore into it. "She's thirty, Mildred. Leave her alone."

"It's indecent," said the woman who had Ruby out of wedlock and had been forty-five and only wanting a baby.

Oh Ruby had fought this fight her whole life. Her mother's insistence of morals, when she'd never even given Ruby the name of her own father. This was how her mother attempted to control Ruby. By making up rules, which her mother clearly didn't live by, she'd kept Ruby at arm's length most of Ruby's life. Living with a boy was indecent? What was having a baby with a man and not telling him? There were so many other...

She stopped herself from getting more worked up. She wasn't going to let this fight ruin what she had—and that was the joy of living with a boy.

"Mama, he's a good guy," Ruby defended. "He's a family guy. He and Lisa are headed to England next week to see his family. It'll be great for them."

"Then you should stay here. You'll be all alone," her mother countered.

The last thing Ruby wanted was to stay in the cluttered little house with her mother and aunt.

"I've lived by myself for years, Mama. I'll be fine."

Jose bit into her scone. "You're not making it with the doctor?" she asked with her mouth full.

Ruby's mother slapped her sister's arm, and Ruby wondered if her face betrayed her as she lifted her cup again to sip the coffee. God, this wasn't a conversation she wanted to have.

"Jose, I swear," her mother scolded. "Ruby's a good girl. Leave her alone."

That seemed to end the conversation, and Ruby was grateful. If they only knew how much she'd *made it with the doctor*, her mother would lock her in a closet and keep her there—no matter how old Ruby was.

CHAPTER EIGHTEEN

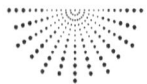

Ruby had become comfortable enough with the sounds of Jason coming and going at odd hours, that she hadn't even heard him walk into the condo. It didn't startle her when his body slid up behind her, and his arms came around her.

It only stirred her enough to settle into him, which had become their way the past three weeks.

"What time is it?" Ruby asked softly in the dark.

"It's five."

She rolled in his arms to face him, but her eyes remained closed. "Five? You're not supposed to be home for hours."

"We had enough staff. I decided to take the opportunity to come home and snuggle up with you." He pressed a kiss to her neck.

"I'm going to miss this," she said softly.

"I'll be back before you know it."

Ruby opened her eyes to find his dark ones staring back at her. "I took off Wednesday and Thursday," Ruby said and the corners of Jason's mouth turned up in a smile.

"You took off to be with me?"

"Of course," she said.

"That makes me happy. And you're sure you can't—"

"I can't go with you."

Jason kissed the tip of her nose. "You can't blame me for asking again."

Ruby rolled again so that her back was pressed up against Jason and his arms came around her. "I get to sleep for another hour, and then I have to go to work."

"You don't get to work from home whenever?"

Ruby chuckled. "I have team meetings today, and I'll be late coming home."

Jason nuzzled his chin into her neck. "Then I'll make the time we have left this week worth it," he said rolling her under him. "I'm going to call you every day."

"You'd better."

He brushed a kiss over her collarbone. "I'll hurry back to you."

"You'd better," Ruby said again with a laugh that fizzled out on a sigh as he kissed her and her body went pliant beneath him.

"God, Ruby. I do love loving you," he said and she let it warm inside of her as he began to peel her from the T-shirt she wore. She'd dissect that later—when he was gone.

* * *

"Ruby?"

Her head snapped up, and the pencil in her hand snapped in two.

"When do we need to follow up on that?" her boss asked as he bore a look into her that had her sucking in a breath.

Follow up on what? Shit!

"I'm sorry, can you repeat that?" she asked, setting the pieces of the pencil down on the table.

He studied her for a long moment before leaning back in

his chair and looking around the room. "I think we're good for today. I'll want all of your reports by next Monday. You're doing great, team."

Everyone else around the table gathered their notes and hurried out of the room. As Ruby gathered hers and stood from her chair, Gus Grant, her boss, stood and moved to the chair next to hers.

"Ruby, sit for another moment, won't you?"

She swallowed hard and sat back down, keeping her stack of notes and her computer on her lap.

"Everything okay?" he asked.

"Everything is great."

He nodded slowly. "Listen, you're a valuable asset to us. So I want to make sure you're doing okay. If this project is too much, we can—"

"It's not. I mean, it's the perfect amount of much."

Gus chuckled. "I've never seen anything distract you this much."

"It's not the project," she admitted. "I'll make sure there are no more delays."

He continued to sit there nodding. Crossing his legs, he rested both hands on his knee casually. "Anything else going on that I can help you with? Or ask your team to help you with?"

"No."

"Things at home are okay?"

Ruby nodded and made sure a smile was plastered on her lips. "Things at home are great."

"Leslie is still working out as a roommate?"

Ruby dropped her shoulders, set her items back on the table, and blew out a breath. "Leslie moved out months ago," she admitted and assumed that Gus would have known that since he'd been the one to send her his daughter's best friend when Ruby needed a roommate.

His brows narrowed. "Really? I hadn't heard that."

Ruby shrugged. "I don't keep roommates long. She moved out without a word. So, I'm not sure what went wrong."

"Maybe something came up."

"Maybe."

"Are you in need of a new roommate? Rent assistance?"

"Oh, no. No," she said quickly. "My best friend's brother moved in."

Now Gus' brows rose. "Oh. And how's that going?"

"Good. He's great. He's a doctor. He's lived in England most of his life, and came back to work here. He's great."

Gus' lip twitched as if he were trying to ward off a grin.

"That's fantastic," he said. "He's not a distraction to your work?"

Gus' grin never did surface and Ruby felt a twisting in her gut. This little thing she had going on with Jason was causing problems in her life, and she was going to have to figure out how to deal with it. When he was gone, she'd get everything pulled together.

God, if only she could talk to her friends about it—well, all of her friends. But for the moment, Mindy was the only one she could confide in. When they returned from England, both of them, then they'd spill it.

Gus reached out and patted Ruby's hand which lay flat on the top of the table. "You're a wonderful asset and a great team leader, Ruby. I know whatever is going on outside of work that is distracting you, you'll get it worked out."

"Yes."

"And I'll have those reports followed up by next Wednesday?" His eyes were wide and focused on her.

"Of course."

Gus nodded, stood, and walked out of the conference room. Ruby let her head drop to the table.

The secret affair with her roommate was costing her sleep, focus at work, and was simply confusing her.

He'd told her multiple times he loved loving her. What did that mean? Was it only the sex? Was she convenient? No. They'd talked about that. This wasn't casual.

She squeezed her eyes shut. In three days he'd be gone for weeks. They could focus on other things for a bit, and she could pull her head out of her ass and not be so distracted. Then, when he got home, they could decide what they were really doing. Again, she figured she'd better save some money to pay for his part of the lease. Surely, she'd be roommateless again soon.

CHAPTER NINETEEN

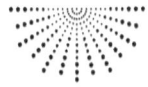

"It had to be the top floor, right?"

Jason snapped his head up from his job of packing up his suitcase when he heard Richard Gere's voice echo through the condo.

"It's the best," Julia Roberts replied.

He chuckled as the rest of the scene played out more quietly and then the sound disappeared.

Stepping out into the living room, he watched as Ruby gathered her laptop and earbuds.

"Do you watch rom coms when you work, too?" he humored.

She looked up at him, her eyes glossed over, her earbuds in her hand. "What? No. Oh," she said as if she remembered what she'd been listening to. "I don't watch them. But some people listen to music, I listen to movies."

Jason grinned. She was the most adorable woman he'd ever known in his entire life. But the past few days she'd been distant.

He'd been forcing himself to look past it. He was a doctor

and perhaps over-analyzed her moods. Maybe it was exhaustion, they'd hadn't been getting much sleep, he humored to himself. Or maybe it was PMS. But the man trumped the doctor, and he knew better than to mention it.

"Are you done working for the day?"

Ruby nodded, easing back against the couch. "Yes. I'm sorry. I meant to not be working, but—"

"You have deadlines. I get it," he said moving toward her and dropping down onto the couch next to her.

He took her hand and interlaced their fingers.

"You seem distracted," he said and she actually groaned.

"You sound like my fricking boss."

"He says you're distracted?"

"Yes. I'm not getting any sleep. I'm confused. I'm unorganized. I'm—"

Jason pressed a finger to her lips. "You'll have three weeks without my distraction."

"Don't say it like that. Don't say that," she nearly shouted as she got to her feet and paced in front of him. "I mean, I don't know what the fuck we're doing here. I've never been in a situation like this."

Jason leaned his elbows on his knees and watched her. "What situation? You've been in relationships before."

"Not one that was going to cost me so much when it ends."

That stabbed right into his chest.

"Ends?" his voice cracked when he asked.

"I mean—well, you know—shit!" Ruby fell into the chair next to her and kicked her feet up on the coffee table.

"Are we ending?"

She shook her head. "No. I just figure you'll—"

"You don't get to figure out things for me. I do that. And us, we figure that out together." He waited for a reply, instead he watched her wipe tears from her eyes.

Jason stood and reached for Ruby's hands. Pulling her to her feet, he gathered her into him. "Ruby, if what we're doing is distracting you at work, then let's figure out how to not distract you."

"You're leaving. This isn't what you need right now," she said softly, her breath warm through the fabric of his T-shirt. "I'm okay. I'll have three weeks to work through this."

"I don't want you working through anything without me. Ruby, we're a couple. Tell me where you're struggling."

She eased from his arms, took a deliberate step back, and crossed her arms in front of her. "We're a couple?"

He narrowed his gaze on her, studying her. "Well, yeah. Ruby, I thought we agreed that—"

"You're right. We did."

"We can tell everyone. I'm not opposed to that."

"I know. I know." She dropped her arms. "I don't want Lisa to hate me. I don't want her to treat me like Tina treated her. I don't want you to decide I'm not worth your time."

"What the hell?" Jason moved to her and gathered her back into him. "Where is this coming from?"

His T-shirt grew damp as Ruby's tears absorbed into the fabric. "I just…" she didn't finish.

Jason kept her in his arms and kissed the top of her head. "Oh, Ruby. This isn't just some lurid affair, honey."

She drew in a deep breath and looked up at him. "What do you mean when you say you love loving me? Is it just sex? You love doing that? It takes your mind off of—"

He eased her back until she was an arm's length away. His skin stung from heat that prickled it. "Are you kidding me with this?"

Under his hands, he could feel her tremble. "I mean, no one wants me around long term, and—"

"Fucking-A, Ruby. Don't you get it? Don't you know what

I'm saying when I say that to you? Don't you know how I feel about you?"

"I'm just waiting for you to walk out. For your room to be empty. For you to not—"

He yanked her back to him, perhaps a little too hard, but she didn't resist.

"Ruby, when I say that, I'm trying to tell you how I feel without scaring you away."

"How you feel?"

"Damn, Ruby. You're everything to me and have been since the very second I saw you. I'm so goddammed lucky to have you as my friend, my roommate, and loving you is—"

"Right there. Loving me. You mean having sex with me. You mean the convenience of having me whenever you're near."

His jaw had gone slack and he stared down at her. "I can't believe that's what you think."

"I can't help it."

Jason cupped her face in his hands and locked his gaze into her eyes.

"Ruby, when I say I love loving you, I mean I love you. I love you so much it's hard to breathe sometimes. Getting to love you is an honor. Getting to make love to you..." He sucked in a breath. "God, Ruby, getting do that, that's only a bonus to the love I have for you."

"You shouldn't say that. This is new. This is—"

"This is a relationship, Ruby. This is a man and woman loving each other and working through these feelings together." He brushed her hair back from her face and cupped the back of her neck with his hand. "You don't have to say you love me. I feel it when I'm with you. And Lisa isn't going to freak out about this. She's going to be happy."

"And if she's not?"

"And if she's not, she's going to have to learn to be. She's my sister. She doesn't get to hate me or push me away. And you—you're her sister too. She loves you and the girls as much as any family. If she's not all in, she'll get over it. I love you, Ruby. I don't plan on going anywhere."

CHAPTER TWENTY

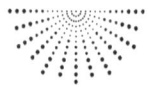

Ruby was sick watching Jason set his suitcase by the front door, check his passport, and again making sure his tickets were on his phone.

His mother had called three times the night before, and Ruby could hear the joy in her voice. Mama Rose was ecstatic that her baby was on his way home to visit. Ruby hoped that Jason would record his mother's reaction to Lisa walking out with him.

Standing in the kitchen, a mug of coffee in her hand, she leaned up against the counter with her hip. Every time Jason had turned around, Ruby had cried. No doubt she hadn't hidden it well, but she couldn't help herself. There was something about watching him leave that made her ache.

Deep inside of her an insecurity stirred, and she knew the moment he walked out of that door, he was gone for good. This was the end of them being roommates. This was him leaving and never coming back.

This was her mind playing jokes on her because somehow she'd driven every roommate away, and he'd already been there longer than most.

"Ryan just texted and said they're on the way," Jason checked his pocket for his passport one more time.

Ruby nodded and sipped her coffee, which had gone cold as she'd stood there.

"Are you going to put on shoes? Brush your hair?" He grinned at her.

"I'm not going," she said and watched as the disappointment flashed over his face.

Jason moved to her, took the cup from her hands, and set it on the counter before gathering her to him. "You're not coming?"

"I can't," she said, her voice cracking with tears that now flowed down her cheeks—again. "I can't go and watch you walk away. Lisa will see right through that."

"She's going to know eventually. Let's just tell her."

Ruby shook her head and eased back to wipe her eyes. "Let her have this trip without worry. She's never had anything quite like this. She's going home to her mother as much as you are, and I don't want to have anything to do with that not being just perfect."

Jason blew out a breath and wrapped his arms around Ruby. "I love you. You're an amazing friend to think like you do."

"I'm a wreck."

"I'll be back," he promised.

Oh, she wasn't so sure. But if he did come back, she had to hold on tight because it would break her to have him back only to have him disappear in the night.

Before Ryan and Lisa arrived, Ruby had brushed her hair, changed her clothes, and made herself presentable. She'd let Jason wrap her in his arms, and they'd had a moment of farewell on her bed a bit hastily.

"They're here," he'd called back from the front door as Ruby closed her bedroom door hoping that Lisa wouldn't come into the condo and figure out what they'd just been doing.

Jason closed the front door, pulled Ruby in, and kissed her until her head spun.

"I'm coming back. I'll be back in three weeks. And when I do, we're telling everyone about this," he said just a moment before the front door burst open and they stepped apart.

"I have to pee," Lisa ran in and straight to the bathroom.

Ryan walked through the door a few moments later. "Have fun with that," he teased. "She's so nervous that I found three cups of coffee, all in different states of being drank. So she's going to be a pain in the ass to travel with," he laughed.

"There's nothing to be nervous about," Jason said.

"I think it's mostly the flying, but surprising your mom is some of it too."

The smile that settled on Jason's mouth warmed Ruby to her core.

"Mom is going to be so happy."

Lisa bolted back out of the bathroom. "Okay. I'm ready." She looked at Ruby, a hint of concern on her face. "You good?"

Ruby nodded. "A bit emotional watching you both get ready to leave."

Lisa pulled her in for a hug and whispered in her ear. "He'll come back. Don't pack up his stuff yet," she teased, but Ruby wondered if Lisa knew the impact of her words.

"Of course he will. I'm the roommate of the year," Ruby laughed, but she wasn't sure it resonated that way.

Lisa stepped back and clapped her hands. "I'm ready. Let's go. I'm ready," she repeated and Ryan wrapped his arm around her.

"I think there are more cups of coffee laying around the

house than the ones I found, aren't there? If you don't settle down, they're going to use your energy to fuel the plane."

Lisa exchanged glances with Jason. "I'm nervous."

"I can tell," he laughed. "You should have let me prescribe you something."

Lisa shook her head. "I've waited for this day since I was sixteen." She blew out a nervous breath. "I'm ready. I'm ready." She laughed. "I'm ready."

Ryan kissed the side of Lisa's head and then moved to the door. "Is this your only bag?" he asked Jason.

"Yeah."

Ryan picked it up and headed outside.

Lisa moved back to Ruby and kissed her cheek. "I love you. Keep the girls in line. Mindy is watering my plants. Make sure she remembers."

"I will."

"No rom com nights without me."

Ruby laughed. "We wouldn't dream of it."

"I'm going to see my family," Lisa sighed out the words.

Ruby took Lisa's hand and gave it a squeeze. "You deserve this. Have the best time."

Lisa kissed her again and then followed her husband out the door.

Jason watched his sister disappear down the steps before he moved to Ruby and pulled her to him. "I love you. Three weeks. I'll be home soon."

"Call me when you land."

"And a thousand times while I'm gone," he promised before dipping his head to kiss her one last time. "I left a pile of shirts for you," he said grinning as he backed toward the door. "Wear them."

Ruby couldn't speak now. She only nodded as the tears rolled down her cheeks.

"I love you, Ruby. I'll be right back."

CHAPTER TWENTY-ONE

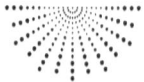

They were an hour into the flight when Lisa startled awake, grabbing Jason's arm.

"Hey," he said softly. "Easy there."

Lisa's fingers still dug into his arm as she got her bearings. "How long have we been flying?"

Jason chuckled. "An hour."

On a huff, Lisa pressed her back into her seat. "God, we haven't even made it to Missouri yet."

Jason pulled his earbuds from his ears, and tucked his puzzle book into the pocket of the seat in front of him. He took his sister's hand and held it in his. "I had no idea you were going to be such a wreck."

"I hate flying."

"I'm learning just how much," he grinned at her.

"I used to save for this. And now, here I am. I'm flying to London."

"I'm sorry you had to wait so long. We wanted you with us all along. Don't ever forget that."

Lisa nodded. "I think losing all of you was the hardest thing I ever went through. It was hard because for the first time, I knew I was loved. And I was loved nearly as much as you and Ken were."

"Oh, as much if not more," he said, nudging her with his shoulder. "Mom was a mess when we lost my sister. But when we got you, she had some spark back. Ryan flying them out to be there for your wedding was the greatest gift she'd ever been given. I can honestly say I've never seen her smile so wide as the day she walked you down the aisle."

"Your brother has children. I'm sure that her grandchildren bring out that kind of joy."

Jason shook his head. "My statement stands. You're her little girl. My brother and I understand our place."

She laughed at that, and he watched as her shoulders eased. "Do you think Ruby was acting weird?"

Now it was his turn to stiffen as she abruptly changed the subject. "I don't know. Why do you say that?"

Lisa turned in her seat slightly to face him. "She's afraid you're not coming back. Or, if you do, you'll move out."

"I'm not going anywhere," Jason admitted, considering that it would be easier to tell his sister what was going on. But, he agreed with Ruby. This trip needed to be about Lisa seeing her family. There was time to tell her.

"I don't know what she does to her roommates that makes them hightail it out in the middle of the night after a few months. She's no stalker. She's not horribly messy. She's fair. She shares her food and makes enough money to pay for her half of things, though she doesn't even need a roommate if you ask me."

Jason laughed. "She is easy-going."

"Right? I mean, she's genuine. Ruby is that breath of fresh air. A little crude sometimes, but always saying what everyone else is thinking."

"She's been the perfect roommate."

"I think she needed you," Lisa said situating herself back

in her seat, her hand still in his. "She has us girls, but we're all married or engaged. She needs someone around that she can be friends with when we all can't be there for her."

Jason bit down on the inside of his cheek. "I'm happy to be her friend."

"How many rom coms have you had to watch?"

Jason snorted out a laugh. "I've lost count. You know she listens to them like some people listen to music?"

That made Lisa laugh. "That's our Ruby. She's a good person. Someday, she's going to make some man very happy."

Letting his shoulders drop, Jason eased back in his seat. Ruby was already there. She made Jason stupid happy, and it was right where he wanted to be.

* * *

MINDY WALKED THROUGH THE FRONT DOOR WITH CHINESE carry out and a box in the crook of her arm.

"True love is the man of your dreams offering to babysit his sisters' kids so they can go out, and then encouraging you to go have dinner with your friend," she said as she carried everything to the kitchen.

"Or, were you so worried about my mental health that you ditched him with a house full of kids to eat sodium rich food with me?"

Mindy wrinkled up her nose. "I promised him two hours tops, and I didn't want pizza."

Ruby laughed as she took the food from her. "What's in the box?"

A smile spread on Mindy's face. "That's a starter box, compliments of my mother."

Ruby's lips flattened. "Oh, no."

"Oh, yes," Mindy laughed as she set the box on the counter. "Open it."

"I'm afraid to."

"Nope. Starter box. You have to see what it is."

"Mindy, if I open this box and doll heads roll out on my counter, your fiancé is going to have to find your body before he can marry it."

Mindy laughed. "Just open the dang box, Rube."

Mindy's mother had an addiction to Christmas trees. She had them in every room of her house, and each one had a different theme. There was some torment over the Christmas trees and Ruby's particular dislike of the one that boasted small ceramic dolls. Though Mindy often reminded Ruby that her mother had that tree just because Ruby found it so appalling.

Carefully, Ruby opened the box and looked inside. Reaching in, she pulled out the ornaments. A TV. A cat, to which Mindy shrugged. A red car that could, sorta, resemble Ruby's Lexus, which she'd named Joellen. A doctor's coat and a stethoscope.

Lifting her eyes to Mindy's, Ruby narrowed her gaze.

Mindy raised her hands in surrender. "I didn't tell her anything." She made a criss cross sign over her heart. "I promise."

"Then why?"

"She assumes, as she said, that Jason will live here for a long time and you needed new ornaments for your Christmas tree."

"I don't put up a Christmas tree," Ruby reminded her. "I don't enjoy Christmas."

"Maybe this is my mother's way of telling you that you should. It's all in fun, Rube."

"It's August."

"It's never too early, according to my mother."

Ruby looked at the car ornament. "Now I have to get a tree."

Wrinkling up her nose again, Mindy shrugged. "I was sent with a tabletop one to get you started. This is important to her."

"And you didn't tell her anything?"

"Not a thing," Mindy promised again.

Ruby shook her head. "I guess there is no time like the present. Go get the stupid tree."

CHAPTER TWENTY-TWO

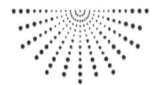

IT WOULD NEVER CEASE TO AMAZE JASON THAT PEOPLE recognized his sister on the streets—or in security lines at airports in London.

Lisa had been stopped twice. One woman wanted an autograph, the other a selfie.

"I didn't realize you were an international sensation," Jason mused as Lisa grabbed hold of his arm and giggled.

"I didn't either. That's so exciting. Not only do I make money on YouTube videos, but people actually watch them."

"Of course they do. And you're about to come face to face with your biggest fan," he said, noticing his father in the crowd of people waiting. Then he noticed the top of his mother's head. "How do you want to play this? I don't think he's seen me yet."

"I'll fall back a few steps. You get your hugs in and I'll walk up on you."

"Okay," he said as Lisa let go of him and disappeared into the crowd behind him.

As he neared his parents, Jason watched his father move

his mother into his line of sight, as if to give her the first run at him. When she could, that was what she did.

His mother took off toward him, nearly bowling him over with a hug.

"I've missed you. God, I've missed you," she said as she kissed his cheeks.

"I've missed you, too," he said, lifting his mother off the ground in an embrace.

As he set his mother down, his father's arms came around him, pulling him in and nearly smashing his mother between them.

"I've missed you too," his father said. "But now that you're here, she'll calm down a bit," he teased and Jason's mother slapped his father on the arm.

"I'll never get used to you with a beard," she said rubbing his unshaven cheeks.

"This is just a travel beard," he said. "But don't you think I'm handsome in it?"

"I don't care what you look like. I think you're handsome." She drew in a breath and scanned another look over him. "You couldn't convince her to come, huh?" his mother asked and he had to bite down on his lip because he'd seen Lisa skirt the crowd.

"He couldn't have kept me away," Lisa said from behind his parents, causing them both to turn around.

This time his father was faster, and he picked Lisa up off her feet and hugged her, just as Jason had done with his mother.

When he set Lisa on her feet, his mother had her in her tight embrace and he could hear her sob.

Lisa looked at Jason from over his mother's shoulder.

"My comment about knowing my place still stands," he teased as his mother held Lisa tightly against her.

. . .

JASON WASN'T SURE IF HIS MOTHER HAD TAKEN A BREATH FROM the time they'd left the airport until the moment they'd pulled up to the house.

"Okay, don't think I'm crazy, but I set up the guest bed in Ken's old room for you. Just in case he could convince you to come," his mother said as she opened her door.

"That was very thoughtful of you."

"No, it was selfish and fraught with the million wishes I sent into the heavens. I'm so happy you're here."

"So am I," Lisa said, and Jason's father opened her door and helped her from the car.

Jason moved in to help his mother from the car. "Take Lisa inside with you and I'll get her bags."

"Oh, I'm not being a very kind mother, am I?" She looked up at him with worry-filled eyes.

"It's okay. I wouldn't have brought her if my feelings were going to be hurt. She's our family. I know that. And you had me for years. And you'll have me in a week when she goes home."

His mother nodded her acceptance of that as Lisa cleared the back of the car and came to stand with them.

"C'mon, darling." His mother looped her arm through Lisa's. "I know you're exhausted, but let's have a cuppa."

Jason watched them walk up the front steps and into the house as his father opened the back of the car and began to unload their luggage.

"How'd you get her here?" his father asked. "I thought she was terrified of flying."

Jason chuckled. "She still is. She had a few moments on the plane. But Ryan made it all happen to get her here. He was fully supportive of it."

"He seems like a great guy," his father said, setting down the heavy suitcase and reaching for the other.

"He is. He and his brother became quick friends of mine. I've been part of some very big moments in the past year."

"I'm glad. We miss you like crazy, but I'm proud of you, son." His father lowered the hatch and stood there for another moment. "She's going to cry for the better part of three weeks. She's happy for you, and she got lots of practice not having you around when you were military. But she misses you."

"I know she does."

"She's missed Lisa too—for years. You bringing her is a gift I could never give her."

Jason swallowed hard. He knew his father had worked for years just to make ends meet for them, and as hard as he tried, he just couldn't make it so that they could bring Lisa with them.

"I think that it's just the start of her visits," Jason promised. "Now that she's flown here, she knows it's not too bad. And with it only being you and Mom, you can come out and see us too. We have her back."

"We owe that to you."

"No, I'm just lucky to be part of her day to day. She wants to be part of all of this, the girls want that for her, and luckily so does her husband. I think we're whole again, Dad. It just took a little while to make it happen."

Jason picked up his bag as his father struggled with Lisa's, proudly making it to the front door and just far enough inside to drop it.

"Go have some tea with your mother and your sister. I'm going to go call Ken and let him know you arrived."

Considering his father's words, Jason took his phone out of his pocket and texted Ruby. *We're here and home. Mom hasn't let go of Lisa since she saw her. I'll call you later. I love you.*

Tucking his phone back into his pocket, he took a

moment to breathe in the scents of the home he'd spent so many years in. Somehow having Lisa there with him made it feel different. He'd meant what he'd said to his father. As a family, they were whole again.

CHAPTER TWENTY-THREE

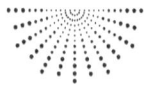

THE CONVERSATION IN THE KITCHEN WAS LIVELY. THERE WAS laughter, and Jason's mother hiccupped with tears.

Jason leaned himself in the doorjamb, crossing his feet at the ankles and his arms in front of him. The smile on his face was genuine pleasure at seeing the two women together, at home.

His mother had dreamed of this moment for so many years. He was glad he was there to witness it.

His mother reached for a napkin from the holder and dabbed at her eyes. "I can't believe you're here. I can't believe I've seen you twice in a year," she sobbed and laughed. "I'm so happy for you. I watch your cooking channel every day. I rewatch old videos when there are no new ones."

That had Lisa laughing and now wiping tears from her eyes, to which his mother pulled out another napkin and handed it to Lisa.

"And your husband? Everything is good in your marriage?" his mother asked.

Reaching for their mother's hands, Lisa held them in hers as she inched closer to her. "Everything is perfect. He's everything I could ever have dreamed of," Lisa said. "And he's why I'm here. I'm mean, aside from him making sure I had a ticket. I wanted to come and share something with you."

"What's that?"

Lisa drew in a breath and Jason watched as her face lit and her smile widened. "I wanted you to be the first to know that we're expecting a baby."

As his mother gasped and sobbed, pulling Lisa into her, Jason stepped into the kitchen to Lisa's eyes going wide.

"You're having a baby?" he nearly shouted.

Lisa blinked hard, his mother still wrapped in her arms. "You were eavesdropping?"

"I was fully in the room," he admitted as his mother eased back from Lisa and wiped away her tears. "Neither of you were paying attention."

"I'm so happy for you," his mother sobbed. "You're going to be a wonderful mother."

Lisa wiped her own tears and turned back to their mother. "I hope so."

"No, you *will* be. Sweetheart, your giving heart and compassion for people always astounded me. You had no reason to love or trust, but you did. And now you're going to love your own little one. I'm going to love your own little one."

His mother waved her hands in front of her face as if it would dry the tears.

His mother reached out for him. "You'll be there to help her, right? You'll get her the care she needs?"

Jason chuckled. "She'll be fine, but yes," he agreed, raising his eyes to his sister. "I'll make sure she's taken care of. And now you can visit just like you planned."

The laughter started, and his mother covered her mouth with her hands.

"I'd visit you too, you know," she confessed.

"Yeah, but Lisa's baby takes priority, I know." He moved from his mother and reached for Lisa's hand, easing her to her feet. "So this is why you didn't want me to give you anything for your anxiety?"

She nodded. "We're not even through our first trimester. Everything is iffy."

"Everything is going to be fine," he said pulling her to him. "I'm so happy for you both."

"Me too," she whispered into his ear.

He heard his mother hiccup her sob again as his father walked into the room.

"She's going to be sobbing like this all week, isn't she?" his father asked, placing his hand on his wife's shoulder.

"Oh, I deserve it." His mother lifted her eyes to Lisa, who nodded her consent for her to share Lisa's news. "Our Lisa is having a baby."

"No kidding?" His father moved to Lisa and wrapped her in a hug. "Well, that just made this trip even more special. Congratulations."

"Thank you," Lisa said softly against his chest.

Jason watched as his mother pulled another napkin from the holder and wiped at her eyes. "Our Lisa is having a baby. Ken has a full house. And Jason and Ruby are together. Everything is just—"

Simultaneously, Lisa and Jason turned toward their mother and said, "What?"

She studied them both.

Lisa's eyes shifted from him to their mother. "Ruby and Jason are what?"

"They're together," their mother said. "You haven't told her yet?"

"I didn't tell you that," Jason confirmed.

The smile on his mother's face widened. "Sweetheart, you didn't have to tell me. I talked to the two of you." When her cheeks blushed, he wasn't sure he wanted her to say anything more, but she took a breath and continued. "I saw how she came to your door before you closed it." She paused and lifted her brows. "And then how you kept her close while we talked. Honey, I know what those looks were."

Now he felt his own skin go warm.

Lisa turned to him, a crease deepening between her brows. "Are you kidding me with this?"

Their father reached for their mother. "C'mon, Rosie, let's give these kiddos some time to work through this."

Jason watched as his mother stood, her face carrying concern for what she'd said, but he nodded softly and smiled, hoping to let her know it was okay.

Once their parents had left the kitchen, Lisa's palms came to his chest and shoved him back.

"Are you kidding me?"

Jason found his footing as she came at him again, but he caught her hands this time.

"Why don't you settle down?" he offered.

"Settle down? I have to come to London to find out you're sleeping with my best friend?"

"I don't think that's what Mom said."

"That's exactly what she said," Lisa argued. "You're sleeping with Ruby?"

Jason swallowed hard, Lisa's wrists still gripped in his hands. "I'm in love with Ruby."

Her mouth dropped open and she blinked hard. "You're what?"

"I'm in love with Ruby," he said again, easing his grip. "And yes," he swallowed hard, "I'm sleeping with her."

Lisa opened her mouth, closed it again, and then opened it one more time. "Since when?"

Jason let out a slow breath and moved his hands from his sister's wrists to hold her hands in his. "Since movie night."

Then he wrinkled his nose. "No," he laughed. "That got interrupted."

"This isn't funny."

"No. It's not." Still holding on to one of her hands, Jason pulled out a chair and offered it to Lisa. He then sat down next to her. "I made a move on movie night. It finally happened after dinner with you and Ryan."

Her face still showed nothing but disgust for the situation, but he'd promised Ruby Lisa would be happy for them. So, until she was, he was going to sit there and explain it to her.

"I can't believe this," she said.

"Why not? Ruby's a great gal."

"I know that," she argued. "It's just, well, everyone else seems to overlook her. I mean, they'll flirt with her at the bar and then make a move on one of us." She tossed her head from side to side. "Okay, they used to make moves on us. We don't give off those vibes anymore."

Jason chuckled. "No, you don't."

"You're in love with her?"

"I am." He squeezed Lisa's hand. "Because what's not to love?"

Tears were welling in her eyes again, and she was blinking them away. "You're right. What's not to love?"

"I didn't want to tell you yet because I wanted this to be a special trip. And I didn't know you were going to shell out your own truth bomb."

Lisa pursed her lips and then smiled. "I wanted Mama Rose to be the first person we told. Ryan agreed."

"I didn't mean to eavesdrop."

She leaned in and pressed her forehead to his. "It's okay. It made it a special moment."

"I didn't mean to have it ruined by Mom figuring out what was going on with me and Ruby."

Now Lisa laughed fully, the tears drying as she did so. "I'm conflicted," she admitted holding up a finger and taking a breath. "But I can't think of anyone I'd rather have love Ruby than you."

"That means a lot."

"She means a lot."

Jason nodded. "She sure does."

CHAPTER TWENTY-FOUR

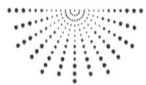

JASON HADN'T SLEPT AS WELL AS HE'D HAVE HOPED TO, BUT waking to the smells coming from the kitchen made him happy. Even better was seeing his mother standing over the stove making pancakes and a pile of scrambled eggs.

"Does Dad get fed like this every day now?" he asked, walking up behind her and kissing her on the cheek.

"This is special. Ken and his family are on their way over and Lisa is taking a shower."

"So I'm late getting up?" He took a piece of bacon from a plate and bit the end off.

"I don't think Lisa was feeling well this morning. I gave her some tea which I always kept on hand for Julie when she was pregnant," she offered, mentioning his sister-in-law.

"That was some news, huh?" Jason took another bite of the bacon.

"The best news. That's going to be one very loved little baby."

The smile on his mother's face made him smile too. Yeah, he and Ken knew their place, he humored to himself, but they knew that Rose Hughes' heart had enough love for hundreds more—that's how lucky they were to have her.

She eyed him cautiously. "You didn't know she was pregnant? What kind of doctor are you?"

He chewed thoughtfully. "A very good one whose sister didn't act pregnant around him." Jason leaned his hip against the counter watching as his mother stirred the eggs. "So, about what you saw with me and Ruby…"

His mother's lips pursed. "I shouldn't have said anything. I didn't have the information, and—"

"I'm in love with her, Mom."

His mother turned her head to look up at him, still keenly aware of her eggs and the pancake she was cooking.

"You're in love with her?"

"I am."

She cleared her throat, which he was sure had clogged with tears. "Are you happy?"

"I am. Ruby is quite a woman."

Flipping the pancake, she then scooped the eggs onto a waiting platter. "And what did Lisa think?"

"She's mad we didn't tell her."

"I'm sorry."

Jason took the platter and set it on the table. "We chose to keep the secret. It was bound to come out. I'm not so sure one of the girls doesn't know. Mindy, I think."

"You don't know?"

He shrugged. "I think I was a little too obvious about my feelings, and I didn't much care who knew," he chuckled. "But Lisa just wants what's best for Ruby."

"And that's you?"

"I sure hope it is."

* * *

THEY'D SPENT THE ENTIRE DAY WITH HIS FAMILY, AND JET LAG was beginning to set in. His mother had nudged him more than once when he'd fallen asleep while they visited and the kids were trying to keep his attention.

When his phone rang, Jason excused himself and walked out the back door. Waiting to be accepted was a video call from Ruby.

"Hey, gorgeous," he said looking at the screen which only showed the ceiling in her bedroom. "Ruby?"

"Hold on. I hit call before I was ready, and you picked up fast."

"What do you need to be ready for?" he asked, sitting on the step.

He watched as the phone was moved and he saw the floor, then the wall, and then Ruby lifted the phone to show him a view of her in the mirror.

She was wearing one of his T-shirts, specifically one he'd bought in Breckenridge the year before when he'd arrived in Colorado and had gone skiing. She had it tied in a knot to her side, and only wore a pair of pink panties.

Every nerve in his body woke at the sight of her.

"What are you doing?" he asked as he watched her model in the mirror.

"I'm missing you horribly. Do you know how many T-shirts you have?"

"No. Did you count them?"

She giggled. "Sort of. I've tried every single one of them on."

Jason adjusted himself, because damn!

"Did you call me to just make me crazy?"

She looked into the mirror, still focused on her scantily clad body, and winked. "Is it working?"

"Uh, yeah," he choked out the words.

"I don't want you to forget me."

"I promise. That's not going to happen."

Ruby turned around the phone. "Are you alone?"

"Yes."

The phone was set down again, this time camera down so the screen went dark. When she turned the phone back over and aimed it at the mirror, she was now only in her pink panties.

"Oh, God, Ruby," Jason growled out the words. "You're killing me."

"Good. But did I surprise you?"

"Yes," the word came out airy and strained.

She focused the camera in on certain parts of her now nearly naked body, and Jason had to bite down on his lip. He was going to need to find some alone time.

Just as he took a breath to say something dirty to her, he heard Lisa from behind him.

"Ruby Jean!" she shouted and he noticed that Ruby's phone had been dropped and was now face down on the floor. His, on the other hand, shook in his hand.

"Don't you dare disconnect that call," Lisa threatened as she sat down next to Jason on the step.

She pulled his phone from his hand and waited for Ruby to reappear, which took at least a full minute. When she did reappear, she had on clothes, and her face was nearly as red as her hair.

"Hey, Lees," she said, but Jason noticed the twitching in her upper lip.

"Do you want to explain yourself?" Lisa asked and Jason nudged her trying to get her to ease off of Ruby, but she held up a finger to him.

"Not really."

"Are you fucking my brother?"

Ruby's mortified look was nearly more than Jason could handle. He had to give her some peace.

"She knows," he said loudly, though Lisa was moving the phone further from him so that he wasn't on camera.

"What?" Ruby shouted.

"I know!" Lisa shouted back, but then her face softened and she actually kissed the phone with a noisy kiss. "I know you're fucking my brother," she said into the microphone, very clearly.

"Oh, God!" Ruby pressed her hand to her forehead. "You told her?" She directed the question toward Jason so Lisa turned the phone to include him.

"My mother outed us."

Now Ruby's eyes went wide. "How? What? Oh, shit! I told you she saw me."

The laugh that now came from his sister was nearly infectious, well, at least to him.

"I think it's wonderful," Lisa said smiling. "I'm mad that you didn't tell me, but it's okay."

"Lisa, I—we—didn't want to hurt you. I didn't want you to feel like Tina did when you—"

"I don't," Lisa interrupted. "I wish you had just told me."

"It's new."

"I know." Lisa turned the phone so that Jason was in the picture too. "He's a good guy. I'll vouch for him."

Ruby finally smiled. "I know he is."

"And, since I wrecked his little striptease. I'll let him tell you a secret."

Jason shook his head, but Lisa nodded handing him the phone.

"What secret?" Ruby asked as he and Lisa exchanged understanding glances.

"She's torturing us, you know," he said.

"I can tell."

"She's making me tell you a secret that you can't tell, right?" he asked clarifying, and Lisa nodded. "Okay, so you can't tell anyone."

"Jesus, Jason, what is it?"

He drew in a breath. "My sister is knocked up."

CHAPTER TWENTY-FIVE

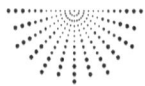

RUBY SAT DOWN ON THE EDGE OF HER BED AND WATCHED AS Lisa punched Jason in the arm for the way he shared her secret.

"You're pregnant?" she asked almost too softly for them to hear over their nudging one another out of the camera's view.

But the camera finally landed on Lisa, and she smiled wide. "I am. I wanted to tell Mama Rose first, and this jack hole overheard."

"Wow. You're having a baby."

Ruby's throat was clogged with tears, and she wasn't sure why they stung. God, she was happy for her best friend —ecstatic.

But something twisted up inside of her that nearly made her sick. Was she jealous? Jealous of a woman who was in a loving marriage? Jealous that Lisa was going to have a baby of her own to raise in a stable household surrounded by love? Jealous that she'd told someone else the news first?

"I'm going to celebrate with the three of you when I get

home. Like the minute I get home next week. Don't tell the girls, okay?"

All Ruby could do was nod, working to keep the tears at bay. This was torture, and this was Lisa's plan.

"Are you okay?" Lisa asked, looking into the camera as if she were searching for something.

"I'm fine. A little more emotional than I thought I'd be with such amazing news, but I'm good."

Lisa nodded slowly. "I love you, Rube. I'll let you have a minute with your boy toy," she laughed and kissed the phone again. "By the way, you'd better treat him nice. Spoil him. Buy him pretty things. Show him a *good* time," she added as Jason pulled the phone from her and she kissed the top of his head before going back into the house.

When Jason had the phone back and was looking at Ruby, she let out a long breath.

"I'm pretty sure I'm going to have a breakdown," she admitted.

"Why's that?"

"Well, your mother knew what was going on," Ruby said, narrowing her eyes at Jason, to which he only shrugged.

"She's an observant kind of woman."

Ruby let out a hum and pursed her lips. "I miss you terribly."

"I miss you too."

"Are you going to let me have my breakdown?"

Jason chuckled. "Continue, ma'am."

"So your mother knows what's going on. Lisa knows what's going on. You're in a whole other country, thousands of miles away, and my striptease went horribly wrong." She let out another breath and the smiled. "And Lisa is pregnant."

Jason smiled back at her. "That's some amazing news."

"She's going to be the best mom."

"I think she will too. And as you might imagine, my mother is over the moon."

Ruby finally laughed though the twisting in her gut tightened. "I'm glad she waited to share that with Mama Rose. That was important for her to do."

"I still can't tell if I ruined the moment or if it was perfect," he admitted.

"I'll bet it was perfect."

Jason nodded and then turned his head toward the door Lisa had walked back through. "I hear little voices looking for me. I guess I should get back inside."

Ruby nodded, now fighting the wave of tears that wanted to break through.

"Yeah. Three weeks, I'll have you all to myself."

"You sure will. Maybe you should take a few days off when I get home. I won't want to be out of your sight."

Ruby was smiling so wide her cheeks hurt. "I'll see what I can do."

"I love you," he said softly, staring at her through the phone, halfway across the world.

"I love you too."

Jason disconnected the call, but Ruby sat with her phone in her hand and just stared down at it. She was humiliated that Lisa had seen what she was doing, and conflicted with knowing Lisa was pregnant and not able to talk to anyone about it.

She squeezed her eyes shut.

She'd brought all of this on herself. She should have made sure that Jason was alone before she started taking off her clothes, and by *sure*, she should have made sure he was alone in a room with the door shut and locked.

Laying back on her bed, she held her phone to her chest. Okay, their secret was out now. Not only did Lisa know she was seeing Jason, but his mother had caught on. God, what had she seen?

Ruby tried to remember the moment. She had on clothes, right? Sort of, she remembered. God, no, she'd only had on a T-shirt, tied up so that her panties were very visible.

She felt sick inside.

Surely, Mama Rose had taken it in stride. Her son was old enough to have an adult relationship.

Ruby cringed. She was a ho! Mama Rose thought Ruby was a ho!

She shook the thought from her head. No.

They'd exchanged the words. Jason loved her. She loved Jason. They were consenting adults.

Ruby sat up, brushing her hair from her face.

She needed a movie.

Taking the quilt off her bed, and grabbing her pillow, Ruby walked to the living room and deposited the bedding on the couch. Then she walked to the kitchen and made herself a cup of coffee and devoured a granola bar.

Walking back to the living room, she smacked her shin on the end of the couch, sloshing coffee onto the quilt.

The tears came right away. Not because of the pain in her leg, or the spilled coffee. She was lonely.

Ruby set the mug on the coffee table and fell onto the couch, kicking the damp quilt on the floor.

"This is ridiculous!" she shouted to herself.

Refusing to wipe away the tears, she just let them fall. She'd been lonely for thirty years, this shouldn't faze her. But loving someone and not being able to just reach out and touch them, seemed to be suffocating to her. And knowing Lisa's secret, now that was a shit move.

Laughter broke through the tears.

Actually, Ruby deserved that.

She picked up the remote and turned on the TV. Scrolling through her list of movies, she settled on *Failure to Launch*, and pressed play. Some asinine Matthew McConaughey rom com humor was exactly what she needed.

As the opening credits began, Ruby carried the quilt to the washer and shoved it in. Once the washer was started, she went into Jason's room and stripped off his comforter. She needed to be wrapped in him today, which was going to be a quiet thoughtful day. Though her thoughts were dark and self-deprecating.

She was going to be joyous for Lisa, and grateful that she was the only one who saw Ruby's striptease.

A laugh finally bubbled from her as she wrapped the comforter around her and fell onto the couch.

As the movie started, Ruby picked up her phone and scrolled through Jason's Instagram again. Her lip trembled when she realized he'd done some housekeeping. Gone were any pictures of him with anyone other than Ruby, Lisa, his family, or times when he was with Ruby and her friends and their significant others.

Squeezing her eyes shut, she held her phone to her chest. She was the only woman in his life, she considered, outside of family. Ruby was that important to him that he'd erased any other women.

God, she was in deep now.

Rolling over to her side, she set her phone on the floor and watched the movie in the dimly lit condo.

Was she ready to be someone's *only*? That was a stupid question. Of course she was. Wasn't that what she'd always wanted? It just never had worked out that way for her.

And was that need to have it what made her jealous over Lisa's pregnancy news? Was she jealous? Yeah, she was.

It wasn't that she wanted or needed a baby—it was that she wanted that kind of love.

The knot in her stomach grew tighter. She had that kind of love.

Jason loved her. He loved her just as Aaron loved Tina, Ryan loved Lisa, and Vic loved Mindy.

She sat up on the couch and inhaled the scent from his comforter.

Jason loved her.

And she loved him.

The next three weeks were going to go by so slowly that it was going to kill her.

She lifted the comforter up over her head and stayed that way while Sarah Jessica Parker tried to convince Matthew McConaughey she was in love with him in order to make him move out of his parents' home.

CHAPTER TWENTY-SIX

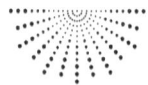

WITH HER PURSE SLIDING OFF HER SHOULDER, A STRAY STRAND of hair tickling her nose, her phone clutched in one hand, and her coffee cup clutched in the other, Ruby managed her way into her office.

"Corporate is calling for a meeting at nine," Will, Ruby's assistant followed her into her office.

"Why?"

"I didn't ask questions. I just answered the phone," he said reaching for her coffee to help her set down her items without spilling it.

"We are on time and under budget."

Will shrugged. "Caitlyn is setting up the call, Brandy went out for donuts."

Ruby shook her head. "Cuz that's going to keep us focused?"

"Everyone is just trying to help."

"Maybe we should be focused on the project. That would help. I mean corporate wanting a call isn't a positive, right?"

A crease formed between his brows. "I don't remember

you being so pessimistic. I would have thought if you ended up in a relationship, it would boost your spirits."

Ruby dropped her purse in her chair and clenched her phone tighter in her hand. "I beg your pardon?"

Will shook his head, set her coffee on the desk, and turned toward the door. "We have fifteen minutes before the call. Pull yourself together and we can have this discussion later."

Will closed the door behind him, leaving Ruby alone in her office.

She could fire his ass, she thought as she picked up her coffee, and set it right back down, afraid she'd spill it because her hand shook.

Will was blunt and honest. Usually, she appreciated that, but today, not so much. Besides, how did he know she was involved with someone? Who the hell did he talk to?

She only had a few minutes left to collect herself. Corporate could just be calling to congratulate them on the work they were doing.

Yeah, she would put her positive spin on it. She had to or she'd go crazy.

Just as she collected her most recent notes, her phone rang, and she answered it without even looking at the name on the screen.

"Yep," she answered as she sorted through her notes.

"Ruby Jean, is that how we answer a phone?" Her mother's voice rang in her ear and she winced. God, she didn't have time for this right now.

"Mom, I'm headed into a meeting and—"

"You're always too busy for me."

Ruby set her notes on the desk and picked up that coffee. "What are you talking about? I was at your house yesterday."

"Yes, but I know you're home alone every night, and you don't come by."

"Mom, I see you four or five times a week."

"You only come over to take things out of my house. I'm missing a set of teacups."

Ruby picked up her purse, dropped it on the floor, and sat down in her chair. "Mom, I took them. Aunt Jose gave them to me. She said you had multiple sets."

"Oh, that bitch!"

"Mom!"

"She's always giving my stuff away. That's why I told her to never come back here."

"She lives there."

"Well, not anymore. I'm calling a locksmith to change the locks."

Ruby's office door opened and Will poked his head in and tapped his finger to his wrist.

She nodded and he shook his head before shutting the door again.

"Listen, Mom, I have to go."

"Of course you do. You don't love me. You never visit."

Ruby felt her jaw go slack and before she could respond, her mother had ended the call. *Shit!*

Squeezing her eyes shut tightly she swallowed down the lump that was forming in her throat and choking her. Her mother needed her. Something was wrong. But if she didn't get her ass into that meeting, everything in her life was going to spiral out of control.

A moment later her phone buzzed in her hand again. This time it was Jason. All she wanted to do was answer his call, but because she could see Will pacing in the hallway, she silenced the ringer, picked up her notes, and headed to the conference room.

. . .

THE CORPORATE CALL WASN'T TO CONGRATULATE THEM ON doing a great job, no, it was a complete blind side change of goals and procedures to Ruby's project. *Her project.*

It was a shitty start to her week, and even shittier was the call she'd received before the meeting. Ruby should have been on her toes, instead, she worried about her mother. What in the hell had all of that been about?

Ruby dropped her notes on her desk, picked up her phone, and called her aunt.

"Ruby, she's resting. She's fine," her aunt assured her.

"Fine? She was hysterical when she called me less than an hour ago. She was going to kick you out of the house and change the locks. She was accusing me of only visiting so that I could take things out of her house."

"I know," her aunt sighed. "She's done this a few times."

"What? Why don't I know that?"

"There's nothing to worry about."

Ruby ran her hand over her face. "She's seventy-five-years-old. Yes, there is something to worry about," she argued with her aunt. "Listen, I'm in crisis mode at work. I can't drop it to come over right now. She's safe and resting?"

"Yes."

"I'm coming over the moment I leave here. Don't let her go anywhere."

"I promise."

"If something happens, call me."

"I will, darling."

"I'm going to make her a doctor appointment for tomorrow. Can you take her?"

"Ruby, she's fine."

Ruby's entire body shook. "If you can't take her, I'll—"

"Of course I'll take her. Ruby, I just don't want you to worry about this," her aunt said. "Our mother went through this too."

Ruby leaned her head back against her chair and closed her eyes. She remembered her grandmother vaguely. Ruby had been very young when she'd died, but she remembered thinking her grandmother was fun. Fun, because she was childlike. Only as she got older did she learn that her grandmother had dementia, so what had seemed silly and childlike was actually a disease taking the life from her.

Swallowing hard, Ruby composed herself. "Auntie, I'll be there this evening. Just take care of her. Don't leave her alone."

"I promise, sweetheart."

"I love you."

"I love you too."

CHAPTER TWENTY-SEVEN

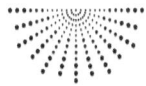

AT HER MOTHER'S KITCHEN TABLE, RUBY SIPPED THE HORRIBLY strong coffee her aunt had made her to start her morning.

She'd slept on her mother's couch for the past two nights, and as she tried to force herself to wake up, she scrolled through her phone.

I miss you. I love you. Let me know you're okay.

The text had come in sometime during the night, but Ruby had never heard her phone buzz. Of course, she hadn't actually fallen asleep until nearly one, and here it was six and she needed to be focused.

Her mother's episode from Monday had been forgotten, by her mother, but Ruby couldn't forget it. She also couldn't get her mother a doctor's appointment until Friday. Therefore, she was sleeping on her mother's couch because she wasn't fully sure she could trust her aunt to not brush off another of her mother's episodes.

"Since when did she stop getting up at the crack of dawn?" Ruby asked as she scrolled through the other texts that had come from Jason during the night.

If it's any consolation, Lisa doesn't handle morning sickness well, he'd texted and added a laughing emoji.

She needed to respond to him. She just didn't want to fall apart when she did. But she'd been ignoring his calls for days.

Jose walked toward the table, carrying her own cup of coffee. "She's become something of a night owl."

"That's not like her."

"She wanders the house until the wee hours and sleeps in," Jose said, as she poured ample amounts of sugar into the bitter coffee.

"You didn't think that was a bit weird?"

Jose shrugged. "My sister has always been on the odd side." She winced as if she reconsidered that. "I mean that she changes. Her sleep schedule, her eating schedule, her moods."

"I don't remember her being quite this bad."

"She's going to be okay, Ruby," her aunt promised, resting her hand atop Ruby's.

"I'm just not so sure about that," Ruby said as her phone buzzed again.

Call me when you can. I love you.

"I'm going to take a walk before I get ready for work." Ruby stood and kissed her aunt on the top of the head.

After putting on her shoes, and tying a sweatshirt around her waist, Ruby headed out of the house with her earbuds in and phone in her hand.

Because she wanted to see his face, Ruby video called Jason.

"Hey," he said before his face even came into view. "Tell me you're okay."

Ruby studied his bearded face, and immediately began to cry.

"Whoa," Jason's voice soothed through her ear buds. "What's going on?"

Ruby realized that in the two minutes that she'd been walking, she'd nearly been running she was walking so fast. She slowed, and sniffed back her tears.

"I'm sorry I didn't return your calls or texts."

"Just tell me I didn't do something wrong," he said, and she watched as he climbed into a car and closed the door. It humored her when she realized how small the car was, how big he seemed, and that he was on the wrong side.

At that point, she actually let out a little chuckle.

"There's just been a lot going on."

"Okay, tell me about it."

Ruby shook her head. "Really it's nothing. I miss you."

"I miss you too. Now tell me what's been going on."

She couldn't walk any further because she was ready to have a breakdown. Turning at the next corner, she headed toward the small neighborhood park and sat down on the bench as she spilled the news to him of everything that had been happening the past few days with her job and her mother.

"Ruby, that's a lot to handle. Have you talked to Mindy or Tina?"

She shook her head. "I've been focusing on Mom and trying not to lose my shit on my team."

Jason let out a slow breath. "I'm going to come home with Lisa."

"Like hell you will. If I knew you were going to say that, I wouldn't have called you. Don't you dare," she realized she was nearly shouting when the group of middle schoolers standing at the bus stop, much too early she thought, looked toward her. "You are there to be with your family. I'll kick your ass out if you come home early."

"Ruby—"

"I mean it. Don't you dare. This is all stuff I can handle. I'm just overwhelmed at this very moment."

He nodded. "You have appointments with her doctor? They need to know."

"Friday."

"Okay. Document it all. Your instincts are right, none of this is normal," he said calmly, but she understood what he was telling her.

Jason watched her, a smile finally curling up the corner of his mouth. "You're beautiful."

"Bullshit," she coughed out the word on a laugh, and then realized that was much too loud when a parent with the kids looked at her.

Ruby stood and headed back toward her mother's.

"I appreciate that," she said as she walked. "And I like the beard."

"Do you?"

"I do. It's sexy."

"As sexy as that bra you had on the other day?"

Ruby felt her cheeks heat as she passed by more kids walking toward the bus stop. "Maybe we can revisit that someday."

Jason sighed. "Maybe someday very soon, especially if I'm not allowed to come home early."

"Promise me you'll stay with your family. I'm impatient, but I'll be okay."

"I promise," he said. "I love you."

Ruby stood in front of her mother's house. "I love you too."

"Call me again, no matter what time it is here."

"I will."

"I'm going to hold you to that. And don't think I won't call Mindy or Tina to find you if you don't."

Ruby laughed. "I'm sure you will."

"Call them. Let them hear what's going on."

Ruby took in a breath. "I will."

They exchanged a few more *I love you*s, and Ruby walked up the front steps of her mother's house. She stopped at the top and texted Mindy and Tina.

Can you girls meet for lunch downtown today?

Before she'd even made it into the house, she received a reply from each of them.

Yes! Tina had sent.

I'll be there. Everything okay? Mindy added.

Ruby stepped into the house, kicked off her shoes, and leaned back against the door after closing it.

It will be after I spend some time with both of you.

CHAPTER TWENTY-EIGHT

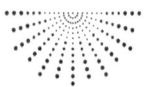

Ruby had left the office early and claimed a booth at the diner down the street. Tina wasn't currently working, and Mindy had a very flexible schedule, so she knew having them meet her near her office wouldn't be too hard.

Her hands had shaken all day, and though she'd been delighted to have checked off many of the items on corporate's new list, she still felt as if she hadn't done anything at all.

She'd called her aunt every hour since she'd left the house to check on her mother too, who hadn't climbed out of bed until eleven. That was simply unheard of in Mindy's world. As a tired teenager, her mother wouldn't let her sleep past eight.

Ruby looked toward the door just as her friends walked in. The tears that had been sitting in her chest rose to her throat and threatened. God, she wasn't some fricking baby! But she just couldn't stop crying.

"Hey," Tina gleefully scooted into to booth followed by Mindy.

"Where's your daughter," Ruby asked.

"My mother wanted some time alone with her," she said grinning. "I'm free for a few hours."

"I'm only free for one," Ruby admitted and picked up the menu she not only knew by heart, but that she'd been reading for the past fifteen minutes.

Mindy looked over the menu. "Are their salads good here?"

"You can eat a real meal," Tina said, never looking at her.

"I just bought the most expensive dress I'm ever going to own, and I'm damn well going to fit into it."

Tina shook her head. "Trust me. You will."

Ruby listened to the banter and suddenly, those tears broke through the dam.

Both women across from her dropped their menus. Mindy slid out of her booth and right around to Ruby's side, wrapping her arm around Ruby's shoulders.

"What's wrong?" Mindy asked, reaching for a napkin and handing it to Ruby to wipe her tears.

"I'm just having a week. I didn't mean to burst into tears like that."

"It's okay."

Tina pushed her water closer to Ruby. "Take a sip."

Ruby lifted the water with her shaky hands and sipped. Then she let out a steadying breath. "I'm okay. Really."

"Jason?" Mindy asked softly, and then when she did both she and Ruby looked at Tina when she gasped.

"Did the bastard move out and move back to England?" Tina growled.

For a moment Ruby just stared at her friend realizing now that Tina was the only one not in on it. She batted her stinging eyes, and her lips twitched until they turned up into a smile. Then she laughed.

Mindy laughed too.

"What's going on?" Tina asked. "Seriously. What does all of this have to do with Jason? Your roommate, right?"

Ruby and Mindy exchanged glances, and Ruby nodded, giving Mindy permission to give up her secret.

"Ruby's been shagging her roommate."

Tina's eyes went wide, and then grew wider. "Are you kidding me?"

Ruby shook her head.

"Lisa is going to kill you."

Ruby let out a slow and calming breath. "She knows."

Mindy eased back. "She does?"

Pursing her lips, Ruby tried to keep her smile from surfacing, but now it was too funny. "I was kinda trying to be sexy, and I video called him and took off my clothes."

"And she saw?" Tina leaned in on the table.

Nodding, Ruby bit down on her bottom lip, and wiped her cheeks with the napkin. "Yes. I seem to not be too stealthy. His mother was the one that outed us, because she saw me open his bedroom door in my underwear," she winced.

"No!" Mindy covered her mouth with her hands. "You slut."

Ruby couldn't even take offense to it. Instead she laughed. She laughed hard, and for the first time since Jason had left, she felt lighter.

The waitress came and took their order, and they were all still laughing after she'd walked away. But when they'd caught their breath, that crushing feeling took over again.

"This is more than missing your sex toy," Mindy said.

"He's not just my sex toy."

Tina took a sip of her water. "This is serious?"

"I think it is. He says he loves me."

Placing her hand on her chest, Tina batted her eyes that welled now too. "That is precious."

Ruby nodded, and then wiped her damp eyes again. "Work is really hard right now, but there's something going on with my mom too."

Mindy ran a hand over Ruby's hair, then clasped both her hands in her lap. "What's going on with your mom?"

"She's confused."

"Like, just because she's old, confused?"

Ruby shrugged, picked up the water and sipped. "I don't know. Right before a big meeting yesterday she called and accused me of stealing things from her house. Then she was going to kick her sister out of the house and change the locks."

"Something's wrong. You're right. That's strange behavior for your mom. When people get older, and their behavior changes like that, it's usually a sign. You need to have her seen," Tina said as she rearranged the silverware on the table as if it were her nervous habit.

"I know. Jason says something is wrong too. I couldn't get her into the doctor until Friday. So I've been sleeping on her couch."

"No wonder you look exhausted." Tina's lips twitched again before a smile spread. "That or because you're doing stripteases in the middle of the night because your sex toy is out of the country."

Both Mindy and Ruby watched Tina after she'd made such an uncharacteristic comment. Her cheeks flushed, and she sucked in her lips to keep from smiling.

"Sorry," she managed before breaking into another fit of laughter. "Oh, God, I'm sorry."

Ruby, joining in the laughter, reached across the table and took Tina's hands. Yes, this was just what she needed. It would only be better if Lisa were there with them, but Ruby's heart didn't ache as much as it had when she'd arrived.

And just because Lisa wasn't there, Ruby considered outing her secret too, but she couldn't betray Lisa's trust.

On Saturday they'd do movie night at Tina's and Lisa would be home. In two more weeks her *sex toy* would be home too. The project at work was tougher now, but not impossible, and her mother—well, they would work through that. Whatever her mother needed, Ruby would make sure she had. But at the moment, Ruby needed her own support, and that was exactly what she had.

CHAPTER TWENTY-NINE

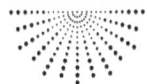

It was stupid early o'clock when Ruby's phone chimed.

She's on her way home to you. I sent her with presents.

Ruby rubbed her eyes and read the text again and again. As she settled back onto the couch, and against her pillow with her phone, her body felt lighter.

You don't happen to be in her suitcase, do you? Ruby typed then thought better of it. That sounded needy. As she moved her semi-working thumb toward the delete button, she hit send.

Shit! She sat up, feeling the need to scramble and rethink what she'd said. She wasn't going to be that woman. The one in a new relationship that needed a man to be in her presence at all times.

I considered it, he texted back, and that put her at ease, until the FaceTime app rang.

Oh hell no. She wasn't going to turn on that camera, but she really wanted to look at his handsome, bearded face.

Taking her blanket and draping it over her head, she finally pushed the connection button.

"Hey there…" he paused and looked at the screen. "Why is it so dark and you're under a blanket?"

"Well, stranger from another land, it's only four o'clock in the morning here, and I'm on my mother's couch," she whispered just loud enough for him to hear her.

He chuckled. "Right. Rookie mistake." He leaned back so she could see him better.

Leaned up against the headboard of his bed, she knew he must be alone in his room. At least whatever she said this time might not be overheard.

His beard was fuller now. It gave him a distinguished look, and made him look older, but not in an unfortunate way.

"I can't believe you grew that beard in a week."

Jason ran his hand over his chin. "I'm not sure my mother is sold on it."

Ruby bit down on her bottom lip. "You had a beard when I met you."

"I did."

"I was thinking, I'd really like you to keep it."

"You would?"

She nodded. "At least until you come home. I know you probably can't keep it with your job, but—"

"I'll wear it home," he humored her. "So you're still staying at your mother's?"

"Her appointment with her doctor is this morning. I took off to take her," she said, and that gnawed at her too. She didn't have the luxury of time away from her project, yet, her mother needed her. And her mother's needs outweighed anything else in Ruby's life.

"Call me when you're done and let me know what they say."

"I will," she promised.

"Make sure to mention all the changes in her schedule and mood. They need to test her. Blood work, scans, and—"

"I'll mention everything," she interrupted, not wanting to talk to the doctor, but wanting to have her boyfriend on the phone only.

Then they were silent, but he watched her, the corner of his mouth turned up into a smile. "What are you thinking?" Ruby asked.

"That it's very early there, and no one is up. You're under your blanket fort, and I'm all alone in my bedroom, with the door shut and locked."

Now Ruby smiled back at him. "And what are you asking of me, Dr. Hughes?"

He let out a moan. "Well, shit. You've never called me that, and now I think it sounds dirty. I can't possibly go back to work and listen to people call me that all day without thinking about you."

"Maybe that was my plan," she said as husky as she could while being as quiet as possible. "Tell me what you want."

"Remember what you were doing the other day?"

She lifted a brow, though she was sure he couldn't see that. "You mean when your sister, my best friend, caught me."

Now he chuckled. "Yep."

"You want me to do that again?"

"Yep."

Ruby licked her lips. Her mother had been up until one in the morning, before Ruby was able to get her settled into bed. Her aunt wouldn't wake for hours.

There was a flitter of giddiness that moved through her when she thought about being naked in the living room, and at any moment she could be caught. These were the things she should have had the opportunity to do when she'd been a teenager, but her life wasn't like that. Her mother hovered and kept her close. Ruby didn't have boyfriends, or even friends when she'd lived at home. There was no room for her mother and others.

That was a gift she'd been given when she went to college —friendships that were still the very core of who she was, and a few *adult* relationships along the way.

"You're thinking too hard," Jason's voice shook her from the trance she'd put herself into.

"I was just thinking this is the kind of thing teenagers do. And then they worry about getting caught."

"Is this a worry from previous experience?"

Ruby frowned. "I was an experienceless teenager, thank you very much."

"Seriously?"

"Why do you sound so surprised?"

"Because you're the sexiest woman I've ever known in my whole life. So I can't imagine that you didn't have guys falling at your feet."

Ruby's entire body warmed with his words. He believed them too, she thought. That came through loud and clear.

"No one wanted any part of this when I was younger, trust me." Though she thought, yes, that had a lot to do with her mother hovering over her like a warden.

"Well, I want to see it now, and later, and forever," he drew out the last word.

Ruby let that resonate through her for a moment.

"If I get caught and grounded—"

"I'll fly home immediately and break you out."

"It's worth testing that theory," Ruby said lifting the hem of her shirt and pulling it up.

Just as she heard him hum, and the shirt was almost over her head, she heard the crash come from the other room.

She let the shirt fall back into place. "Shit! Mom?!" She dropped her phone, kicking herself out of the blanket wrapped around her, and ran down the hallway.

Pushing open the door, her aunt right behind her, she found her mother sprawled on the floor.

"Mom!" Ruby ran to her as her aunt turned on the bedroom light.

"What happened?"

"I don't know. I just heard the crash." Ruby knelt down next to her mother and rolled her over. "She's bleeding. She hit her head. Call 9-1-1."

Her aunt nodded and ran to get her phone as Ruby reached for the towel her mother had left draped over a chair and pressed it to her mother's head.

Her mother moaned.

"Hold on, Mama. We're getting you some help."

CHAPTER THIRTY

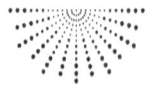

IT WAS CLEAR THAT SOMETHING HORRIBLE HAD HAPPENED.

Jason had kept the call connected, even though he was looking at the ceiling in Ruby's mother's house.

He'd heard loud, muffled voices. Ruby's and someone else's, her aunt he remembered. A few minutes later someone had hurried through the room, and he knew that paramedics had arrived.

Jason disconnected the call and stared down at the blank screen. He swallowed hard. As a doctor, he didn't usually feel helpless in emergency situations. He was trained to take care of the situation and get the person to safety. But this, this was heart-wrenching and he couldn't do anything about it.

Swinging his legs over the edge of the bed, he raked his hands through his hair and kept them there as he leaned his elbows on his knees. He had to go home—home to Ruby. She needed him.

Jason opened his phone again and scrolled through his contacts. He couldn't call Lisa, and what help would she be anyway?

Instead, he scrolled down to Ryan's phone number, and

realizing just what time it was in Colorado, he decided to text.

Need your help. Ruby's mom had an accident and I need to get hold of Mindy and Tina. Can you have them get in touch with her and go to the hospital?

Jason sent the text and stared down at it. Only a minute later his phone rang in his hand. It was Ryan.

"What's going on?" Ryan's voice was shaky and full of sleep.

"I'm sorry to wake you, man. Ruby's mom, something happened. I was on the phone with her and she heard a crash." Now he heard his own voice shake. "The paramedics came, but I haven't talked to Ruby since. Can you help get the girls in motion? I don't have their numbers. I think she's going to need them."

"Yeah, I can do that." There was silence between them before Ryan spoke again. "Are you doing okay?"

"I'm a little freaked out. I'm usually in control of situations like this. Sitting from a position where I can't help, I don't know what to think."

"Listen, I hope you don't mind, but Lisa told me about you and Ruby."

"No, I don't mind at all."

"I'll get the girls moving. What else can I do?"

"Just let them know to have Ruby call me when she's ready."

"Will do."

They said their goodbyes and Jason laid back on his bed. His stomach knotted and his heart pounded in his chest. He wasn't sure when he'd ever been more uncomfortable.

JASON COLLECTED HIMSELF. THE TEXT FROM RYAN SAYING that Tina and Mindy were en route to be with Ruby helped.

He opened his bedroom door and walked down the hallway. His mother was in the kitchen, and he stood at the door watching her move about the small space.

Her only complaint, other than having to leave Lisa behind when they'd moved, was that everything in England was small. The houses, the cars, the kitchens, everything.

"Oh, Lord!" she shouted when she turned and saw him in the doorway. "I forget there's another man-sized person in this house." She laughed. "I'm so happy you're here though."

Then she saw it. He knew the moment she'd seen the worry in his eyes.

"Sit," she ordered as she took his arm and led him to the small kitchen table. Without another word, she started the kettle and took down two cups. In each, she put a bag of tea. When the kettle whistled a few minutes later, she filled the cups, and set them on the table. Then she went about gathering all the items to make the tea palatable, as Jason always considered the process.

When his mother finally sat down next to him, he was calmer.

She lifted her eyes to meet his. "Something happened. Something's wrong. What is it?"

Jason covered his mother's hand with his and smiled. "I have missed you."

She sighed. "And I've missed you something terrible. Even more than when you were with the military," she admitted. "But this isn't about you being home or us missing one another. Something has you very troubled, and you didn't look like this this morning when we took Lisa to the airport."

One of the main reasons he and his brother never got into trouble was because his mother's keen sense of her children usually botched any plans they might have had.

"I was on the phone with Ruby and something happened to her mother," he said.

His mother's eyes widened. "What happened?"

"I'm not sure exactly, but I assume she fell from bed. She has been showing signs of possible dementia," he said, and he noticed his mother's eyes moisten. "Ruby's been staying with her, even though her aunt lives with her mother. They were supposed to go to the doctor today, but while I was talking to her, there was a crash and Ruby ran off. She didn't disconnect the call, so I heard the paramedics arrive."

His mother turned her hand over in his and held it. "Oh, sweetheart. Is she okay? Is Ruby okay?"

Jason shrugged. "I'm waiting for word. I've talked to Ryan and he put Mindy and Tina into motion to go be with her."

There were tears in his mother's eyes now. "We need to make plans for you to get home."

She stood, and he eased her back into her chair by the hand he hadn't let go of. "I'll go home when it's time."

"No," she said shaking her head. "You'll go home as soon as we can get you a flight."

"Mom—"

"Hush," she said, finally pulling from him and walking to the counter where she had her iPad set up as if she'd been looking at a recipe. "Ruby needs you. She's the woman you love and you need to be there."

"But I'm supposed to be here with you and Dad."

"Jason Paxton Hughes, get over yourself," she scolded, and he actually laughed.

When she looked back up at him, her face stern, he held up a hand in surrender.

"Mom, you don't have to do this."

"I most certainly do." She began to type into the iPad. "You love her, right?"

"I do."

"I knew that. I knew it the moment you landed on American soil and you met her."

"You did not," he argued, and his mother raised her brows.

"*Hey, Ma,*" she mimicked him. "*I just met Lisa's friends. Ruby. Ruby. Ruby.*"

Now Jason laughed harder. "I didn't do that."

"You most certainly did. I even know Mindy's mother has a Christmas tree full of porcelain dolls at her house because Ruby thinks its freaky."

Well, maybe he had talked incessantly about her. Maybe it was only a surprise to him and Ruby that they were destined to be together.

"I love her," he said confidently and his mother smiled.

"I know you do."

"Who do we love?" His father's voice boomed from behind them.

"Ruby," his mother said without skipping a beat.

"Right. I knew that," his father said as he walked through the kitchen, resting his hand on his wife's shoulder. "What are you doing?"

"Sending Jason home."

Jason shook his head. "Really, Mom—"

"One more word out of you and you'll row back."

Jason eased back in his chair. "Thanks."

CHAPTER THIRTY-ONE

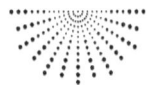

Mildred Norton had a stroke.

Ruby listened as the doctor explained their findings while her Aunt Jose sobbed next to her.

Every muscle in Ruby's body was rigid, which made her chest hurt when her heart kept beating as hard as it was. Until they did more assessments, they wouldn't know how severe the stroke. Until her mother woke up, they wouldn't know what was lost. Until—until—until, the doctor kept repeating.

Hand in hand, Ruby and her aunt walked back to where they'd been assessing her mother in a private room. They each sat in a chair, still with their hands clasped together.

The TV was on, and the morning news was silent, only subtitles scrolled across the screen. The clock in the corner of the TV screen said that it was just past six in the morning.

"I need some coffee," Ruby decided, and said it aloud at the same time. Perhaps she just needed to hear her own voice. And she needed to hear something positive. Coffee was positive.

"Go. I'll stay here," Jose said.

"I'll bring you back some."

Jose shook her head. "I'm already shaking, honey. Coffee won't help me."

"I'll get you something. We need to take care of ourselves. We're in for a very long day."

Ruby stood, rested her hand on her aunt's shoulder as if it might give her some comfort. Then, before leaving the room, she moved to her mother and kissed her forehead. "I'll be right back, Mama."

Ruby wrapped the sweater she wore around her tighter. She'd grabbed it as they'd run out the door. A bit of modesty, she'd decided, since she didn't have a bra, and no one wanted to see her in her shorts and T-shirt without a bra on.

Rubbing her eyes, she pushed open the door to the main waiting room and was surprised when she looked up to see Mindy and Tina sitting there.

They both jumped up and hurried to her.

As they wrapped their arms around her, the tears that had been clogging her chest and her throat flooded from her.

She didn't ask questions right away.

She didn't even speak.

She took all of the love and support her friends showered her with silently. This was family. This was sisterhood. This was love.

As they all eased apart, she looked at Mindy with her hair pulled back, fresh faced, and eyes full of sleep. And Tina, with a hat on. Had Ruby ever seen her with a hat on?

"Where is your baby?" she asked Tina.

"At home with her daddy," she confirmed as she brushed a stray hair from Ruby's face. "How's your mom?"

The tears were back, and Ruby used the sleeve of her sweater to wipe them away as fast as they fell.

"Stroke."

Mindy's hand came to her mouth. "Oh, Rube."

"We don't have any news really. She's still out. She has a huge gash on her forehead which they've had to stitch up."

"What can we do?" Tina asked.

Ruby shrugged. "I don't know. I don't know what I'm doing." She let out a breath. "What are you doing here anyway?" she asked as if she'd now realized she hadn't called them.

"Jason reached out to Ryan, who called Aaron," Tina said smiling. "He wanted to make sure we were with you."

More tears fell, but this time they were because of the man she'd fallen in love with.

"I suppose I should tell him what happened," Ruby said. "You two should get home to your families. I don't know what they'll do, or where we'll go from here."

Tina opened her purse and pulled out a small bag of diaper wipes. She handed them to Ruby. "Here, take these. Wipe your face."

Mindy then mimicked Tina's movements, pulling a small brush from her purse. "Here, tame that fire on your head," she teased.

For the first time since her mother had fallen, Ruby let out a little laugh. She looked around the waiting area for the bathroom.

"While I'm in there, do you think you could come up with a bra?" she teased.

"I'd let you have mine," Tina said grinning. "But it's milk damp."

Ruby gagged and walked toward the bathroom with the brush and wipes in hand.

When she returned, hair in place in a high messy bun, face sans sleep, and old makeup, she felt a little more ready to face the day ahead.

Tina waited for her with two cups of coffee in a tray. "It looked better than the stuff in the vending machine," she said noting the logo on the side of the cup from the coffee shop on the corner.

Mindy handed her a bag with egg sandwiches inside, and another bag with junk food from another vending machine.

"I didn't realize I was in the bathroom that long," Ruby teased as she handed Mindy back the brush.

"Looks like you had another cry while you were in there."

"Yeah, I don't see that stopping."

"It's okay." Mindy pulled Ruby in for a hug. "It's all going to be okay," she whispered, and Ruby nodded, though she wasn't sure it was going to be okay.

"Thank you."

Tina hiked her purse over her shoulder. "We're going to stop by your house and get you some things. A bra, some pants, a hat," she teased, and all three of them laughed.

"Thank you."

"What does your aunt need?"

Ruby looked back at the doors that lead to the emergency ward. "For her sister to recover."

Tina reached for her hand and gave it a squeeze. "We'll bring her some clothes too. Well, your clothes."

Ruby nodded. "Hey, get that Oxford shirt that's hanging on my doorknob. Bring that back."

Both of her friends nodded, kissed her one more time on each cheek, and then she watched them walk out.

She loved them. How had she gotten so lucky?

Looking at the bounty in her hands, she sat down in the nearest chair, setting the tray and bag on the seat next to her. Pulling out her phone from the pocket of her sweater, she looked down to see that Jason had texted only once.

Call me when you can. I hope everything is okay. I love you.

Ruby blew out a breath. She'd left him on the call when she'd run for her mother.

She knew she couldn't call him. She didn't have the

strength for it right now. If she heard his voice, she'd break down. No, her mother and her aunt needed her to be strong.

Mom had a stroke. They are still trying to assess how bad the stroke was. She hit her head and has six stitches too. Thanks for sending the girls to me. That helped. I'll talk to you soon. I love you too.

CHAPTER THIRTY-TWO

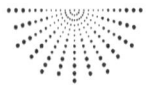

THEY MOVED MILDRED NORTON OUT OF THE EMERGENCY department and to a hospital room, but she hadn't awoken yet. Mindy had delivered a bag of items to Ruby, and more snacks and bottles of water. Her friends were good to her.

Mindy promised they'd both be back in the afternoon, so if Ruby or her aunt needed anything they'd bring it by.

How was she ever supposed to thank them for everything?

She wasn't, she knew that. That was what true love was—never having to repay the favors that weren't asked for. They did it out of love, and Ruby knew that even though she'd had an adventureless youth, her girls had made up for that in her adult life. Now she sat in the red Oxford shirt she'd asked for, dressed in a pair of her favorite yoga pants, and her teeth had been brushed. Yeah, she couldn't have asked for more.

THE REST OF THE DAY, THE DOCTORS RAN TESTS, DID assessments, and when they sat down with Ruby and her aunt, their prognosis wasn't good.

"The stroke was severe. Until she becomes more fully aware, we won't know just how much it's impacted her, but we think it will be best if she goes to rehabilitation and perhaps a care facility after that. Her care will be extensive."

Jose had covered her mouth with her hands and begun to sob at that.

"She has plans for that," Ruby said with her voice trembling. "She had plans for long-term care."

The doctor nodded. "That's good. Was there a family history of strokes?"

Ruby looked at her aunt who shrugged.

"I don't know," Ruby said.

"I'll have someone come in and talk to you about care options. We're going to keep her for a few more days and see how things progress."

All Ruby found that she could do was nod. She was numb.

JOSE HAD A FRIEND PICK HER UP AND TAKE HER HOME. SHE wanted to sleep in her own bed, put on some clean clothes that were hers, and Ruby was sure she just wanted a few moments to lose it.

Ruby had taken to losing it whenever she went to the bathroom or took a walk down the hall.

Her mother still hadn't awakened, and Ruby didn't take that as a good sign. It was nearly midnight and Ruby was curled up on the recliner with a warm blanket over her, staring out the window into the darkness.

How is she? The text flashed on the screen of her phone silently.

Ruby ran her fingers over the words as if it brought Jason closer to her.

Still unconscious.

Those little bubbles popped up and she knew he was texting again. *Where did they take her?*

Denver Health, Ruby replied as the door opened and a nurse walked in to check her mother's vitals. Ruby slid her phone into her pocket and focused on the nurse who had come into the room.

"She hasn't moved or anything," Ruby said to the nurse. "Shouldn't she have woken up by now?"

The nurse made notes in the computer, her expression unchanged. "All strokes are different. Has the doctor talked to you about it?"

Ruby nodded, but she knew the nurse knew more than that. She had to. None of it made sense. Ruby understood that her mother would have issues going forward, but why hadn't she woken up?

Over the next hour, the nurse returned more often, followed by the doctor.

"What's wrong with her?" Ruby asked, the blanket wrapped around her, standing next to her mother's bed.

"We're just watching her vitals," the doctor said. "She's showing some signs of stress, so we're monitoring her."

"What do you mean she's showing signs of—"

That was all Ruby had said before the nurse pushed a button on the wall, the doctor began moving around the bed and working on her mother. A moment later, the room was flooded with people.

And the monitor screeched, the lines no longer jagged.

"What's going on?" Ruby stood at the edge of the room. "What's happening."

A nurse broke from the crowd around her mother. "Honey, we need to tend to her. She's stroked again. We need you to step out in the hallway, and I'll come to get you."

"What do you mean—"

"I'll come for you," the nurse said again, this time opening the door and waiting for her to walk through.

Ruby looked back at her mother one more time, before stepping out into the hallway.

* * *

THE SECURITY GUARD ONLY LET JASON TO THE ELEVATOR because he'd flashed his credentials, even though they were from a different hospital.

Lisa had sent him the information on where to find Ruby. She'd planned on visiting her in the morning.

The hall was dimly lit, as it usually was in the middle of the night. Most of the patients were asleep, and the nurses hovered at the station catching up on charts.

He saw her, at the end of the hall, a blanket wrapped around her. She was staring out the window, leaned up against the wall.

As if Ruby sensed him, she turned.

The blanket dropped, and she ran at him.

Jason moved toward her, and without slowing, she slammed into him, clinging to him. Her body slid down the front of him, dragging him down until they were both on the floor.

"Ruby. Baby."

She sobbed against him. Her entire body shook, and she fought for breath.

Jason held her, piled on the floor. He soothed his hand over her hair and kissed the top of her head.

His body instinctively rocked back and forth as if he were comforting a baby or a child. "Shh," was the only sound that came from him, though he didn't care if she cried. Something had broken in her when she'd seen him.

As Ruby's breath began to shudder, she eased back only

slightly and looked up at him. Her eyes were red and so were her cheeks. Every part of her trembled against him.

"Oh, sweetheart." He pushed her hair back from her face and then held it in his hands so he could just look at her.

"You came back."

He nodded.

"My mother put me on a plane immediately."

Ruby smiled briefly before another wave of sobs rushed through her. Jason pulled her to him tightly.

"I'm right here, sweetheart. I'm going to be right here with you. I'll help you take care of—"

Pulling away from him, Ruby wiped her tears away with the sleeves of her sweatshirt and shook her head.

"She had another stroke." Her breath shuddered and she gasped for air. "She's gone."

CHAPTER THIRTY-THREE

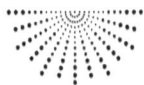

JASON HAD WAITED FOR RUBY AND HER AUNT TO SAY GOODBYE to her mother. They'd finalized what they needed to at the hospital, and then Jason drove them home.

Ruby needed to be at her mother's house, with her aunt, and Jason would see to it that they were both taken care of. But seeing her broken, twisted him up. The vivacious light that always sparkled in Ruby's eyes was gone. It was understandable. Jason often walked families through death. There was nothing quite like telling a family member that their loved one had died. It was gut-wrenching and undeniably one of the worst parts of his job. The difference was, he didn't love any of the family members mourning their losses, as he loved Ruby.

Admittedly, he didn't know a lot about her family, and that bothered him. He should know. But what he did know was that her mother and aunt were all she had.

And though her mother was older, and Ruby knew that her time with her mother was limited regardless, this had come out of nowhere.

It was six o'clock in the morning when Jason's phone dinged with a text.

Are you kidding me? I got a text from Ruby in the middle of the night. Her mother DIED?

Jason read the text, picked up his mug of coffee, and carried it outside to the back porch where he sat at the small table. The air was chilled around him, but he needed that chill to keep him awake as jet lag settled in.

He pressed the contact button for his sister, and listened as the phone rang only once before she frantically answered.

"Jason?"

"What happened?" His sister asked, her voice filled with tears.

"She had a second stroke in the middle of the night."

"Poor Ruby." Lisa sniffed. "Okay, I've texted with the girls. We're headed that way this morning after Tina secures someone to watch the baby."

"I don't know, Lees—"

"You're right. You don't know. She needs us more than she needs even you."

That stung, he thought. "She's a mess."

"She needs us. How's Jose?"

Jason set his mug down, and leaned his elbow on the table, resting his head in his hand. "She's lost."

"Tina just texted. Our mother-in-law is going to watch the baby. We'll be there by eight."

"Seriously, I don't know—"

"Seriously, you're right. You don't know," she said again. "I love you. I'll see you in a little bit."

The call was over.

Jason set his phone on the table, and kept his head in his hand. His eyes drifted closed and then he felt the hand on his shoulder.

Opening his eyes, he looked up at Ruby. She had her hair

down, and it nearly covered her face. A blanket was wrapped around her shoulders.

"Come sit on the porch swing with me?" she asked, holding out her hand.

Jason took her hand, stood, and followed her to the swing. He sat down, and Ruby curled up on his lap, resting her head against his chest.

They sat in silence as Jason moved the swing with his foot. Every so often Ruby would sniff back tears, and he'd kiss the top of her head.

"Thank you for coming back," she said softly against him.

"You can thank my mother." He brushed another kiss over her hair. "She didn't even give me a chance. She had my ticket bought and my dad had my suitcase in the car within an hour of our call."

"I'm sorry I just dropped our call and never came back to you."

He lifted her chin with his finger and looked her right in the eye. "Never be sorry for that. She needed you."

Ruby lifted her hand to his face and stroked his beard. "You kept it for me."

"I told you I would."

"You look tired."

Jason blinked hard and his eyes stung. "I didn't sleep on the flight."

"You should go home."

He ran his index finger over her bottom lip. "My sister is on her way with the girls," he said and Ruby smiled.

"I expected that."

"Did you?"

She nodded. "When one of us is in need—"

"You're all there."

"It's always been the way of it."

"I envy that."

"You flew all the way from London to be with me, and you didn't even know what happened. You're part of it."

Jason smiled at her. "I'm here for all of it. I'll help with arrangements, and whatever comes after. I'm all yours."

Ruby inhaled deeply. "You mean that, don't you?"

"I do."

Tears came again, and Ruby leaned into him. "My mother never had this—what you and I have. I mean we were friends first. We have a history through Lisa. We have each other."

"We do have each other." He pressed his cheek to the top of her head. "Didn't she have this once? She has you."

Ruby shook her head. "All she wanted was a baby. She was forty-five and she got me. I don't even know who my father is. I'll be honest, I'm not sure she knew him either. But I don't know."

"I didn't know that."

Ruby nodded and the tears flowed again. "She'll never see me get married or have kids." She hiccupped a sob.

He had no words for that.

"I knew she wouldn't be here forever. I just thought—"

"I know, sweetheart," Jason kissed her cheek. "I know."

"I'm glad that you met her."

Jason grinned and held her a little tighter. Oh, he'd met her. There had only been a few times, but they would all be memorable.

There was the time she'd dropped by with food for Ruby, because she'd been sure that Ruby wasn't eating enough. She hadn't announced herself, Ruby wasn't home, and she'd walked in on Jason in the shower.

He'd gone with Ruby to dinner at her mother's house exactly twice. That was moral support when the girls couldn't make it, he considered now. Mildred Norton had been cordial, but exhausting. It had been clear that Ruby was her entire life, and she did everything she could to keep some control over her.

The patio door opened, and Ruby's aunt stood there, looking every bit as lost as Ruby did.

"Honey, your friends just pulled up," Jose said weakly.

Ruby nodded. "I'll get them."

Jose nodded and ducked back into to the house.

Ruby moved from his lap. "Your babysitting session is over," she said teasingly, but a tic in her cheek told him she'd be happy to just sit on that swing, on his lap, all day.

He'd argue and ask to stay, but the day of travel and stress was hitting him hard now. Jason knew he wasn't going to be any help to her if he didn't get some sleep.

Hand in hand, they walked back into the house, and straight to the front door where his sister and her friends stood on the front step with a box of bagels, donuts, trays of coffee, and bags of groceries.

Ruby ushered them in, hugging them around the items they carried, and he knew she was in good hands. Those girls were there to help her process in a way he'd never be able to help her.

CHAPTER THIRTY-FOUR

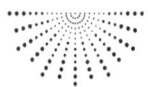

R<small>UBY SAT ON THE COUCH, CROWDED IN BY HER BEST FRIENDS</small> who were also in yoga pants and T-shirts, wrapped in blankets and watching stupid Adam Sandler rom coms. They were into their second movie, *50 First Dates*.

Jose had even joined them, curled up in the oversized chair eating a bagel and drinking spiked coffee from her favorite coffee mug.

"I have to assume most of these movies are just adlibbed," Ruby commented with her mouth full of donut. "Seriously, it's like he says something and waits for a reaction."

Mindy had to press her fingers to her mouth to hold in her donut. "I've always thought that too. This one seems to be a bit more scripted, but..."

"We didn't choose these movies for their romantic quality. We picked them *because* they're stupid," Tina admitted.

Ruby chuckled. "You hit the nail on the head with your choices."

Jose sipped her coffee and looked at the four of them

piled on the couch. "Is this how you do your movie nights?" she asked.

Lisa pressed her head to Ruby's. "Mostly. This is recovery mode."

Tina nodded. "Which really means its sans real food, wine, facial masks, and toenail polish."

That caused the four of them to laugh.

Jose picked up her donut and took another bite. "My sister was always jealous of the relationship the four of you had," she admitted and all four sets of eyes were on her. "Maybe jealous is a harsh word. Envious?" Jose shrugged. "She never had friends. I think if she'd had some, she wouldn't have been such a controlling and sad woman."

Her aunt's depiction of Ruby's mother struck a nerve, and every muscle inside of her tightened. Jose was right. Ruby's mother never had friends. She never had someone, other than Jose, that she could trust. And yet, Jose, being her mother's younger sister by fifteen years, she'd been as controlled by Mildred Norton as Ruby had been.

Ruby kicked her legs free from the blanket that was over her, stood, and moved to her aunt. Jose put down her coffee mug and donut and stood letting Ruby wrap her arms around her and hold her.

It was another moment where Jose and Ruby fell into one another's arms and sobbed. They had each other, and they needed to draw on that going forward.

LISA HAD SENT RUBY AND HER AUNT TO BED AFTER THE MOVIE. Funeral arrangements could be made later, she'd said, and Ruby agreed.

But while she rested, her friends stayed and cleaned the kitchen, tended to the laundry, organized the refrigerator with the food they had brought, and just took care of Ruby and her aunt so that they could tend to themselves and her mother's arrangements.

Growing up without friends, Ruby realized just how lucky she was, getting that scholarship that allowed her to go to college, where she met her friends. Without those girls, whom she could hear quietly move through her house, she'd have been a lost soul, just like her mother.

Now she even had a man who loved her.

Swallowing hard, she wondered if she was worthy enough for Jason Hughes to want to be that man forever. Ruby had never had a man in her life. No grandfather. No father. And certainly no man who had found her worthy enough to work on a relationship with her.

She rolled to her side, in her mother's bed, and wrapped her arms around her mother's pillow.

She might not have ever had a man in her life, but the one she had now, he'd left his visit with his family and flew all day long to be with her. He'd stayed with her. He'd held her.

Right now, she needed to stay in her mother's house, support her aunt, and organize her mother's final plans. But all she wanted to do was be home in Jason's arms. She wanted the normal they'd created, even before they'd fallen in love.

Ruby smiled, as warm tears slid down her cheeks. Since he'd moved back to Colorado, Jason had always been there for her. The very thought of him being there forever gave her the peace she needed in that moment. She closed her eyes, and let herself relax.

* * *

JASON HAD FALLEN ASLEEP SO QUICKLY, WHEN HE'D RETURNED home, he hadn't even changed out of his clothes. It was almost three o'clock in the afternoon when he'd awoken, needing to use the bathroom.

Checking his phone, he realized that Ruby hadn't reached out to him. That either meant she was giving him time to recuperate, or she had plenty of support.

His mother on the other hand had been blowing up his phone for hours.

It would be nice if you told me you were home safe.

Did you make it through customs okay?

Jason?

Is Ruby's mother okay?

Seriously, call me!

I JUST TALKED TO LISA! CALL ME!

Please give Ruby my love. My heart breaks for her. Let me know what plans are for her mother's funeral.

Jason, if you don't call me soon, I'm going to send the police to check on you.

He laughed. Well, he might have won boyfriend of the year, but he'd certainly lost his placement as favorite son at the moment.

Instead of texting, he called his mother.

"This better be you calling me and not the police telling me something happened to you and they have your phone," his mother answered the phone and rattled off her spiel to him.

Jason chuckled. "I'm fine."

"Oh, well good," her tone was sarcastic, and then she let out a sigh. "Ruby? How is she?"

"Broken," he said, letting his head fall back on the couch. "This was sudden."

"Where is she now?"

"She's at her mom's and the girls are with her."

He heard his mother laugh. "We should all be so lucky to have a team like that. How is my Lisa?"

Jason loved that his mother always referred to her as *my Lisa.* He couldn't remember a day when he or his brother felt jealous over the term either. They had always been keenly aware of how much Lisa needed to be loved.

"She seemed to be fine. I didn't spend much time with her before she swooped in and took over my girlfriend."

His mother laughed. "It's what they both needed, I'm sure."

"I think you're right. But thanks for sending me back. To be with Ruby in that moment was special. And I mean that in the sincerest of ways."

"I know you do. You'll keep me updated on plans?"

"I'll let you know."

"And will you call me next time you fly home? I mean when you land? I am your mother after all, and I'll worry myself sick."

Jason laughed as he scrubbed his hand over his face. "I promise. I love you, Mama."

"I love you too, son. Take care of Ruby."

He had every intention to do so.

CHAPTER THIRTY-FIVE

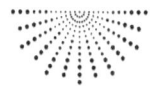

Ruby was on her fourth cup of coffee when Will opened her office door carrying a huge bouquet of flowers.

She startled and then cried.

She'd been in her office since six that morning just trying to catch up. Seeing Will's sweet face, and the flowers, undid all the calm she'd mustered just to show up.

"These are from everyone in the office," he said, his commuter bag still draped across him. "They wanted to send them to your house, but I know you well enough that I knew you'd be here."

"They are lovely."

"I'm sorry about your mom," he said setting the flowers down and then taking a step back. "And, I don't think you should be here."

Ruby lifted her stinging eyes to meet his. "And where should I be?"

"You should be home, mourning."

"Yeah, well, projects don't get done that way, do they?"

Will scratched the back of his neck and then bit down on his bottom lip. "You know, you've trained your team really well. I mean, we've been with you on this project since its inception, and the six prior to it. There isn't anyone on this team that can't pick up a little slack because our leader needs some personal time."

Ruby's eyes had dried as Will gave his little speech.

Her lips twitched, wanting to turn up into a smile. Pride swelled in her chest as he laid it out for her. Her team felt well equipped to take over because she'd made them that way. And they weren't pushing her out because she was overbearing. They were asking her to take the time she needed.

Ruby walked around her desk, and Will took another step back.

"You all think you can handle this? We have all that new stuff corporate threw at us."

Will nodded. "We can do it."

"And *everyone* is on board with me not being here?" she asked with a raised brow.

"Even Jefferson McKnight," he said, naming her boss' boss. "He's the one who suggested that we're all fine if you're not here. I mean, it's complimentary."

The smile formed now. "I really appreciate that."

She had thought diving back into work would help her, mentally. But the past few hours had been stressful. Maybe a week to sort through some things would be better for her. Besides, Jason was still off work for two weeks, and she had a lot of healing to do.

"Okay, I'll go. But you have to promise me that you'll call me for anything. I won't be but a call or email or text away."

"I promise," Will said, holding his hand up as if taking a vow.

She wanted to hug him, but that would be bad form, she decided since he kept taking steps back.

Looking at the flowers and then back up at Will, she

pressed her hand to her chest. "Thank you again. You don't know what it all means to me."

* * *

JASON CARRIED EMPTY BOXES INTO MILDRED NORTON'S HOUSE at Ruby's request. He wasn't sure if she had him running random errands, or if she truly needed his help.

When he walked into the house he heard the yelling.

Jose and Ruby had been going at it for days, and he wasn't sure what he could do to help calm them. They'd made arrangements for Mildred on Monday when Ruby had been sent home from work. Her mother's wishes were to be cremated, and then it was left to Ruby to decide what to do after that.

She wasn't talking about it. No matter how many times he'd tried to get her to talk, Ruby wasn't going to discuss plans—the truth was, she didn't have any.

"Why do you have to do this now?" her aunt's voice raised and echoed down the hallway.

"This all killed her. Her need to hold on to every goddammed thing in the world killed her," Ruby argued back.

"You're just throwing away her memory."

"I'm giving you a fresh start," Ruby yelled as she stepped into the hallway and looked up at Jason standing there with boxes. "Hey," she said softly, a huge contrast to the volume she'd been using.

"Hey."

"You brought the boxes?"

Jason nodded, the flat boxes still tucked up under his arm. "I have more boxes in the back of my truck too."

"Good. We need to pack all of this up."

Jason set the boxes down and moved to her. He reached

187

for her hand, lacing their fingers together. "Why don't you take a break for now. You've been at this for days."

Ruby pulled back her hand. "My life isn't on hold for this. I have things to do."

"You need to process what happened with your mother. You need time to—"

"I need to go through all this shit and give Jose a fresh start to live her life free of all this crap."

"That's Jose's decision, isn't it."

Her eyes were wide and nearly wild. "What do you know? You don't even know me."

Ruby turned to go back into her mother's bedroom, and Jason followed.

She was taking things out of a closet that was overflowing with clothes on hangers, boxes, and bags. Jason leaned against the door jamb, his arms crossed in front of him. He watched as she raged, pulling out clothes and throwing them on the bed.

"Why have all of this? She never went anywhere," she spat out the words, though he was sure she wasn't speaking them to him, she was just venting.

"Boxes of shoes and purses. Unopened. Sure, why not hoard this shit?"

Ruby continued to go through the boxes.

Jason noticed that Jose had closed her bedroom door and turned up her TV.

"Have you eaten today?" Jason asked as he watched her.

"Sure." She ripped dresses off of hangers and tossed the dresses into a box, and the hangers into another box.

"Sure? Maybe that means you need a break. Why don't we go out to dinner?"

She lifted her eyes to him. They were wild with what appeared to be anger, and her hair curtained them. "I don't have time to go to dinner. I have to go back to my life next week. I need to tend to this life she didn't fucking bother to live!" Ruby was yelling, but Jason didn't flinch or move.

"You might have to go back to work next week, but we have weeknights and weekends. Jose isn't going anywhere is she? We have time."

"We have time? *We*? When did this become *your* problem?"

"The minute I told you I love you and you said it back to me," he said without even a tremor in his voice. "Why don't we focus on the funeral Saturday."

Her eyes narrowed as she ripped another dress off of a hanger. "You have no idea what needs to be done here. If you're not going to support me, then why don't you go home?"

Jason shifted from his stance and walked toward her. Her eyes followed him until he stood right in front of her. "Push all you want, sweetheart. I'm not going to run from you. And if you want me to spend my last week off of work helping you pack up your mother's life, then that's what I'll do. But I think you should take some time for yourself to process all of this."

"Process? Isn't that what I'm doing? I'm processing the fact that my mother lived in this house without having a life. Last week she accused me of coming in here and stealing from her. What in the hell would I steal?"

Jason reached out for her hand. "Ruby, take a breath."

"Go home."

"Home is where you are. And you're here."

"You're not hearing me. I don't want you here."

Jason let that sink in. "Maybe Jose would like to have me here so you don't attack her."

Ruby's eyes went wide and then filled with tears. She dropped the dress in her hand and stared up at him. "I didn't attack her," she choked out the words.

"She lives here, Ruby. This is her home. You have to let her process it too. Maybe she finds comfort in all the stuff. Maybe she needs a few days to absorb what's happened." Jason took her hands in his and kissed her knuckles. "Come home with me tonight and sleep in your own bed. Let me hold you."

She fell against him, and he was sure grief and exhaustion had finally taken its toll on her. He held her to him until she'd cried out all her tears for the moment. Then, when his knees had locked and his arms had gone numb, he kissed her atop the head. "Let's go home."

CHAPTER THIRTY-SIX

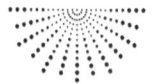

SHE HAD SLEPT IN HER BED, IN HIS ARMS, AND NOW RUBY couldn't muster the strength to get up.

While he'd held her all night, her mind kept her awake. Why had her mother let her health go? Ruby now knew the strange behavior was a lead up to the stroke, but could it have been prevented? If she'd just left the house, had some friends, enjoyed the things she collected, would she have lived longer? Was seventy-five years a long enough life?

Ruby's pillow was wet from the tears that had leaked from her eyes all night.

She was alone now.

Completely alone.

When Jason had finally climbed from bed, when the sun had come up, Ruby stayed. She never moved. She was numb.

"Hey," Jason's voice broke through the silence and Ruby noticed he was dressed and carrying a cup of coffee.

She could smell him, the cleanliness of him. His soap. His shampoo. His cologne. She'd missed him so badly in the week he'd been gone, and now, here he was back just for her, and she missed him still.

He set the cup of coffee on the nightstand and sat down on the bed next to her.

"It's almost one o'clock."

Ruby blinked hard. "One o'clock? It's light out."

A smile turned up the side of his mouth. "In the afternoon."

So, somewhere she'd fallen asleep. Maybe that was good. Of course, her body told her a different story.

"Why don't you get up and get showered. I'll make you something to eat, and I cued up a movie for you," he said, lifting his hand into her hair.

"I don't need some stupid rom com to save me," she snapped.

He winced, but didn't pull away from her. "There are millions of movies. We could watch episodes of Lisa's cooking show." His smile grew, but Ruby didn't find humor in what he said. "Come be with me, Ruby. Let me hold you all day."

She took his hand and pulled it away from her head. "I want to go back to Mom's."

Jason chewed the inside of his cheek. "Maybe a day away from—"

"I'm going. It doesn't matter what you say to me. I have shit to do. You can pull this cuddle crap and mourning shit all you want. Just because you're a doctor doesn't mean you know anything about what I'm going through."

He blinked hard. "You're right. I don't know what you're going through. I only know that I love you, and I want to take care of you."

"Then leave me the hell alone."

* * *

RUBY SAT ON HER MOTHER'S BED, SURROUNDED BY ALL OF THE things that she had pulled from her mother's closet and drawers.

When she'd told Jason to leave her the hell alone, he'd kissed her gently and walked out. Walked out of the room. Packed a bag. And then walked out the front door.

Ruby wiped the tears, which wouldn't stop falling, from her cheeks.

It was better this way, she decided. She'd never needed a man. Her mother had never needed one. So, if Jason just left, it would be easier.

A fresh flood of tears began.

Fuck it.

This was what she had to tend to. This was only her mother's bedroom. There was a spare room, a basement, a garage, the dining room, the kitchen, and closets all over the house.

Jason had thought it so wise to throw Jose into his fight, but Ruby was thinking of Jose. She didn't deserve to live in the shit pile that was her mother's collections of, well, nothing. And here, Ruby had busted Mindy's chops for years because she hadn't remodeled her house after her grandmother had died. Maybe it was because she didn't want Mindy to end up like Ruby's mother.

Her chest hurt now, and she pressed her hand to it.

This was how it started wasn't it?

Ruby didn't remember her grandmother, not really. But after she'd died, her mother had taken everything her grandmother owned and stored it in their house. Including her sister. Wasn't Jose taken in so that Ruby's mother could take care of her? She'd thought it was going to be a fresh start when her mother and Jose moved into the house they lived in now, but obviously it was only a fresh start to collect more things.

God, she needed to free Jose.

Ruby's mind swirled, and she wanted to escape. But where to?

She'd fielded all of two calls to her team, because they were competent and doing the job she trained them to do.

Her friends had been there in the moments she needed them, but they had families—real families that they needed to tend to. Ruby came after that. She understood that.

But then she thought about it. She'd pushed Jason out the fucking door. Just like she'd done with all of her roommates without even knowing it.

When the door to her mother's bedroom pushed open, as far as it would go with the mess that Ruby made on the floor, she looked up to see the loving gaze of three sets of eyes upon her.

Lisa shook her head. "This is a mess."

And why when she said that had it made Ruby laugh?

Her friends walked into the room, stepping over boxes and clothes to get to the bed and sit next to her.

Mindy picked up a sweater and looked at it. "This is cute."

That had the tears that were rolling down Ruby's cheeks roll faster, but this time with laughter attached. Sure, the girl with the shrine to her grandmother would think that Ruby's mother's outdated wardrobe was cute.

"What are you guys doing here?" she finally asked.

Lisa took her hand and held it. "My brother just moved into my spare bedroom."

The laugher was gone and the tears were back.

"I pushed him away," Ruby said.

"He's not there permanently. You know that right? He loves you. He's giving you what you asked for."

"He should stay permanently. I'm no good for anyone."

Lisa squeezed Ruby's hand and narrowed her eyes. "You can shut the hell up right now." She kept her eyes on Ruby for a beat. Just enough that Ruby felt it in her stomach. "We're here to help you. If this is what's important to you to move on, then we're here to help. If you needed to spend a week wrapped in a blanket watching movies, we'd be there. Jose is sorting through the front closet."

"She shouldn't be—"

"What? Mourning too? This is her home and right now it's in shambles, her sister is gone, and her niece is miserable. She's taking her lead from you. When all of this shit is boxed up, she has to make her life here."

"Maybe I should move in and—"

"Bullshit. For the first time in your life, Ruby, be selfish. Fucking be selfish," Lisa scolded standing to face her. "My brother loves you. Do you know what a gift that is? Let me tell you. From someone who doesn't know why her parents gave up on her and let the state take her away forever, let me tell you what a gift it is to have someone who loves you like my brother loves you and Ryan loves me. Let me tell you what you're thinking about giving up."

Lisa placed her hands on the tiny swell of her stomach.

"There's more out there. More beyond all of this shit that you're obsessed with cleaning out. Mourn. Your mother died. Cry. Your mother died. Remember her, Ruby. Remember the fond things and forgive the missteps. But remember that for the past decade, the three of us have always had your back, and now my brother wants to make a future with you."

"He walked out."

"To give you the space you demanded. So don't you dare turn this around on him."

Mindy reached for her hand. "We're here for you, honey. Let us be here for you."

Tina took her other hand and drew in a deep breath. "Where do we start?"

Ruby looked around the room at the mess she'd made. Why was this important?

"I've made a mess of this."

Lisa nodded. "You have."

Laughter broke through the tears. "Okay, let's go through the clothes and pack them up for donation. Or let Mindy go through them for her wardrobe."

"I like that sweater," Mindy said reaching for it.

Ruby laughed harder. "Thank you."

"We will never not be here for you, bitch," Lisa said as she grabbed Ruby's head between her hands and kissed the top of her head. "Now let's get to working on this. You have a dinner date at seven, and you'll need to be ready."

CHAPTER THIRTY-SEVEN

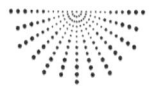

They'd cleaned for a few hours, and Ruby was surprised at the dent they'd made in her mother's bedroom.

Tina had gone to help Jose, and they had managed through the front closet.

Ruby realized that it was going to take more than a week to sort through the house, and she and Jose needed to sit and have a long talk about the house.

Watching her friends sort through her mother's things, Ruby had realized that anger had her in that room tearing everything apart. Her mother deserved so much more than just junk in boxes, and Ruby didn't want that for herself or her aunt. They deserved better than what her mother had allowed herself in life.

Tina left early to head home to nurse her baby. Mindy had a small box of sweaters and knickknacks to take home with her when she left. Lisa waited for Ruby to clean herself up and change her clothes.

"No matter what I do to myself to look presentable, I still look horrible," she said running gloss over her lips. "Look at my eyes. They're red and swollen. My skin is blotchy."

"You look beautiful. You look like you've been crying over the death of your mother. And I know you know who will be at dinner. He isn't going to care," Lisa said, leaning against the doorjamb of the bathroom.

"Do we have to go out to dinner? I mean, I could cook something, do take out."

"Ryan and I will be there. The point is to get you out for an hour. And Jason wants to be with you."

"I shouldn't have gotten so mad."

"He understands. He deals with death on a daily basis, Rube."

Bracing her hands on the counter, Ruby drew in a deep breath. "I didn't think about that."

"He's a patient man. He'll wait for you."

"He shouldn't have to wait for me. I shouldn't have pushed him out."

Lisa smiled at her. "Get through the funeral, and then let us all be here for you to help you with this."

Ruby nodded. "Thank you."

"Love means never having to say thank you."

Ruby laughed. "I thought it was never having to say you're sorry."

Lisa shook her head. "You owe me a million apologies and my brother a million and one."

She pulled Ruby to her and held her there.

Ruby was going to make it through her grief, and she owed her friends for that.

* * *

JASON MOVED HIS NAPKIN, REARRANGED HIS SILVERWARE, AND took a long pull from his beer.

His mother reached across the table and placed her hand on his. "Why are you so nervous?"

He swallowed. "I guess I'm worried she won't want to see me."

"She's coming isn't she?"

Jason nodded. "She is. Though I'm not so sure that Lisa hasn't tied her up and thrown her in the trunk."

It was Ryan that snorted out a laugh. "That would be a sight for sure."

When the door to the restaurant opened again, he saw his sister walking in, Ruby right behind her.

"Excuse me," Jason said as he stood and hurried to the front of the restaurant.

Lisa touched his arm as she passed by him. Ruby stopped and looked up at him.

"I'm sorry," she said, and he could already see the tears that began to shimmer in her eyes.

"Can we take a minute outside?" he asked, and Ruby nodded.

She turned and walked back out of the restaurant and he followed. When they cleared the front of the restaurant, Ruby turned into his arms and pressed herself against him.

"I'm sorry."

Jason chuckled as he ran his hand over her hair. "Don't say that. You're reacting to a stressful situation. And you're surrounded by love, so let us all love you."

She nodded as she pulled back and wiped her eyes. "You don't have to stay at your sister's house."

Jason brushed his thumb over her cheek. "I want to give you time."

"I think I need to realize how loved I am. I mean the woman who loved me my whole life is gone, and I'm mad, but I need to embrace the family I made for myself over the years."

"I want to be part of that family, Ruby."

She looked up and into his eyes. "You are."

Jason pressed a kiss to her lips. "I'm glad you're feeling good about family, because I have a surprise for you inside."

Ruby lifted a brow. "A surprise?"

"Yeah, c'mon."

RUBY TOOK JASON'S HAND AS THEY WALKED BACK INTO THE restaurant. When she noticed Lisa and Ryan at a table in the back, she pulled Jason closer.

"Are your parents here?"

He grinned at her. "They flew in for your mother's funeral."

"Are you kidding me?"

"You mean something to me, Ruby. Therefore, you mean something to them. When I say we're all here for you, I mean *all* of us."

She wasn't going to cry, she promised herself.

Mama Rose stood from her seat and moved to them, enveloping Ruby in a hug.

"Oh, honey, I'm so sorry to hear about your mother," Rose said softly in her ear. "We flew out as soon as we could to be here for you."

"Thank you. That means a lot to me."

Rose eased back. "Well, honey, you mean a lot to us and our family." She smiled at her and then shifted her smile to Jason.

John Hughes stepped in and kissed Ruby on the cheek as well. "My condolences."

"Thank you."

As his parents sat down, Ryan moved to her and kissed her cheek as well. But he didn't have any words. Instead, he took her hand and gave it a squeeze.

Jason pulled out her a chair as everyone sat down around the table. Conversation picked back up, and Mama Rose and

Lisa talked about the plans for the nursery for the baby, Ryan and John talked soccer, and Jason rested his hand on Ruby's thigh.

"I can't believe they flew here. No one will be at her funeral," Ruby whispered.

"You'll be there, and they're here to support you. If I have any say in the matter, someday you'll be their daughter too, so it means something."

She had to remind herself to breathe. He didn't ask her to marry him. In fact, he didn't even use the word, but Ruby's whole world spun. Not only would her mother miss all of that, she'd miss getting to see how much she and Jason actually did love one another.

There weren't going to be any tears tonight, she promised herself.

Taking her napkin from the table, she set it in her lap and breathed through the threat of tears.

If Jason had his way, this would be her family. And she knew, for a fact, that she and Jose would always be welcomed.

CHAPTER THIRTY-EIGHT

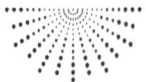

Ruby had ordered dinner for Jose, and asked Jason to go on home after he'd dropped her off at her mom's house. She promised she'd be home, but she wanted a few moments with her aunt while she was thinking clearly.

Jose was on the couch, wrapped up in a quilt and watching reruns of *Murder, She Wrote.*

"They still play this?" Ruby asked, handing her aunt the container from the restaurant.

"It was one of our mom's favorites. Your mother couldn't stand it."

"She wasn't a fan of Angela Lansbury."

Jose shook her head. "Who in their right mind doesn't like Angela Lansbury, I ask you."

Ruby chuckled as she sat down next to her aunt. "I guess that says a lot. Who in their right mind."

Her aunt shifted her eyes to meet Ruby's. "She tried, honey. Life was just tough for my sister."

Ruby nodded. "I know. And I know I'm the gift she gave herself. I had a good life. I'm just angry that she didn't take care of herself or this house, and that she didn't have a better life."

"As long as you had a good life, she'd have thought her life was well lived."

Jose handed Ruby the remote. "Here, find one of your movies. I'd rather be happy."

Ruby clicked through the channels until she came upon *Sleepless in Seattle*.

Her aunt smiled at the TV. "No one wrote rom coms like Nora Ephron, eh?"

She was right. They always ranked high on Ruby's list of favorite movies.

Jose took the sandwich from the box and took a bite. "Thanks for this."

"You're welcome." She eased back on the couch. "Jason's parents were at dinner."

Covering her mouth, Jose said, "They live in England."

Ruby laughed and snatched a fry from the box. "They flew out for the funeral."

"No one will come to the funeral," Jose admitted, just as Ruby had said to Jason.

"No one except family." Ruby ate the fry and noticed her aunt's eyes tear up.

"Your friends."

"Yeah. My friends, and my boyfriend's parents."

Setting the food on the coffee table, Jose pulled a tissue from the box on the side table and blew her nose. "You're a lucky girl, Ruby. He's a catch. And I don't mean just looks, though, he's not unfortunate in that area either."

Ruby smiled at her aunt. "No he's not."

"Well then, how special is that? My sister will have a special memorial after all."

Now Ruby's eyes watered. "She sure will."

They watched Meg Ryan's character stand in the middle of the street and watch Tom Hanks' character kiss his actual wife. Ruby thought it funny that the common knowledge of Tom Hanks and Rita Wilson being married, never distracted from the movie, yet it always came to mind. Was that proof that everyone was always willing to suspend reality just for that happily ever after?

"Are you going to stay here?" Ruby asked her aunt when she'd picked back up her food and started eating again.

"Why wouldn't I?"

"I don't know. I just don't know what part of your life my mother dictated and what part you chose."

Her aunt's eyes went wide. "You think she dictated my life?"

Ruby shrugged. "I think she did everything she could to keep the two of us near. Maybe dictate was harsh."

Her aunt took a thoughtful bite of a fry. "I guess I honestly never thought of it that way. She took me in when our mom died. She fed me and made sure I always had a home. I guess I was just comfortable."

"But you're still young—"

"I'm sixty, sweetheart. That's not young."

"Sure it is. You can still do a lot of things. Travel. Go to school. Start a new career. Get married."

Now Jose laughed and held up a hand. "Okay. Let's get a few things out in the open. I never, ever want to get married."

"Why?"

"I'm not attracted to anyone. I have friends, but I've never felt the pull to need a partner. And don't feel bad for me," she continued when Ruby took a breath to talk. "I'm happy."

"I'm glad to hear you say that."

"I think I'll stay here. I helped pick this place out when your mom and I moved here. She didn't do all the choosing."

"She took over though."

Jose looked around the cluttered house. "She did. And now, after her funeral, you and I are going to sort through it in our own time." She lifted her brows to drive home the point.

Ruby nodded, accepting that.

"I knew she was hoarding herself into this house. That's why I always sent you home with things. But it brought her joy. So let's respect all this crap as we give it away or throw it away. It was well curated."

Ruby laughed at her aunt's analogy of the mess ahead of them. "You're being very kind."

Jose took one more fry and then set the food back on the table. Her face grew serious, and she turned to look at Ruby.

"Let me be honest too. We need to go through this house carefully." She took a breath and let it out slowly. "I have explicit instructions to find a box your mother couldn't put her hands on. I was asked to never let you have it, and to just make it go away if something happened to her."

Ruby pressed her hand to her chest. "Why?"

Jose scratched the side of her neck and wrinkled her nose. "First I'm going to tell you that I'm not going to honor that."

"O-kay," Ruby drew out the word.

"The box has the only information your mother has about who your father is in it."

Ruby picked up her aunt's glass of soda and took a long sip. She'd gone lightheaded hearing that, and she didn't know what to say.

"I don't know who he was," Jose admitted. "I don't know anything about him. She didn't want you to know either. You were hers and that was her plan."

"So why keep the box?"

Jose shrugged. "I don't even know. And, maybe she long ago got rid of it. But if it's here, I'm going to give it to you."

Ruby nodded slowly. "Well, then," she let out another long breath. "I guess we'll take our time and sort through all of this. There seems to be a treasure buried here, and I may or may not be rich when we find it."

CHAPTER THIRTY-NINE

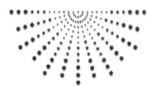

It rained on Saturday.

Ruby thought it was most appropriate that while she and her aunt held hands, in the small chapel at the cemetery, and they said goodbye to her mother, it rained.

Tina and Aaron were there, sans their daughter. Mindy and Vic sat in the pew with Mindy's parents, who had also come to support Ruby. Lisa, Ryan, and Jason's parents sat behind them. Lisa often rested her hand on Ruby's shoulder to give her support.

Jason sat next to Ruby, because she'd asked him to. He'd offered to sit with his parents, but after what he'd said at the restaurant, about if it was his choice she'd be part of the Hughes family, she knew he had to sit with her and Jose. He was part of her family too.

The minister who performed the service was one her mother had known in passing. She hadn't been a churchgoer, but she'd known this man who talked kindly of her.

She was interred next to her own mother, and when the ceremony was over, Ruby stood with her aunt alone as her aunt pressed her hand to Ruby's grandmother's name, on the wall with others who had gone before them.

"I feel as if I should be sad that I'm alone," her aunt said. "But I feel them with me all the time. And, I know I'm not alone. I get the honor of still being here with you, Ruby. We are family. We have each other."

Ruby wrapped her arms around her aunt's shoulders. "We are."

"And we have a much bigger family," Jose said, turning her head to look at the others that huddled not far from them. "I'm grateful for your friends. I know over the years they've given you a lot of comfort. But, they've given me comfort too."

"They're some pretty fantastic, bad ass women."

Jose laughed at that. "They sure are."

"You know what would be good?"

"What's that?" her aunt asked as she patted Ruby's hand.

"We need a Rom Com Movie Club night."

"We do?"

"Yes. Today is about friends and family and being together when someone needs you. It's about remembering those we've lost, and cherishing those who stood by you while you mourned."

"I like that."

"And you need to be there," Ruby confirmed. "So does Mama Rose, and Mindy's mom."

"You're up for that?"

Ruby nodded. "Mom's favorite rom com was *The Shop Around the Corner*."

"Stewart?"

"Only the best."

Jose drew Ruby in for a hug. "I think you're right. That's exactly what we need to do."

* * *

THE WORDS ROM COM MOVIE CLUB WERE SYNONYMOUS WITH
the second Saturday of the month. But just the string of
words also meant the assembly of the sisterhood.

Ruby offered the house. Mindy offered the wine. Lisa had
plenty of items in her refrigerator and pantry to serve at a
moment's notice. Tina could manage a bottle of nail polish,
but she'd have to bring the baby, but that was always now a
given and welcomed. Mama Rose made Jason take her to the
Target down the street, she was going to buy a fun pair of
pajamas and supply the facial masks.

Mindy's mother couldn't keep a straight face when she
offered to bring something that would be the hit of the night,
she promised, and left it at that.

They would reconvene at seven that night, and the men
were left to plan their own evening.

JASON WATCHED, AS HE HAD MANY TIMES BEFORE, RUBY'S
friends file into their condo. When his sister and his mother
arrived together, he thought it was a sight he'd never tire of
seeing. It wouldn't be every day that it would happen, but it
would happen more often. In retirement, his parents would
fly back and forth between Ken's family, and Lisa's family.

He looked at Ruby setting out wine glasses on the counter
while her aunt moved about the kitchen, either trying to find
a place to be or staying out of the way.

Every time he looked at Ruby, his pulse kicked up a little
more. His body grew warmer. Love pulsed through his veins.

As he watched her, he realized his mother would be there
for their family too. And in that moment, he knew they
would eventually have a family. It was what he wanted, and
what he hoped Ruby wanted.

When she had mourned enough, they'd talk about it.

"I didn't see you buy the big tub of cheese puffs," Jason said as his mother walked through the front door carrying the oversized tub.

She laughed. "Ryan sent these. He said his wife can't stop eating them now that she's pregnant."

Lisa shook her head. "I'm going to gain sixty pounds."

"Honey, you deserve to indulge and enjoy. Ryan knows that," his mother said as she carried the tub to the kitchen.

Mindy and her mother arrived next, and Corinne Baldwin carried a large box.

"Can I help you with that?" Jason moved to take it.

"No. I've got it. I just need to set it out of the way for a bit."

Jason pointed to the corner of the dining room. "I guess you could set it over there by the Christmas tree that just showed up one day."

Corinne laughed. "She set it up."

Mindy shook her head. "She was afraid. Very afraid."

"Hmmm," Corinne said as she set down the box.

Tina carried her crying daughter up the front steps, juggling her purse and the diaper bag.

Jason's mother swiftly moved from the kitchen and right to the door.

"Honey, let me take her," she reached her arms out to collect Tina's daughter, holding her against her shoulder. "You come sit with Grandma Rose," she cooed at the baby and sat down with her, which seemed to calm the baby.

"I need that skill," Tina whined as she dropped the bags.

Lisa moved to her and hugged her. "You have it. I have no doubt that you'll be able to take my baby and calm them while I freak out about it."

"You're not going to freak out about it," Tina assured her.

"Sure I am. Your daughter is the only baby I've ever been around, and I'm freaked out," she admitted and Tina laughed.

Jason closed the door and walked to the kitchen where Ruby added charms to the stems of the glasses.

"I'm going to head out. Dad and I are going to meet Ryan and Aaron at the bar and have a few beers."

Ruby nodded and looked up at him.

Her eyes were red from tears that came and went, but she smiled at him.

"You're okay? You're sure you want to do this?" he asked.

"I am. I wish I could have convinced Mom to come to a few of these nights. They would have been good for her. But I know they're good for me, and it'll be good for Jose too. Besides," she said as she slid her arms around him, "I promised your mother a rom com movie night. It seems like the perfect time to do it."

"I love that they're here," he said, wrapping his arms around her too and pulling her in closer. "I think we'll see a lot more of them."

"I'd like that." She rose on her toes and kissed him. "And I can't wait to go back and see where you grew up."

"I promise to take you."

"Maybe if things work out for us, we could go for our honeymoon."

Jason eased back and scanned a look over her beautiful face. "Oh, ya?"

She shrugged. "I guess that wouldn't be very romantic for you, would it?"

"I don't care about romantic getaways. I was more focused on you saying honeymoon."

She smiled. "Maybe someday we could talk about it."

"Someday we will."

CHAPTER FORTY

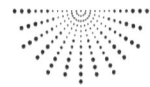

Jason took a long pull from his beer and looked at the three men that sat at the table with him. His brother-in-law and his brother, and Jason's father. The moment would only be more perfect if his brother Ken were there with them, and of course if his father wasn't there because Ruby's mother had just died.

Taking a breath, Jason set his beer on the table and wrapped his hands around it.

His father's hand came to Jason's arm. "Everything okay?"

"Yeah. Just appreciating this moment," Jason said. "I'm just sorry for the reasoning behind it."

"That was quite a blow for sure. Your mother didn't hesitate. She sent you back, and the moment you said her mother had passed, she had us tickets. All I heard on the flight over was *poor Ruby*, and just how happy she was that you were in love."

Ryan shook his head. "Moms are sappy, aren't they?"

Jason lifted his eyes to his brother-in-law. "Mine is super sappy."

"Yeah, I've caught a few conversations between her and

Lisa. I've never seen two women who can laugh and cry so much at the same time."

Jason's father laughed as he eased back in his seat. "Rose is sappy, especially over Lisa. She always was. The day she came to live with us, after Lisa had hugged her goodnight on that first night, Rose came to bed sobbing."

"I didn't know that," Jason admitted.

His father shrugged. "Lisa didn't have memories of living with her own parents, and had very few of her grandmother. Your mother's heart was broken for her. She swore she'd give her the best life. When we couldn't take her with us, Mom went into a deep depression."

"That I remember."

"Knowing now that she's happy and in love, and of course the baby, well, Rose is in seventh heaven."

Jason noticed that Ryan had to blink extra hard after hearing that. No doubt it had hit a sensitive nerve.

"I'm not sure I even rank up as high as Mama Rose does when it comes to people Lisa loves. In fact, I'm down the list quite a ways when you add the girls into that equation," Ryan laughed. "Shit, once the baby comes, she might forget my name."

They all laughed at that and Jason's father lifted his bottle to salute Ryan. "And yet, you still love her."

"Yes, sir, I do. I had no idea when I moved back home that my life would change for the better."

Jason let that simmer for a moment. He'd come home too. Of course, he'd left as a boy, and not by choice. Oh, he'd had a great life in England. None of his Colorado friends had ever played cricket or competed in rowing. Military and an Oxford education, it wasn't something many of those friends would even understand. He knew that coming back to Colorado, but there was a pull to be where he was born.

He'd had offers from three different hospitals in America,

but there was no contest when he saw the hospital in Denver was hiring. Lisa would be nearby, and it just had to be where he landed—back where he was born.

But, much like Ryan, he never would have imagined that when he took the position, he'd move in with the most amazing woman he'd ever met. It might have taken her a hot minute to fall in love with him, but Jason had fallen, and fallen hard the moment he met Ruby.

It was laughable now. The nights he would lay in his room, listening to her move about their condo just being Ruby. The rom coms cued on the television, the curses that would fly just because she was having a conversation with herself as if no one else were there, and the fact that she kept a clean house, but her laundry never landed in the hamper.

This time he laughed out loud and all three men turned to look at him.

"Sorry," he said, lifting his beer to his lips.

"I missed what happened," his father said.

"Nothing. Just thinking about something," or someone, he thought. And when he thought about her, he couldn't help but smile. Even in the last week when she'd been hurting so bad and tried to push him away, she still completed him.

Jason swallowed down the beer and laughed again. God, now he was thinking in rom com quotes. And because he couldn't help himself, he texted the fiery redhead that consumed him.

You complete me.

* * *

RUBY STARED DOWN AT HER PHONE.

"What's wrong?" Jose asked, tight lipped because her facial mask had hardened.

"Nothing," Ruby answered, equally as tight lipped.

"Is that my son interrupting your night with the girls?" Mama Rose asked, her face pink from having just washed off her mask.

Ruby nodded, and her mask cracked when she smiled. "I think I've gotten under his skin. He's quoting rom coms."

That warranted a laugh from everyone.

Rose sat down and picked up her wine. "My boys are sloppy sentimental. So is their father, but he'd never let anyone else see that side of him," she said and sipped her wine.

Lisa emerged from the bathroom with her face clean, and sat down on the arm of the chair where Rose sat. "I remember John being sentimental. It was refreshing. And Ken and Jason, they were just crybabies."

Rose elbowed her gently and laughed. "You were kind of a bully when you came to live with us."

"I was not," Lisa protested. "Seriously though, they were crybabies because they were sentimental, in a really good way. I guess that's why Jason's a doctor. He always just cared for people. He wanted them to be well—not happy, but well." She wrinkled up her nose. "Does that make sense?"

Ruby nodded. "It does. He's patient. I gave him every reason to leave me this week, and he did," she said. "But he ran to your house, so that doesn't count."

"And I sent him right back."

"But he was there for me. He let me scream and yell at him. I bossed him around. I cried—a lot."

Mindy rested her head on Ruby's shoulder. "Your mom just died. You're allowed all those things."

"He knew that. God, if this was any one of you, I'd have been knocking down your door and making you take a walk."

Lisa raised her hand. "Been there. Done that. When I'd

have an anxiety attack, there she was. Busting down my door and yelling at me to get out of bed or off the couch."

All of the women laughed, and Ruby smiled at her dear friend.

"And when you think you can't handle that baby, I'll be knocking down your door."

Lisa reached for her bottle of water on the table and took a sip. "Maybe we should handle it together. You could also get knocked up and we could have babies at the same time."

Rose tapped her fingertips together in a silent clap. "Two babies would be nice."

"You're not supposed to side with her," Ruby said to Rose who grinned back at her. "I'm not having any babies."

Rose shrugged. "I'm too old to be worried about old fashioned ideals. But I know how my son feels about you."

Ruby's heart felt as if it were swelling in her chest, even as she laughed with everyone.

She loved the freedom they all had when they were together to talk how and about whatever they wanted to. And having Corinne, Rose, and Jose there, only made it that much better. Rom Com Movie Club officially had new members—not to mention, Tina's daughter as well.

CHAPTER FORTY-ONE

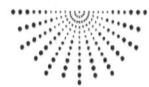

THEY SLEPT IN HER BED, IN ONE ANOTHER'S ARMS.

Jason peppered her shoulders and her neck with small, thoughtful kisses as she stirred awake.

"Mom texted and said she made reservations for brunch," he said softly in Ruby's ear.

"For this morning?"

"Yes."

Ruby took a moment to assess how she felt.

There was calm with Jason's arms wrapped around her and his breath on her skin. Her chest ached when she thought of Jose waking up alone in her own house. She thought of the dream she'd had where she'd called her mother and talked to her on the phone.

A single tear rolled down her cheek and into the pillow.

"What time is it?" Ruby asked, not yet willing to move from bed.

"Seven."

"What time is brunch?"

"Eleven."

She grinned, turning to face him, his arms still wrapped tightly around her.

"That makes it lunch."

"Not if they serve eggs and pastries too," he humored.

"I'll get ready," she said, running her fingers gently over the small tuft of hair on his chest.

"How do you feel this morning?" he asked as he brushed small circles on her back with his fingertips.

"I dreamt about her. We talked on the phone." Ruby drew in a breath. "I'm sad that Jose is alone."

"I think she'll be just fine."

"I know she will. In fact, she's never been on her own. So, it's like at sixty, she finally gets to be an adult. But I don't like how it came about."

"I know." Jason brushed her forehead with a kiss.

"I need to spend some time over there the next few weeks after work. She said there is something in the house we need to find."

"What's that?"

Ruby chewed on her bottom lip contemplating the box Jose had told her about.

"My mom kept a box with information about my dad. She asked Jose to make it disappear if something happened to her."

Jason rose up on his elbow and looked down at her. "You don't know *anything* about your dad?"

"Nothing. I don't even know his name. She always said she didn't know anything either, but I guess that wasn't the truth."

"And she didn't want you to have the information?"

Ruby rolled onto her back. "I guess not. She wanted Jose to make it disappear. See, that house *is* a mess, because Mom couldn't find it or it would be gone."

"But Jose told you about it."

Ruby linked her fingers with his and rested them on her stomach. "She did. And now, I want to know."

"I'll help you. I have one more week off from work, and then I'll help in between shifts. I want you to have everything you need to make your life whole."

Ruby gazed up into his dark eyes and smiled. "I have that."

"I mean it."

"So do I. I'm glad you moved back home," she admitted.

"Me too."

His hand was warm in hers, rested on her belly. She laughed and he eased back slightly.

"What's funny?"

"Your sister, one of my dearest friends in the world, told me I should get knocked up too, so that we could go through all of this together."

The corners of his mouth turned up into a sexy grin. "No kidding?"

"Your mother backed her up."

Now the laugh erupted from him, and she felt it resonate through her. "You live your life trying to not knock up girls, only to get to an age where your mother condones it."

Ruby shrugged. "Adulthood is weird."

"No kidding." His face grew serious and he his eyes scanned over her face. "It wouldn't be the worst thing."

Narrowing her eyes on him, she shook her head. "I'm not going to get knocked up," she told him directly. "Let's find out who I am before we recreate parts of me."

Jason moved so that he was poised atop her, his hands on either side of her shoulders, and his body between her legs.

"I know who you are, Ruby Jean Norton. And, in time, if I do get to knock you up, I'd be honored to be your baby's daddy—with all your good and bad parts mixed with mine."

Her heart fluttered, but she refused to let that cloud the path they were on.

"I'm not ready for that. Not even if your mother is."

He nodded slowly, letting his body press to her. "I know you're not. I'm not going to rush you. I'm here, Ruby. I'm here for the long haul. I'm programmed that way. There isn't a single thing about you that I don't love."

She couldn't help but giggle when he said that, and he eased back just slightly. "I doubt that very seriously."

"Don't," he said quickly, and she sobered from her laugh. "Love means you adore, accept, and understand every little part of someone."

"Wow." She lifted her hands up into his hair. "Someone has been watching way too many rom coms," she said before she began to laugh again, and now she couldn't control it.

Jason locked their legs, and rolled them until Ruby straddled him.

"I'd memorize every one of them if it meant making you understand just how much I love you."

Ruby leaned down and kissed him softly. Her hair curtained them.

"I wish my mother had this kind of love. The kind you're willing to give. The kind you were raised with."

"We all make our choices, Ruby. She made hers, and she gave that love to you."

"You're right. She did." She kissed him again. "I love you, Dr. Hughes."

Jason tunneled his fingers into her hair. "Oh, there you go talking all dirty to me, and we were having a sentimental talk," he growled.

"All this talk about love and knocking people up, it makes me a little anxious."

"What should we do about that?"

Ruby sat up and pulled her T-shirt up and over her head, dropping it off the side of the bed.

"We should practice, without success, that is. The knocking up part."

Jason's hands moved up her sides and to her breasts, cupping them. "Practice. No knocking up."

"Right."

"I've had good success with that."

"Show me."

CHAPTER FORTY-TWO

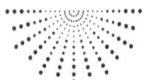

THERE WAS NO NEED FOR SURPRISE AT THE COMPLIMENTS RUBY received from the upper management. She'd taught her team everything about the project, and they'd all worked together on multiple other projects. But knowing that her entire life fell apart over a week ago, and she hadn't been able to pay any mind to her work, and the project was still on track and everything looked good, well, it did surprise her—and terrified her. Did they even need her?

That was just self-doubt, and it always crept into Ruby's life. She might as well face that no matter what, it would be there always.

She maneuvered her way through the spreadsheets on the computer comparing numbers and timetables. Grateful for the distraction from the past few weeks.

After she'd stopped by her mother's—aunt's—house that morning for coffee, she felt confident that Jose was going to be okay on her own. But, Ruby was going to still be a constant, and that wasn't something Jose would ever be rid of.

Ruby looked up from her computer when there was a tapping at her door.

Expecting part of her team to be standing there, she felt a rush of warmth move through her when she saw Jason standing in the doorway. He leaned against the doorjamb, his ankles crossed, and his hands tucked into his front pockets. A smile curled up one side of his mouth, and Ruby eased back in her chair. God, he was sexy.

"There is little to no security in this place," he humored.

"We don't have a lot of threatening people wanting to compare financial statements and production timelines."

He chuckled and moved from the doorway to her desk. "I thought I'd see if you had some time for lunch."

"You got your parents off to the airport?"

He nodded. "They fly out in an hour, but they've been at the airport now for two hours."

"I enjoyed having them here. I still can't believe that they came here for me."

Jason moved around her desk to stand in front of her, and she swiveled in her chair to look up at him.

"Anything for you," he said brushing his fingers over her cheek and gazing lovingly at her. "Lunch?"

Ruby smiled up at him. "I need ten more minutes."

"I have all day."

* * *

RUBY FOUND THAT HER MOTHER HAD OCCUPIED A LOT MORE OF her time than she had thought. And that realization wasn't bad, it was just fact. Time seemed different now, somehow. Every now and then, when she'd realize it, it would cause tears to be shed, or there would be a full-on meltdown where she'd need some kind of recovery, such as a night with her girls, or being wrapped in one of Jason's T-shirts while he was at work.

It had been a month, and everyday had some ease to it, but it crushed her as well to know that when she had something she wanted to tell her mother, she wasn't there.

One of the newest coping mechanisms, since her mother had passed, was the weekly calls with Mama Rose, where she would call Ruby when Jason was at work.

It was absolutely comforting.

"I think my calls with Mama Rose kept me sane," Lisa said as they sat at Ruby's mother's kitchen table going through a box of old papers. "She'd call me every couple of days when they first moved. She made sure I understood how to set up my apartment, and how to pay my bills."

"You were sixteen. That's exactly when you needed a mom most," Ruby said, throwing an old receipt from a tank of gas, a large soda, and a donut from ten years ago, away in the trash.

"Yes, but my point is, she takes care of her own, and now you're one of her own."

Ruby shook her head. "I'm not. I'm just the girl her son is sleeping with."

"You don't really believe that do you?"

Ruby flipped through a handful of receipts and then threw them away too. "No. I just feel as if I'm a hot mess all the time. Not that it was any different than before my mother died. I am the hot mess friend."

Lisa made a pile of the items she'd pulled out of the box. One pile for receipts, another for correspondence, many of which were outdated flyers that had come in the mail.

"I think we can all agree that Mindy is now the hot mess friend," Lisa said, resting her arms on the table.

"Yes, well, she's not a bridezilla like Tina was, yet not as easy of a bride as you were."

"My point exactly. A hot mess."

They both laughed. "I need to make some time for her," Ruby said. "I don't feel as if I'd lived up to my maid-of-honor duties lately."

Lisa rested her hand on Ruby's. "You've been preoccupied. Her wedding isn't for three more months. You have time to be more involved. Besides, she understands."

"Three more months?" Ruby scanned a look over Lisa. "We did account for your weight gain for this wedding, right?"

Lisa swatted her hand at Ruby. "That's a mean way to say it."

"Honestly, it was. I just said it that way to make myself feel better. Why when someone dies, and you swear you don't eat at all, you gain ten pounds?"

"It's stress. Trust me. Unless you're knocked up," Lisa grinned and Ruby shook her head.

"I'm most certainly not knocked up. Though you and your mother-in-law seem to glamorize that a little too much."

"You're sure you're not?"

"I had my period last week, thank you so much for this beautiful conversation."

Lisa shrugged. "I'm just saying. You're thirty. You're in a good relationship that's going to end in marriage. And I don't like to do things alone, and—"

"You can stop right there." Ruby held up a hand. "I love him. That's enough for now."

Lisa let out a little hum. "Fine. But you'd look cute pregnant."

"It's not a reason to bring a child into this world."

"I'm not forcing you. I'm just having some fun." Lisa ran her hand over the tiny rise of her stomach. "For someone who never had family, to now, not only having one of my brothers living here, and having one of my best friends as my sister-in-law, I'm giddy with anticipation that you'll be another one of my sisters-in-law. Or fake-in-laws as I'm only an honorary Hughes."

Ruby smiled at her. "You're more than that to them, and I think you know that."

"I do."

"You do know I'm not engaged to him, don't you?" Ruby pursed her lips that wanted to smile as she threw away the pile of receipts that Lisa had sorted out.

"I know. Again, I'm hopeful."

"Ruby," her aunt's voice had both Lisa and Ruby lifting their heads to see her standing the doorway.

She held a Nike shoe box in her hands and her face was pale.

"What's wrong?" Ruby asked as she stood and her aunt walked toward her.

Her aunt set the box on the table and backed away from it as if whatever was inside could hurt them all.

She lifted her eyes to Ruby's. "I found it."

CHAPTER FORTY-THREE

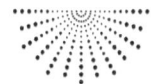

Ruby sat and looked at the box as if when she opened it a spell would be cast on all of them.

Lisa reached for the lid and Ruby slapped her hands down on it.

"What's wrong?" Lisa asked, pulling her hands back.

"I'm not ready. I don't want to open it."

Lisa's eyes went wide. "Seriously? Aren't you curious?"

Jose eased down in the chair next to Lisa. "Ruby, it's okay."

Ruby shook her head and pulled the box to her, as if she were keeping it safe. "I'll open it when I'm ready. I'm not ready." She squeezed her eyes shut and then opened them. They stung with tears and every muscle in her body tensed. "This is bullshit. This box is bullshit," she spat out the words.

Jose wrung her hands together. "Sweetheart, she saved it for a reason."

"Its whole purpose is bullshit. My whole being is bullshit."

Lisa's shoulders pushed back and her face grew serious. Ruby had seen that look enough times, but she didn't care.

Nothing Lisa had to say would mean anything in this moment.

"You have answers in that box. Answers to questions you've always had," Lisa said.

"And now you, too, are full of bullshit."

Lisa licked her lips. "I am not."

"When have I ever asked questions about my father? Huh? When?"

"Are you sitting here telling me that you don't care."

"That's what I'm saying," Ruby argued, even though just holding the box made her heart race.

"I don't believe you."

"I don't give a shit," Ruby said pulling the box to her and standing. "I'm not ready for this."

"That's a lot different than you not wanting to know."

"What's in here has nothing to do with me. There's a reason my mother didn't want me to know this."

Jose wiped tears from her cheeks. "Sweetheart, I wouldn't have—"

"Nope," Ruby interrupted. "You don't have to be sorry. You shouldn't have been given this task. If she didn't want me to know, she shouldn't have kept this fucking box in the first place. She should have thrown it out, or never had it. Instead, she kept it in this house, buried in shit where she couldn't even find it. What kind of life do you have to have to bury secrets in a house and not find them?" Her voice had risen and her aunt flinched.

Irritation coursed through Ruby. This wasn't Jose's fault. This wasn't Ruby's fault either. But this stupid box she held was the bane of her existence. Had her mother kept it to torture her? There was no reason to put Jose in the position that her mother had.

Ruby had been angry with her mother since the moment she died. Anger was part of grieving, and she knew that.

Jason had explained it to her. The counselor at the hospital had told her that. Even the mortuary had sent someone to talk to her after her mother died.

Yes, she was mad because her mother had wasted a perfectly good life burying herself in her house. The only time her mother did anything was when they'd go on vacation, but the more that Ruby thought about it, even then she'd lock herself in the hotel, or on a small section of beach. She'd wasted her life hiding.

And now, from the grave, she gives Ruby information that she'd kept her whole life? Where did she get off telling Jose she was in charge of that?

Ruby wanted to scream, but instead she stood in front of her best friend and her aunt and shook.

Lisa reached for her. "Ruby, sit down. Let me get you some water."

"I'm fine," she shouted, her voice shaking as bad as her hands did. "I'm fine. I need to go."

Lisa shook her head. "I don't think you should drive."

Ruby agreed, but she couldn't tell her that. "I know how to drive home angry."

"Yep, and I'm not going to let you. So here are your choices. You can give me that box and we can look in it, or you can hold it while I drive you home." She ran her hand over her belly and pursed her lips. "Or, I can tape your ass to that chair and leave you here."

Jose hiccupped a sob and a laugh at the same time, and both Ruby and Lisa shifted their eyes to her.

"Ruby, let her take you home," Jose said.

Lisa touched Ruby's arm. "Jason will be home soon and you can talk to him about all of this. But you're going to let me drive you home. You're going to calm your ass down. And you're going to forgive your mother for her shortcomings, because dammit, she loved you and that's all you ever needed."

* * *

RUBY HAD GIVEN IN AND LET LISA DRIVE HER HOME.

She sat on the couch in the dark. *Steel Magnolias* on the TV, and an open bottle of wine on the coffee table.

The box her aunt had found sat on her lap, the lid still on top of it.

She didn't move when Jason opened the front door and dropped his keys on the table. Without turning to see him, she heard him pause and take in the sights around him. No doubt, Lisa would have called him.

"Ruby? Everything okay?" he asked softly.

"Fine."

Jason skirted the back of the couch and came to sit next to her. "Is that it?" He looked at the box.

"I see your sister told you everything?"

"Ruby, if you didn't want me to know about that box, you would have hidden it or thrown it away."

Okay, so he called her out. She deserved that.

"Yes, this is the fucking box that my mother felt necessary to keep even though she had no intention to share the information with me."

Jason nodded, his patience warm in his expression. "Where is your wine glass?"

"Who needs a fucking glass?"

He chuckled. "Can I join you?"

"Whatever you want."

Jason picked up the bottle and took a pull from it.

It was so ridiculous that Ruby found herself chuckling. "Get a glass."

"If a glass is too good for you, then it's too good for me." He smiled and she found that it eased her.

She set the box on the table. "I don't know what to do with it."

"I don't have answers for you. And you don't have to tend to it tonight. You can sleep on it."

"What if I know his name? What does that do for me?"

Jason shrugged. "It gives you a name on both sides."

"His name isn't even on my birth certificate."

"You don't have to open it."

"Give me one positive."

"This is the doctor talking, but you'd know both sides of your medical history if you had something to go on. Lisa doesn't remember her parents and has very little memory of her grandmother, but at least she knows her medical history," he said and that was the only thing that seemed to click with her.

"I'm scared."

Jason cupped her face in his hands and held her gaze. The love that resonated through him calmed her.

"Then don't open it. Nothing in that box changes who you are or how I feel about you. And, likewise, it shouldn't change a thing about who you think you are. You are a brilliant and caring woman. You are loved by so many. You're whole with or without that box."

Ruby let out a slow breath.

"I want to know."

Jason lowered his hands and covered hers. "Then we open it. And I'm right here with you."

"What if it's bad?"

"It's just a name, Ruby. Again, Lisa is proof that family doesn't have to be blood."

Ruby nodded and leaned in to kiss Jason softly.

As she eased back, she kept her eyes locked with his.

There was a flutter in her stomach and a lightness in her heart as she felt his fingers on her skin. This man—this glorious man—he loved her. No matter what was in that box, he'd love her forever, and he'd said that.

"Can I ask you something before I open it?"

Jason nodded. "Anything."

"You'll love me regardless, right?"

"That box doesn't change how I feel about you. So, yes. I'll love you regardless."

"Do you really want to be with me forever and have a family?"

His smile widened. "Yes."

"It's very evident that I'm not easy."

"It's evident that you feel deeply about a lot of things."

God, he was perfect.

"Will you marry me?" Ruby asked and surprise lit in Jason's eyes.

"Are you proposing to me?"

"I am. Before I find out what's in this box, I want a commitment from you."

"Nothing's going to change."

"Okay, so then answer me. Will you marry me?"

Jason lifted his hands to her face again and locked eyes with her. "There is nothing I want more in the world than to marry you. So, yes."

Ruby wrapped her arms around his neck and kissed him hard on the mouth.

"No take backs."

Jason laughed. "Never."

CHAPTER FORTY-FOUR

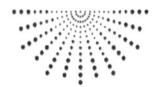

JASON OFFERED TO ORDER A PIZZA BEFORE HE TOOK A SHOWER.

Ruby had brought out two wine glasses and filled them.

And the orange box sat on the coffee table and waited.

Ruby picked up her wine glass and sipped.

She watched the box as if it would disappear if she took her eyes off of it.

Did she really want to do this? Did she really need to open it?

The calm that Jason had brought to her still held.

And with that calm she knew her answer.

Yes, she did want to open it.

No, she didn't need to, and that made all the difference.

When Jason joined her back on the couch, he picked up the full glass of wine and sipped. "I enjoy when you're still up when I get home from work."

She laughed. "It's nice when you get home and it's not in the wee hours of the morning."

"I agree."

Comfortable silence fell between them, but the box on the

table kept their attention. Each of them sipped their wine, the box the focal point, but neither of them said a word.

When Jason's phone buzzed, he looked down at it. "Pizza will be here in five."

"I'm glad. I didn't realize how hungry I was."

"Because I'm sure you haven't eaten all day."

She smiled up at him. "You're right."

The doorbell rang and Jason nipped her lips with a kiss before setting his glass on the table and standing. He walked to the door and opened it.

"The pizza needs ten more minutes," Lisa said. "I couldn't get it finished in your time frame."

Ruby watched as Lisa blew her a kiss and walked past her to the kitchen.

"What did you do?" she asked as Jason stood by the door as Mindy and Tina walked through.

"I have that wine from France that you like," Mindy said holding up the pink bottle.

"I pumped so I could have some too," Tina added as Jason shut the front door.

Tina and Mindy followed Lisa into the kitchen as Jason walked back to the couch and held his hand out to Ruby to help her to her feet.

"If you have any doubts about how everyone feels for you, I hope this shows you that nothing in that box matters," he said.

"I don't deserve you."

"Don't sell yourself short. Besides, you're stuck with me now. You asked me to marry you, and I won't let you back out of that."

"She what?" Mindy stood only a few feet away, the bottle of wine she'd brought in one hand and a glass in the other.

Tina moved in next to Mindy with her glass of wine. "She

what what?" Tina asked looking at Mindy's dumbfounded look and then at Ruby's wide-eyed expression.

"I think they're engaged," Mindy whispered loudly.

"What?" Was Lisa's reply from behind her friends.

Ruby felt the heat rise in her cheeks as Jason pulled her close and she buried her face against his chest.

"Sorry," he whispered in her ear.

"Don't be. I would have texted them all in the middle of the night anyway." She eased from his chest, and wrapped her arm around him as they both faced her friends. "You are all so nosy."

"You're engaged?" Lisa asked and her voice cracked with tears.

Jason pulled Ruby in tight to his side. "It just so happens that she proposed to me and I said yes."

A laugh broke from Mindy, and she quickly covered her mouth with her hand. "She proposed to you?"

"Yeah, so?" Ruby snapped.

"I love it. God, that is so you and it's awesome." She shifted her glance to Jason. "And what did you say?"

"How could I possibly turn her down? Of course I said yes," he said tipping her face up and pressing a gentle kiss to her lips before her friends rushed them and enveloped them in a group hug that was filled with laughs, tears, and a few friendly jabs.

JASON WATCHED AS THE GIRLS SETTLED IN AROUND RUBY. Plates of pizza and glasses of wine filled the coffee table, and the orange Nike shoe box sat in the center of the table, not quite forgotten, but not as important as their friendship.

"So you'll have to plan your wedding for after my baby is born and before Mindy gets pregnant and Tina starts on her second baby," Lisa said as she lifted her pizza slice to her mouth.

"You assume I'm going to get pregnant right away?" Mindy asked.

"You should. You're not getting any younger."

"Now you sound like my mother." Mindy looked around the room. "Did you ever open the box my mom left for you when we did movie night here?"

Ruby's brows lifted. "What box?"

Jason moved to the dining room. "I forgot she brought it with her. We set it over here by the tree," he said picking up the box that had been pushed into the corner and forgotten. He handed it to Ruby who eyed it carefully.

"I'm afraid to open this," she said and Mindy laughed.

"Why? She gave you a perfectly good tree with nice ornaments," Mindy defended.

"True." Ruby lifted the flap on the box and was noticeably surprised when she opened the box and there was garland. "She's bound and determined that I'm going to have a tree, huh?"

"You set it up already. She was pleased."

Ruby pulled out the garland and a silver star. "I guess it's time for new traditions."

The next layer had ornaments in green and red, and what looked like another ornament wrapped in tissue paper. Ruby picked it up and unwrapped it, and then let out a scream unlike Jason had ever heard.

His first instinct was to move to her until each of the girls burst into laughter.

"Oh my God!" Lisa cackled. "She gave you a doll head."

Ruby's eyes were wide as she set the head back in the box and looked up at Jason.

"I don't understand," he said. "Why would she do that?"

Mindy clapped her hands together. "Oh, it's a joke

between them," she laughed. "My mother has a tree full of doll heads because Ruby thought her doll head ornaments were so freaky."

"It is freaky."

"No it's not," Mindy said wiping tears from her cheeks. "Well, it never was meant to be. But when Ruby told my mom it freaked her out, she built a whole tree around it."

Tina lifted her hand as if to interject for his benefit. "Her mother puts up trees all over the house and they're all themed. They go up on the first of November."

Jason felt the tension leave his shoulders. "I see. Well, my mother loves trees too. But I've never seen a doll head on a tree."

Mindy picked up the doll ornament. "It's holiday themed. See? It's not weird."

Jason shook his head. He wasn't so sure about that.

Ruby replaced the ornament and draped the garland around her neck. In that moment, she looked at each of her friends and smiled before she lifted her eyes to meet his. She didn't have to say a word to him. She was grateful that he'd called them when she needed them most. And she hadn't even opened the shoe box yet.

CHAPTER FORTY-FIVE

THE BOTTLE OF WINE MINDY HAD BROUGHT WAS GONE, AND Jason finished the last slice of pizza that Lisa had brought.

The mood had become somber, and Ruby knew it was time to open the box.

As everyone watched her, she leaned in, pulled the box from the table and wedged herself into the corner of the couch. Her feet were pulled in and tucked under her. Her skin was warm from the wine. Her stomach threatened to reject the pizza she'd eaten, but she knew it was nerves.

Ruby studied the box as if she hadn't looked at it since it was handed to her. There was a small piece of tape that kept the lid on, or perhaps a small piece of security to know that no one had ever gotten into it. That's how her mother thought.

When they traveled, her mother would put out the *Do Not Disturb* sign and put a small piece of tape on the door. Then she would know if the door had been opened. It was a wonder Ruby could sleep alone anywhere without security measures. And to think, since Jason had moved in, not once had she locked her bedroom door.

Taking in a breath, Ruby slid her finger under the tape and lifted the lid.

She wasn't sure what she thought she'd see, but the sight inside was underwhelming.

"What's in there?" Tina asked softly.

Ruby swallowed hard. "Letters," she said as she moved each envelope, then let them fall and pulled out the first one.

Her hands shook as she looked at it.

"Does it have a name?" Mindy asked.

"They're addressed to my mother. The return address says Captain Ruby and it has a military address on it. But it's post marked in North Carolina."

Tina looked around at all of them. "She named you after him? You've had his name the entire time?"

Ruby looked up toward Jason, and her plea must have resonated through her gaze. He moved through her friends, and wedged himself on the couch between his sister and Ruby.

Slowly, she pulled the letter from the envelope. The paper shook in her hand. She was looking at the handwriting of her father, and for some reason she noticed right away that their penmanship was similar.

"It's dated a year before I was born," she said.

Lisa lifted her bottle of water to her lips. "She was seeing him?"

Ruby shrugged as she read the opening to the letter aloud.

"My dearest, Millie," she said and the tears broke through immediately to where she couldn't even see the words. "No one ever called my mother Millie."

Jason's hand rested on her thigh. "You don't have to—"

"I do. I just need a moment."

They all nodded, but each set of eyes was wide and on her.

"I miss you," she continued when she could. "Our time

together was so brief, and I wish I didn't have to leave. I always enjoy when I can spend time with you. I can't tell you where I'll be, that's classified. War is ugly and stupid, and has no place in our modern world. But my men depend on me, so I will lead them."

The letter was short, and was obviously a goodbye after Ruby's mother had been with him. He signed it only, *E.R.*

The next three letters were short as well, and friendly. He couldn't say much about where he was or what he was doing. But he missed her and couldn't wait until he could see her again.

There was a sheet of paper, which looked as if it had been taken from a note pad that grocery lists had been written on. It started with milk, eggs, bread and moved to seven o'clock, Holiday Inn, Fort Benning.

Lisa reached for it. "No date?"

"No."

"Do you think you were conceived at a Holiday Inn on an Army base?"

Ruby noticed the corner of Jason's mouth curling up at his sister's question. She didn't answer Lisa. Instead, she moved to the next letter and pulled it from the box.

But it had her mother's handwriting on it. The letter had been returned. So had the next and the next.

"He stopped taking her letters," Ruby said as she shuffled no less than ten envelopes that had been returned. Her skin grew hot with anger. The bastard had just given up on her mother. No wonder her mother never told her about him.

Ruby pulled each envelope out of the box. *Return to Sender. Return to Sender. Return to Sender.*

"Whoa," Jason said, resting his hand on hers and shifting to lean over and pick something up off the floor. His expression dulled as he handed Ruby the newspaper clipping.

Her mouth went dry, and the anger that had quickly boiled inside of her balled up and landed in the pit of her stomach. In her hand she held an obituary, and she looked down at a picture of her father for the first time.

"Captain Eugene Ruby was killed in combat—" she couldn't continue.

"Eugene Ruby?" Lisa said his name. "Ruby Jean."

Ruby lifted her eyes to Lisa. She hadn't even realized the correlation. Setting the box on the table, Ruby turned into Jason's arms and wept against his shoulder.

Lisa took the obituary. "He died the month before you were born, in Afghanistan."

"Lees," Jason said as if he were trying to shush her, but Ruby shook her head.

"It's okay. Go on," she managed.

Lisa nodded. "He was thirty-five at the time of his death."

"Ten years younger than my mother," Ruby said through her sobs.

Lisa continued, "Preceded in death by grandparents. Left behind his parents, a sister, and a..." Lisa stopped.

Ruby lifted her head hopeful that it would mention her. *And a child due next month*. She heard the words in her head, though Lisa never said them.

"And what?" Ruby asked. "And what?" she asked again, but this time it strained.

Lisa looked at each of them before looking back down at the obituary. "And his newlywed wife of two months, Jessica Mayberry of Raleigh, North Carolina."

The blood drained from Ruby's head and she felt dizzy. She pushed back from Jason, and somehow managed to stand as her head spun from the wine and the information she'd just ingested.

She had no idea how she made it to her bedroom, except that she had to use the walls to keep her from falling over.

When she walked into the dark room, she slammed the door closed behind her and locked it. Then, she slid to the floor and sobbed.

Her father was a bastard and her mother had tried to shield Ruby from that. She didn't want to know any more. No one believed in marriage and happily ever after. No one got second chances and warm reunions. It was all make-believe. Her mother was jilted. Ruby had a name that garnered no purpose. She was worthless.

Lisa's parents knew they'd lost her. Ruby's other half didn't even know—or care—that she was alive.

To hell with it all.

CHAPTER FORTY-SIX

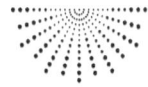

THEY HAD GIVEN UP AFTER AN HOUR OF TAPPING ON RUBY'S bedroom door and trying to gently coax her out.

She'd screamed and yelled at them to leave her alone. And she cried until she fell asleep behind her bedroom door.

When she woke, it was dark. Every muscle in her body ached, her head throbbed, and she could hardly open her eyes. Picking up her phone from the floor next to her, she looked at the time. It was just past one in the morning.

Ruby sat on the floor for a few more moments collecting herself. She'd acted like an idiot. What had she expected? She knew not to open the box. There was a reason her mother didn't want her to have it.

She wasn't going to be mad at Jose about it. Her aunt had been trying to give her something positive in light of the loss of her mother. It just hadn't worked out to be a blessing, and that broke Ruby's heart.

Reaching for the doorknob, Ruby pulled herself up. She unlocked the door and eased it open.

The condo was silent, not that she'd expected anyone to stick around. Then again, she wouldn't be surprised if she walked out to the living room and her friends were sleeping in chairs and on the couch.

She shook the thought from her head. No, two years ago, maybe. But now, they had kids, husbands, fiancés. Things were different.

Ruby looked down the hall and noticed that Jason's door was closed.

Stepping out of her room, she walked toward the living room. The small lamp on the end table was on. Laid out on the coffee table was the contents of the shoe box, and her mother's returned letters had been opened.

Anger surged through her. They'd had no right, no right, to open those letters. Damn them! Oh, she was going to lose her shit on them. Maybe she'd call them. Yeah, who fucking cared about husbands, babies, and fiancés right now? Not her. No, she was pissed.

She lifted her phone as movement caught her eye. Jason stood a few feet away in only a pair of lounge pants, having just walked out of the kitchen and not his bedroom. His hair standing up as if he'd tunneled his fingers through it a million times. He scratched his bearded chin and watched her.

"You opened the letters? Those were private. No one had the right to—"

He held up his hand to stop her as he took another step toward her. "You get to listen before you accuse."

"Accuse? The letters are fucking sitting right there!" she shouted and pointed to the pile.

"And if you keep yelling, you'll wake up your aunt."

Ruby swallowed hard. "My aunt?"

"She's sleeping in my room."

"Why is she here? You called my aunt because I was throwing some toddler-like hissy fit and locked myself in my room?"

"We wouldn't have opened the letters, Ruby. She was the one that was supposed to make the box disappear. She was the only one around when you were born. We felt as if it were her right to help you."

"Help me? I need help now? I'm just some bastard child, and I always was. I mean, what the hell does it matter that I know his name now? He was no more part of who I am now than he was. Sure he's some womanizing, jackass who—"

"Read the letters, Ruby," he cut her off.

"You're pissing me off."

"Read the letters, Ruby," he said again taking another step toward her. "There's more, and you need to know it all."

"I don't want to."

"Then I'll tell you."

"No. I don't need you to tell me anything. I don't want to know. I never should have opened that box. I never should—"

"They had a plan," he interrupted again. "She wanted a baby."

"Stop."

"Read the fucking letters," Jason growled.

"He returned the letters," she yelled again, and when she did, she heard the click of the bedroom door and knew her aunt had stepped out into the hallway.

Ruby covered her mouth to keep the sob from escaping.

"Are you okay?" her aunt asked, standing in the shadows in just her nightgown.

"I'm fine. You should go back to sleep. In fact, you should be in your own bed. I'll drive you home."

Jose shook her head. "I'm not going anywhere. Jason's right. You need to read the letters."

Ruby looked down at the pile of papers that had been in the box. She was afraid to touch them—afraid of what they contained. God, she couldn't handle any more.

She squeezed her eyes shut and dropped herself on the couch while Jason and her aunt watched her.

Fine. She'd read one of the damn letters.

Ruby picked up the letter on the top of the pile. It was dated four months before she was born.

I don't know how long it takes for my letters to get to you, but at some point, it'll find you. You'll be getting married soon, and I wish you a lifetime of happiness. I wanted to tell you that I'm going to have a baby. I wanted to wait until I knew for sure that everything was going to be okay. The baby will be here in April. The doctors are watching me closely because of my age.

I will never be able to thank you for this gift, and as promised, I will keep the baby my secret, but I can't imagine a better person to be my baby's biological father. You've always been an amazing person, a trusted friend, and your wife will be a lucky woman.

Ruby looked up from the letter and right at her aunt. "They were friends?"

Jose shrugged. "I didn't know him, but my sister had a whole life before I started to live with her," she reminded Ruby.

Wiping her eyes, Ruby picked up the next letter.

I'm sending this letter because I've heard some news. I don't want to believe it, but no one has confirmed that you are missing. So I'm going to write to you as if I haven't heard that. God, please tell me that it's not true.

Ruby lifted her eyes toward Jason.

"I did some digging," Jason sat down and picked up his laptop. "There were four of them that were taken prisoner. They were missing for nearly a month."

"That's how he died?"

Jason shook his head. "They escaped, but," he paused and set his laptop back down. "You know what, when you're ready, you can read it. What you need to know is he actually saved his men."

Ruby picked up the next letter.

She's here. You're gone. I know you're gone. But I'm going to send this letter. You can't trust anything, right? Maybe the news we got is wrong. Maybe it's a strategy.

You need to know our baby is here.

I've named her Ruby Jean, after you. She'll carry my last name, but she's a gift. You unselfishly gave me this gift, and I can't share her with you. I realize that was our plan. Your new wife would be broken if she knew she existed.

I miss you. Knowing you're gone has broken my heart. I'll raise her to be a good person, just like you. Thank you, my friend. I will always love you.

Ruby looked at the other letters. "She kept sending them?"

Jose nodded as she sat down next to Ruby on the couch. "I think she was in denial. You were planned, sweet girl. Your mother wanted you, and he was a friend willing to give her that gift."

"His wife never found out?"

Jose shrugged. "I don't know."

"She died fifteen years ago from breast cancer," Jason said. "She had remarried and had a family."

Ruby sat back, holding the letters to her chest. So her biological father wasn't a bastard after all. He was a gracious friend who gave her mother the gift of a baby—her.

"I guess I have a name, right? There has to be information on him out there."

Jason nodded. "I found a few things. I'll help you find more. But he seems to be a good guy."

"Yeah," Ruby said looking down at her mother's handwriting. "Of course he was. I mean, I'm a delight," she said and Jose laughed loudly drawing the attention of Ruby and Jason.

Jose wiped her happy tears from her cheeks. "Oh,

sweetheart, you are my delight. You were your mother's delight. And your father would have been proud of you." Jose reached for Ruby's hand and gave it a squeeze.

Ruby set the letters back in the box and put the lid on top. "I'm sorry about before."

"Oh, honey, you deserve every emotion you've had. But now you know. Remember you're everything your mother ever wanted. Go on with your life, enjoy the love that's being given to you. Be happy."

CHAPTER FORTY-SEVEN

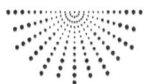

THEY'D BEEN FRIENDS SINCE RUBY'S FATHER WAS TWENTY-FIVE, and her mother thirty-five, Ruby had learned just from internet searches. At some point her mother was a civilian working on an Army base, and they had become quick, and good friends.

Eugene Ruby had been married twice. The marriage before Ruby was born had been his second, and he'd only been married three weeks before he'd been shipped out again.

There were no children born of either of his marriages.

Her father had one sister, and both of his parents were also gone now too. It seemed as if Ruby had hit a dead end, but leave it to Lisa to find a way to get all the answers.

"It's a DNA test," she said as Ruby unwrapped the Christmas present during their movie night in December at Tina's house. "And I know you used to say you never wanted to take one, but you know who you are now. Maybe someone that you're related to knew your father and they can shed some light on things."

Ruby studied the box. "I don't know."

Tina rested her hand on Ruby's thigh. "Listen, it's more than just knowing who your parents were or building a family tree. Jason knows who he is. He knows his mother's history and his father's history. Your mother had a stroke. That's the only history you know. Even your aunt doesn't have a lot of background. But with this test, it can give you genetic clues. So even if you don't have some long-lost brother or something, maybe you can find out that you carry a certain gene for blue eyes, and you'll know what to expect when you and Jason have babies."

Ruby let out a long, slow breath. Tina had a point. Of course she had a point. With motherhood, the woman had become very wise.

Gripping the box in her hand, Ruby read the instructions. "Okay, I'll send it in."

* * *

JASON WALKED RUBY THROUGH THE RESULTS OF HER DNA test weeks later. There was a genetic reason she didn't like cilantro, a gene found that said she had a certain athleticism, to which Ruby laughed right out loud. And she had a first cousin who lived in Missouri who had also taken the test.

A knot formed in her stomach when Jason pulled up the website and the profile for Annette Kirkland of Kansas City, Missouri.

"We can send her a message, it says." Jason looked at her hovering behind him and he scrolled through the site.

"I don't know," Ruby said, chewing on her thumb.

"Ruby, what do you have to lose?"

She thought of the night she'd slept behind her bedroom door. What if she ended up doing that again? What if this time, the information was really bad?

"Maybe it's better that I know I was a wish granted to my

mother, a gift from a dear friend, and that none of this says I might get a disease."

Jason shook his head. "Did you think it would come right out and say that?"

"Tina made it sound like that."

He grinned at her. "Okay, so all of that is true to some extent. But, Ruby, a cousin. You don't have family other than your aunt. Give yourself this gift."

Ruby dropped her hands and then bit down on her bottom lip until it began to hurt. "I don't know."

"Let's reach out and ask to connect. We can even go in and make a new email or something. Seriously, if you get uncomfortable, you can just ghost them."

"That's rude. Have you ever been ghosted?" she asked.

"No. Have you?"

"Lots. So I won't do that to them."

"I vote to send them a message. And, if things go bad, we'll pack up and move in with my folks."

Ruby laughed, moved in toward him, and kissed the top of his head. "Your mother would love to have me live with them."

"She most certainly would. After all, you're going to be her new daughter at some point," he said, strained, since she'd asked him to marry her, but wouldn't commit to a date.

"We'll see how she feels when Lisa's baby gets here." Ruby moved around him and came to sit on his lap. "You'll still love me if we find out my dad really was a bastard?"

"I'll still love you."

"You'll want to have kids with me even if my genetics end up giving our kids warts?"

"I know how to make warts go away," he confirmed.

"You'll still—"

"Ruby, there is no reason in the whole world that I wouldn't be with you forever."

She searched his eyes and decided he was sincere. Of course, he was sincere. He loved her.

Ruby looked at the computer screen. Annette Kirkland from Kansas City, Missouri might have actually known her father personally. She might have remembered him from when he was younger. But thirty years was a long time for someone to be dead and gone.

"Okay, let me write a message," Ruby said as she stood and Jason moved from the chair.

Ruby sat down in the chair and stared at the computer screen. Her hands shook and her heart rate had kicked up.

She clicked the button that led her to a form to message her cousin.

With her fingers hovered over the keys, she tried to formulate words to convey who she was and why she was reaching out. She sat there for at least five minutes trying to decide what to say. Jason had sat down on his bed, and silently supported her.

Finally, she decided on the information she knew. She was Ruby Jean Norton, the daughter of Eugene Ruby, and the website said that Annette Kirkland was her first cousin.

It was short and to the point, she decided, when she finally got the nerve to hit the send button.

Sitting back, she stared at the screen as if she'd expected an automatic response.

"Let's go for a walk, or a drive," Jason suggested, standing and moving to her.

"I'm scared."

"Don't be. No matter what she has to say, or even if she doesn't respond, your aunt and I will forever love you, and so will your friends. You have family, Ruby. This is just an opportunity to expand it if it works out for you."

She averted her eyes from the screen to his face. He was

right. This wasn't important. Those she had around her were important, and the life she was making was important.

Now she wished she hadn't sent the message.

Ruby stood and took Jason's hand. As they walked toward his bedroom door, his computer chimed and he stepped back to look at the screen.

"Um, Ruby, your cousin just sent you a message."

CHAPTER FORTY-EIGHT

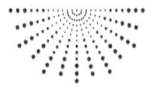

WHAT WOULD HAVE BEEN ROM COM MOVIE CLUB NIGHT HAD become Ruby's support group as she waited for Jason to arrive with her cousin.

Mindy handed Ruby a cup of coffee, then sat down on the couch and watched her as she paced back and forth.

"You're going to wear a hole in the floor," she said.

"Can't help it. I don't remember ever being so nervous," Ruby replied cupping her mug in her hands, but not drinking.

Tina rubbed her daughter's back as she slept on her shoulder. "Do you think she'll be overwhelmed with all of us here? I mean, really, it seems insensitive."

"Go then. Whatever," Ruby snapped, though she hadn't meant to.

Lisa rubbed the small swell of her stomach, her feet propped up on the coffee table. "Settle down," Lisa scolded. "We're used to each other. Tina's right. Your cousin might be overwhelmed."

Mindy pointedly looked at each of them. "We're here to support Ruby. Why don't we see how the introduction goes?"

Ruby stopped pacing and sent a gracious smile toward Mindy. "Thank you," she said plopping down on the couch next to her.

Groundhog Day played in the background, unnoticed. Ruby had chosen it because it was how she was feeling. The same scenario playing over and over. She knew her life, she didn't know her life. She had information, she didn't have information. She understood who she was, she had no idea.

When they heard the key in the lock, and the door opened, Ruby was to her feet and moving around the couch.

Jason smiled as he pushed open the door, his eyes kind and warm as if it were a sign.

A moment later, the woman Ruby had been waiting for crossed into Ruby's home. She too looked up at Ruby and smiled with kind eyes. Eyes that Ruby recognized because they matched hers.

Without even one word, Ruby moved to Annette and enveloped her in a hug.

"Thank you for coming," Ruby said on a sob as the woman in front of her tightly wrapped her arms around Ruby.

"Oh, honey, it's so nice to know you exist," she said, pressing a kiss to Ruby's ear.

They pulled apart, their hands gripping together, and they stared at one another.

Annette, whose hair was lighter than Ruby's with age, she was sure it too had been as red in her youth, lovingly smiled at her. Her own green eyes kind and warm. "You look just like my mother," Annette said. "Or how I remember her from when I was little."

Ruby batted her eyes. "I do?"

Annette nodded. "She was as beautiful as you are. Don't get me wrong. My uncle was handsome, but he was military, so there was a hardness to him that my mother didn't have." She laughed. "Does that make sense?"

Ruby nodded. "It does."

"I brought lots of pictures," her cousin said.

"I can't wait."

Annette let her eyes move from Ruby to the others in the room, and Ruby remembered that her friends were there for her support.

"Oh, hello," Annette said, and Ruby looked at the three sets of eyes staring up at them, as if they too saw the similarities between Ruby and her cousin.

Lisa was the first to move toward them and hold her hand out. "We don't mean to bombard your meeting. I'm Lisa," she said, shaking Annette's hand.

"Annette," Ruby's cousin replied.

"This is Mindy and Tina," Lisa said presenting the other two who moved in to shake her hand.

"It's wonderful to meet you all. You're all friends?"

Ruby nodded. "We've been friends since college."

"That's a wonderful gift. I met my husband and my best friend in college too. I know how wonderful those kinds of relationships are. It's nice that you're all here for Ruby in this big moment."

Ruby was already in love with this woman. She understood Ruby at a level that only the women surrounding her understood.

"Please, come in," Mindy said. "Can I get you something to drink?"

"That would be lovely," Annette said as she followed Ruby's friends to sit.

Ruby moved to Jason who continued to smile at her. "She's lovely, and so excited to be here," he said.

"Thank you."

"All I did was pick her up," he moved in and kissed her gently. "I'm going to go get her things from the car."

Ruby watched him walk down the front steps before she turned and watched her friends busy themselves around her cousin—her cousin. She drew in a breath. In all of her life, she'd only known her mother and her aunt—and one creepy great-uncle. When her friends had cousins, grandparents, uncles, and more, Ruby had her mother and aunt. Now she had a cousin, who had kids, who had known her father.

It was overwhelming.

Mindy touched Ruby's elbow, and she hadn't even seen her move in next to her.

"You're okay?"

Ruby nodded as she looped her arm through Mindy's. "I think I'm going to be just fine."

* * *

ANNETTE'S MOTHER WAS THE YOUNGER SISTER OF RUBY'S father by a few years.

"I was fifteen when news came that he'd died," Annette shared with Ruby, alone at her kitchen table, long after her friends had finally left them and Jason had gone to bed. "Grandma was broken after that. She lived for five more years, but I do think that after he died, she started to die."

"That's very sad," Ruby said, gripping her coffee mug between her hands and scanning a look at all the pictures that Annette had brought, that now covered the table. "It's been hard enough to lose my mother, I can't imagine a child."

"I think if only she'd known you existed," Annette sighed, "well, it appears that no one was to ever know you existed."

"I'm sorry about that," Ruby said, lifting her mug to her lips.

"Honey, this has nothing to do with you." Annette placed her hand over Ruby's. "You are the product of a love that even some married couples don't have. Your mother wanted a baby, and might I say, she chose the right man. My uncle, well, I've only known you a few hours, but you have his heart."

Ruby turned her hand over and held her cousin's. "I wish things had been different," Ruby admitted.

"They weren't supposed to be."

There was a humming in Ruby's ears when her cousin said that. A humming that dulled the pain of Ruby not knowing who she was her entire life.

For some reason, what her cousin said, that made sense. How did those five words zip up a thirty-year hole in Ruby's heart?

"What about your mom? What does she think?"

Annette smiled at Ruby as if deep down there was a secret. "My mother always said that out there in the world there was a part of my uncle no one knew about. It's as if she knew you existed even when no one else did."

"Did she know my mother?"

Annette shook her head. "No. Whatever friendship that my uncle and your mother had, that was all them. But my mom, she just knew."

They talked until the sun came up, and Ruby felt as loved by this woman who had flown in to meet her as she did when she was around her aunt or her friends—and when she was with Jason.

Her cousin told her about the family she'd missed out on, and those who looked forward to meeting her. She told her that her father loved Chinese food and pizza, and never watched a funny movie he didn't quote over and over again. Eugene Ruby was also fond of fart jokes, stupid magic tricks, and the F word was one of his favorite sentence modifiers.

Ruby laughed out loud at that. Her mother didn't often

cuss, but Ruby had always found it to be a part of her, causing her friends to often recoil when she'd say something.

Her father was kind with his time and whatever money he had, and his reasoning for being military was to help everyone in the world.

His first marriage was right out of high school, and doomed from the beginning. They were just too young to be married and apart as they were. It ended amicably. His second wife—well, Annette didn't remember much about her.

By the time they drove Annette Kirkland, a woman that a day ago Ruby would never have known, and now a relative that she looked forward to seeing again, back to the airport, Ruby felt as if she'd been given a whole new life.

CHAPTER FORTY-NINE

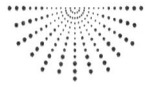

"My father had green eyes too," Ruby said as Jason drove away from the airport after they'd dropped Annette off after her short visit.

"You mentioned that," he laughed.

"Did I tell you that my cousin and grandmother also had red hair? Since there was no red hair on my mother's side, now I know where I got it."

He smiled as he nodded. "Well, no more do you have to field those kinds of questions. Now you know."

"My aunt always said the mail man gave me red hair. When I was little I would follow him down the street to try and catch a glimpse of him. One day he took off his hat. He was bald."

Jason laughed as he took Ruby's hand and pressed a kiss to her fingers without looking away from the road. "Maybe our babies will have red hair and green eyes too," he said.

"Maybe." Ruby turned in her seat to study him. "I want to have kids with you," she said, matter-of-factly.

Now Jason briefly shifted his gaze to her. "You do?"

Ruby nodded. "I know who I am now. I'm not some girl

whose father just disappeared. Well, not really. I mean, I know the plan was just for me to be with Mom. But now I see myself as a gift, just as she saw me. Only now, I have the gift. I mean I didn't get to meet my father, but now that I know Annette, I have a feeling I'll get to know all of my family."

"What does Jose think?"

Ruby bit down on her lip. "I think she's a little jealous, but excited too. Does that make sense?"

"Perfect sense. You're all she has too, Rube, and now *you* have a whole new family."

"No one will ever replace her."

"Of course not."

"And she'll get to be the grandmother to my kids, our kids. That's something, right?"

Jason linked their fingers together and squeezed her hand. "You keep talking about kids. Maybe we should solidify a day to get married."

"I don't want to ruin Mindy's wedding by planning my own."

"A date isn't planning it all out."

"Well, and Lisa's baby—"

"Will come when he or she is ready no matter what we have planned."

"Your parents—"

"Would fly out tomorrow if I asked them to."

Ruby puckered her lips and raised her sunglasses to the top of her head. "What kind of wedding do you want?"

Jason lifted a brow. "I don't know. I've never, ever, thought about it."

"Me either."

"Seriously?" he chuckled.

"I never thought someone would want to marry me. And the more roommates I lost, the more I believed that."

"I've been there a long time. I'm not going anywhere."

"I know that. Or, I know that now." Ruby turned back in her seat and picked up her phone. She scrolled through the calendar.

"What are you doing?"

"Looking for a date."

"Alright then. Do you want to find a venue first? Don't we have to check those dates?"

Ruby looked back up at him, and humored at the look on his face when he thought he was giving her logistics that every bride would have to think about.

"I'm not getting married at some venue," she said.

"You're not?"

"We're not," she laughed.

"And where are *we* getting married?"

"In the gazebo in Mindy's back yard. Well, I guess in the gazebo in Lisa's back yard now."

Jason's smile was wide. "That's what you want?"

"It is. I've never wanted a church wedding. Tina and Mindy can have that. I want only the people I love most around me, and now that includes my Ruby side of the family."

He nodded. "I just need enough time to get my brother and his little family out here too. But if you need to do this tomorrow—"

"No. I'll still have you tomorrow. I don't need anything until everyone we love can be with us."

"I love you," he said, squeezing her hand again. "I didn't know this was how my life was going to end up when I took a job back home."

"I'm just glad you wanted to come back home. You've been an excellent roommate."

"Only because you like to wear my clothes."

Ruby laughed. "Exactly."

CHAPTER FIFTY

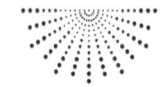

THE T-SHIRT READ *MAID OF HONOR*. THE PAJAMA PANTS HAD big pink roses on them.

Ruby looked around her condo and smiled.

It was going to be crowded.

It was going to be epic.

It was going to put every other bridal shower to shame.

Lisa walked out of the bathroom tugging on her T-shirt. "Did you forget I was pregnant?"

Ruby laughed. "I know you all don't think I'm on it, but I ordered the shirts before I knew you were *with child*."

Lisa laughed. "It did come as a surprise," she said as she rested her hands on her swollen belly. "What else can I help with?"

Ruby shrugged. "I think everything is ready. The cake is out, the food is ready, and the movie is cued."

Lisa shook her head. "*My Best Friend's Wedding?* That's not a bridal shower-esque movie."

"It's a funny play on words," Ruby defended. "Besides, no one is going to watch."

"True." Lisa followed Ruby to the kitchen and pulled a

bottle of water from the refrigerator. "When do we get to do a rom com night for your bridal shower?"

"There's too much to think about. Mindy's wedding. Then your baby. We'll get there."

"Get there sooner," Lisa teased. "The man loves you and wants to marry you."

"I know," Ruby said, grinning at the thought. "I don't want to take away from anyone else's special event."

"Mindy will get hers. She's getting married in two weeks. Done."

"And you're having a baby."

Lisa rubbed her stomach. "Can't deny that. And, consider this, Mama Rose and John are coming back out when the baby is born."

Ruby nodded slowly. "And?"

"Oh, come on," Lisa groaned. "They'll be here in May for the baby and they're staying the whole month."

"Why?"

"Because I have never been around a baby. I have no idea what to do."

"You've been around Tina's."

Lisa snorted out a laugh. "Have you ever held her baby? No. Because Tina is a hands-on mother and her mother and my mother-in-law are always standing on the sidelines to scoop the baby up otherwise. I'm at a loss. I need Mama Rose."

Ruby grinned at her friend. She supposed she was much in the same boat. Ruby had never been around a baby.

The doorbell rang, and Ruby moved to answer it. It was time to celebrate Mindy and forget about setting a date for herself. It would come in time. She absolutely knew that Jason wasn't going anywhere. She knew, just like her rom coms, her happily ever after was here.

. . .

MINDY SAT NEXT TO HER MOTHER AND HER SISTER AS SHE opened her presents. Everyone's toes shined with a bright blue polish, which Ruby had said was Mindy's something blue. However, at the first threat of tears, she'd promised Mindy it was a joke and assured her that all of the bridesmaids and Mindy's mother had pedicure appointments before the wedding.

The facial mask for the evening were designed to look like animals. Again, Ruby thought it was hysterical, and Mindy, being overly emotional, nearly cried.

But she must have finally found some humor toward the end of the night, when she cornered Ruby in the kitchen, drinking wine, and Mindy hugged her tightly.

"This was the best bridal shower ever," Mindy said brightly into Ruby's ear.

"Really? I wasn't sure you were enjoying yourself."

Mindy eased back, took Ruby's wine, and drank it down. She blew out a hot breath and handed Ruby back her glass.

"I wasn't sure what to expect with my mom and Vic's mom together."

Ruby looked past Mindy, out to the living room where Mindy's mother sat right next to her fiancé's mother, deep in conversation. "There's no hairpulling or cat scratching going on. It looks like they're doing okay."

Mindy nudged Ruby. "They are. I didn't expect that."

"That's what you wanted, right?"

Mindy nodded, reached for the bottle of wine, and filled Ruby's glass. She took the glass again from Ruby, and drank. "Things were just so awkward when we found out about Vic's mom and my dad having a past."

Ruby shook her head and let out a snort. "They were teenagers who were screwing around."

"I know. I know." Mindy sipped the wine and handed it back to Ruby, again. "And, nothing *actually* happened."

"Don't let any of that ruin what you have going on. You're getting married to the guy next door. He's a catch. He's everything you ever wanted, and—"

"And my very first kiss."

"Right. How can you even go wrong with a trope like that?"

Mindy nodded. "You're right. And as soon as I'm married, it's your turn."

"I'll get there."

"Yeah, we're going to start planning the minute I get back from my honeymoon."

* * *

ROM COM MOVIE CLUB NIGHTS WEREN'T SLUMBER PARTIES, usually. But in the case of the night before a wedding, it had become one.

All four women, and a baby, cuddled on Lisa's couch and watched *The Wedding Ringer*.

Ruby shook her head through the entire movie. "You chose this for your pre-nuptial night?" She elbowed Mindy in the arm.

"It's funny. I need funny."

"It's stupid."

"In movies, there's a fine line."

Ruby rested her head on Mindy's shoulder. "I guess there is. But I think after watching this, I'm going to need to charge a fee for maid-of-honor services rendered."

Mindy snorted out a laugh. "And you don't think I've paid that up front all these years?"

"Bitch," Ruby whispered.

"Hag," Mindy retorted.

Tina shook her head. "You two are horrible."

Ruby wrinkled her nose. "She didn't hear all the things we called her before her wedding, did she?"

Mindy's eyes went wide. "Rube!"

Tina adjusted the sleeping baby in her arms and handed her off to Ruby, who exchanged frantic looks with Lisa.

"Hold her, you hag, I have to pee," Tina said with a wink.

Ruby looked down at the little girl in her arms. Soft blonde curls framing her cherub face.

In her life Ruby couldn't remember holding a baby, but brushing her fingers along the baby's soft skin twisted Ruby's insides.

A husband and a baby, it was the things dreams were made of—but not dreams Ruby thought would ever come true.

It was going to come true. She was going to marry Jason. They were going to have babies. She, too, would be one of Mama Rose's daughters. If she had a daughter she'd name her Millie, after her mother.

"Are you okay?" Mindy rested her hand on Ruby's arm. "You're crying."

Ruby laughed. "Am I?"

Mindy brushed away Ruby's tears. "You didn't know?"

"I'm happy, Mind. I'm really happy."

Mindy rested her head on Ruby's shoulder. "You should be."

CHAPTER FIFTY-ONE

IF EVER THERE WAS A WEDDING THAT HAD NOT ONE FLAW, IT was Mindy's. Even with the threat of the mothers having a past that could erupt in violence, everything was perfect.

The weather was perfect.

The fit of the dresses were perfect—even Lisa's with the last-minute alterations to accommodate her growing belly.

The caterers were early.

The D.J. only had good music.

The cake was flawless. It was the kind of cake that was too pretty to even think of cutting, Ruby thought. But she'd be the first in line once they did cut it. After all, nothing tasted better than wedding cake.

The wedding itself was so perfect that Mindy hadn't even cried through the ceremony, though Lisa and Tina had. Of course Liv and Corinne had as well. Ruby couldn't help but wonder what kinds of things ran through their minds as they'd watched their children getting married.

Liv, Vic's mother, and Corinne, Mindy's mother, had been friends in childhood, and a little wayward teen angst had gotten between them. The thought had Ruby pursing her lips so she wouldn't laugh through the ceremony, just thinking about how funny karma was.

The woman who was orchestrating everything for the hotel had approached Mindy and Vic as they finished dinner. Crouched down next to them, Ruby could hear her tell them, "We're going to clean up the dinner serving while you share your first dance. Then we'll move into the traditional portion of the evening with the cutting of the cake and bouquet toss and garter toss."

Mindy nodded, turned and looked past Ruby toward Lisa and Tina, and gave them a sharp nod. Then she looked at Vic, and said, "Assemble."

The grin he shot her back was adorable, Ruby thought as she took a bite of her bread.

Mouth full, she nearly choked when Mindy spun to her and yanked her out of her chair.

"Meeting in the bathroom, now," Mindy demanded, and Ruby felt the hands of the other two behind her pushing her in the direction in which Mindy hauled her.

The bathroom just off the banquet room at the hotel was a lounge, really. It boasted a sitting room with couches and mirrors. The bathroom was through another door.

Perhaps it was for times like this, when the bride absolutely lost her mind and gathered her bridesmaids in the bathroom before all the big events of the day.

When they were all in the sitting room, Tina turned and locked the door.

"Are we hiding?" Ruby asked. "If you want to freshen up, I didn't bring the makeup bag or the hair spray." Then she had another thought and turned to Lisa. "You're not in labor are you?"

Lisa laughed. "I'm months away from having this baby," she said, resting her hands on her stomach.

Ruby nodded, and scanned the smiles and sparkling eyes of her best friends.

When the bathroom door swung open, her aunt stepped into the sitting room and gave Mindy a nod, then handed her a canvas bag.

"The bathroom is clear," Jose said.

"Good." Mindy took the bag and gently sat it on the counter.

Ruby pulled her aunt in next to her. "Are you the look out? You're just hiding in the bathroom waiting for the bride to get drunk in the bathroom?"

Mindy shushed Ruby over her shoulder.

With Lisa's help, she pulled out a bottle of champagne and handed it to Tina, who got to work opening it. Then she took out four champagne flutes and grinned when she handed Lisa a juice pouch.

"Geez, thanks," Lisa snorted a laugh.

"You're a big part of this. We can't leave you out," Mindy said, grinning at Lisa as she lined up the champagne flutes.

The pop of the cork off the bottle had Ruby pressing her hand to her chest. She was expecting it, but it still surprised her.

Jose's hand came to Ruby's shoulder. "Got ya, huh?"

"Always does," Ruby laughed.

Mindy filled the glasses and handed one to Tina, then one each to Ruby and Jose, before taking one of her own. Lisa, carefully stabbed her straw through the juice pouch and held it up in victory, careful not to squeeze it.

Ruby noticed her aunt eyeing the door which Tina had locked. Was there something in the food, Ruby wondered? The four women whom she adored were acting very odd.

Mindy drew in a breath and held up her glass. "To sisterhood. I don't know how I would have gotten through the past decade without all of you. You too, Jose," she added and Ruby watched her aunt blink damp eyes.

They all sipped from their glasses as there was a knock on the door. They all grinned when it was Ruby's knock. *Thud! Thud! Tapping of the fingers.* She used it whenever she knocked on the girls' doors.

"Who is that?" Ruby whispered.

"I'll get it," Tina grinned and moved to the door unlocking it.

Through the door, to the women's bathroom, walked Aaron, carrying his own glass of champagne. He sidled up next to his wife and wrapped an arm around her. Ryan followed his brother, glass in hand, and stood next to his wife. He gently rested his hand on her stomach and gave her a gentle kiss on the lips.

Vic, with his tuxedo jacket on and buttoned up, glided into the room, unlike his new wife, who had been shoving Ruby into the room earlier in her flowing white dress.

Ruby took inventory of everyone in the room. The men who had been added into the fold through marriage. Sitting on Tina's mother's lap, in the other room, was the first baby that had been added to the group of friends, and now Lisa carried another.

Love, for each of the people circled in the room, swelled in Ruby's chest.

But when Jason walked through the door, looking handsome in his suit, and the beard which he'd grown again, just for Ruby for Mindy's wedding, that love that had filled her chest, now warmed Ruby's entire body.

"Welcome to our private speakeasy," Ruby said as Jason moved in next to her.

She handed him her glass of champagne, and he took a sip, his dark eyes moving over her.

Tina moved back to the door and locked it again.

Ruby noticed that her friends formed a circle around her and Jason, just as they had done when Vic proposed to Mindy.

"What's going on?" Ruby asked, looking around at her friends and her aunt, who batted away more tears.

"Mindy has some big things coming up out there," Jason said, handing Ruby the glass of champagne she'd given him when he'd walked in.

"What kind of things?" Ruby asked, looking toward Mindy.

"Garter and bouquet," Mindy said, grinning, her head rested on Vic's shoulder.

"What does that have to do with us hanging out in the bathroom?"

Jason looked around the room. "This is really a salon."

"If you say so."

"I say so." He took the glass from her and handed it to Tina before turning back to Ruby. "You do know what the bouquet and garter mean if you catch them, right?"

"That you're supposed to be the next one to get married."

"Right." Jason nodded.

"We're already the next ones to get married. I don't think we need to even join in."

"That's right," Jason considered. "You proposed to me."

"I did. And you said yes," she reminded him.

"I sure did. But we have some things missing."

"We do?"

Jason took Ruby's hands. "A date."

"Is that what this is all about? We're all hiding in the bathroom so you guys can hound me about a date?"

Jason shook his head. "No. You have a date."

"I do?"

Lisa stepped up next to her brother. "My baby is due at

the end of May. Our parents are coming out to be part of that."

"You mentioned that."

"Well, now they're going to come out at the beginning of May, and so is Ken."

Ruby shifted her eyes back to Jason. "I don't understand."

"We're getting married the first Saturday in May," he said.

"In the gazebo in my back yard," Lisa added. "Where I got married."

"But, that's your time. Your time to have your baby and your family here."

Lisa stepped in between Ruby and Jason, pulling Ruby into her arms. "My baby is part of your family now, Auntie Ruby." She kissed Ruby's cheek, then wiped away the lipstick that was left. "I don't care that I'll be as big as a house for your wedding. Our entire family will be here, and it's the perfect time for you to get married."

Ruby blinked hard, and then turned back to Jason. "Really?"

"If you'll have me on that date, I think it's the perfect time."

"I will. I do. I mean, yes," Ruby stammered as she heard her aunt sniff back tears.

"I'm glad you agreed," Jason said as he dropped to his knee in front of her.

"What are you doing? We're already engaged."

Jason pulled a ring from his breast pocket and slid it on her finger. "You needed it all, Ruby Jean," he said with a wink.

"Oh, my, God!" She looked down at the solitaire diamond he'd slipped on her finger.

"Ruby, will you marry me?"

"Yes! Of course I will," she agreed pulling him to his feet. "You didn't have to do this."

"But I did. And even though the venue is small, you have time to invite any of your family that you want to."

"Really?"

"Yes, really."

Ruby rose on her toes and kissed her fiancé. "Thank you."

"Anything in the world for you."

CHAPTER FIFTY-TWO

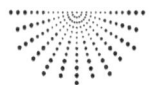

MINDY'S COUSIN HAD TRIED TO WRESTLE THE BOUQUET FROM Ruby's hands, but, as planned, Ruby was victorious in securing the bouquet.

Jason had no problem catching the garter that was taken from Mindy's thigh and shot into the air by Vic. There wasn't a man there reaching for it as eagerly as Jason.

Ruby moved to him, gathering him to her. Her arms slipped around him, and his her. They swayed to the music that played while the cake was readied for cutting.

"And we can make a wedding like this happen if this is what you want," Jason said, looking down into her eyes.

"I don't want any of this. All I want is you and me and our families. Just as you've planned it."

"My sister was insistent. You have to know that."

Ruby smiled up at him. "I know. Everything that happens in her life is an experience, and she's always been willing to share it with us."

"You're beautiful, Ruby," he said, lifting a hand to her cheek. "I didn't move back to America for this. It was so far from my mind. But I'm so happy I chose to land right here."

"So am I." Ruby lifted her arms around his neck. "Thank you, for everything. And I don't mean for the ring or the wedding plans. Thank you for your patience when I needed it. For not letting me push you away, as I did everyone else. Thank you for my family—the one you helped me find, and the one you're letting me be part of." Her lips twitched with the threat of tears, but Jason continued to smile down at her. "And thank you for proposing in the bathroom," she laughed.

"Salon."

"Bathroom."

"You tell your story, I'll tell mine," he said on a laugh as he lowered his hand to her waist again. "Just so you know, I asked your aunt for her blessing."

Ruby stopped swaying. "You did?"

Jason nodded. "There's a lot going on in your world and hers lately. If she didn't think it was a good time, or right for you, I wanted her to have her say."

"And what did she say?"

The corner of his mouth turned up in a grin. "She was standing there when I gave you the ring, wasn't she?"

Ruby pressed her hands to his chest. "What-did-she-say?" she asked again, her eyes narrowed on him.

Jason stopped moving. He took her hands in his, and held them between them. "She said that, I was everything your mother ever could have hoped for, for you. That she's thrilled to know that I love you, and that I will offer you a good life, as your partner."

Ruby's breath shuddered as she drew back the sob that wanted to escape.

"She's thrilled that you have a sister now, one that was always your sister," he continued and Ruby felt the first tear slide over her cheek at the mention of Lisa. "She hopes we'll have lots of kids, because siblings are very important."

Now Ruby hiccupped the sob and held her breath.

Jason's thumb brushed away the dampness on her cheek. "Above all else, she's just grateful that you're happy. Your aunt loves you and cherishes you as if you were her own daughter. And she's ecstatic to know you'll be loved forever."

"Thank you for including her."

"I wouldn't dream of not," he said, bending to place a gentle kiss on Ruby's lips. "Marry me in my sister's backyard. It won't be the start to me loving you forever, because I already do. But it'll be the start of our forever. Cuz, Ruby, I'm never leaving. I'm your roommate for life, and you have free rein over all of my T-shirts."

Now she laughed. "I like the Oxford Rowing Team shirt best."

"It's yours."

"What if you need to move back to England?" she asked, and a pang of panic surged through her.

"Why would I need to?"

"Your family."

"Then we'd discuss it. I wouldn't make that decision without you."

"I hadn't thought about it until now."

"Well, I have," he admitted. "Ruby, the world is a small place, really. I can get back and forth with ease. My life will always be there too. My brother's wife is British. My nephews are British. England is their home. He's never leaving. Part of my life will always be there, even if my parents go somewhere else."

Again, he pressed his lips to hers, then continued, "And you have family in Missouri. We'll have to travel there from time to time."

Ruby's smile widened. "Do you think they'll all want to know me?"

"Every single one of them."

"Okay, then we get married in your sister's backyard, with your family there, my friends, and my family too."

"It sounds like a plan."

"And then Lisa can have her baby."

"As is the plan," Jason said, his body beginning to sway again, and Ruby followed.

"I guess after that, it'll be my turn—and Mindy's," she added as she watched the wedding party move toward the cake and motion for her to join them.

"I'm all for practicing the knocking up. With or without the actual knocking up."

Ruby laughed, took Jason's hand, and pulled him toward the cake.

"Let's practice this part," she said. "Then we can work on the knocking up."

CHAPTER FIFTY-THREE

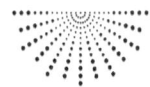

RUBY STOOD IN LISA'S BEDROOM AND LOOKED AT HERSELF IN the long mirror. The mirror was the only original item from the bedroom, which used to be Mindy's grandmother's. The house, which she'd given Mindy so much shit over, was now modern and beautiful—and Lisa's.

Studying herself in the simple white dress, which accentuated her many curves, Ruby thought she was beautiful. Perhaps it was the absolute happiness that tugged at her cheeks when she smiled—all the time now.

Mingling in the living room was her cousin Annette, and the ten other family members she'd brought with her. Many of them who knew and loved Ruby's father.

For the past two days, they'd shared their stories about what an amazing man he was. There was a new pride that Ruby had for being part of the Ruby family. It only made her love her life more.

She was a gift that her father gave to her mother—which had been the plan.

And though Ruby never had the pleasure of knowing her father, and her mother wasn't there to see this moment, Ruby knew that she was shrouded in love from the inside out. Ruby's life was started with love. She was marrying the man she loved, surrounded by the friends she loved. And, when the time was right, they'd consider bringing children into the world, also conceived in love.

"I have the champagne," Mindy held up the bottle and Tina carried in the glasses.

Lisa waddled into the room and closed the door.

Mindy handed Lisa an empty glass and Lisa snorted. "I don't even get a juice pouch this time?"

"I don't have time," Mindy laughed as she filled the glasses. "Just play along."

When the other glasses were full, Mindy set the bottle on the dresser, and closed up the small circle.

"Everyone put your left hand in," she instructed.

Each of the women put their hands into the center of the circle, and each hand was adorned with a ring.

"On an evening in our Freshman year, we walked into a coffee shop to study. Behind the counter was a girl," Mindy said, nudging Lisa with her shoulder. "All I know is that on that night, my life was complete—or I thought it was. Having shared every moment with the three of you has been a blessing I never knew was possible. And now that we're all going to be hitched, and there are babies, and Lisa now has two sisters," Ruby and Tina wrapped their arms around one another's waists, "well, everything feels right," Mindy concluded.

"I didn't know I was going to start a trend," Tina rested her head against Ruby's.

"And I never thought I'd ever get married—or have a baby —or sisters—or have my family here all the time," Lisa laughed through tears that choked her.

Ruby moved her hand so that it piled atop all the others. "And I never thought I'd know who I am. But the truth was, when I met all of you, I was my true self. And only because I could be my true self around all of you could I find a man who loves me for who I am."

"God," Lisa sighed. "You did that without one curse."

"Fuck you," Ruby said and all of them erupted in laughter as they clinked their glasses together.

Then, Lisa winced and all three of them shifted their eyes to her.

"It happens," she defended. "I've been on my feet for hours."

"We have at least an hour to go," Mindy argued.

"We will be fine," Lisa said, running her hands over her enormous stomach. "The baby is out of room and lets me know it."

A smile curled up the corner of Tina's mouth. "Oh, just you wait."

"Shut it," Lisa held up her finger to shush her sister-in-law. "This isn't about me. This is about Ruby."

Mindy let out a sigh. "Our Ruby is getting married."

"Oh, yeah she is," Ruby said as the door opened and her aunt slid through, closing it behind her.

"Are you ready?" she asked.

"I am," Ruby said.

Each of the girls kissed her cheek, and left the room with their champagne glasses in hand.

Ruby looked down at the glass she'd yet to sip from. As her aunt neared her, Ruby sipped and then handed her aunt the glass.

Jose took a sip and winced. "I never was one for the good stuff."

Laughing, Ruby put the glass on the dresser next to the bottle. "And that's the good stuff. Mindy never has bad stuff."

Jose took Ruby's hands in hers. "Thank you for letting me walk you down the aisle."

"You are my family."

"Oh, honey, you have an entire family out there. And when I look around, I see your face on each of those people. And here I thought you looked like my mother," she laughed.

"No one will ever replace you," Ruby said, her voice steady.

"I know, honey. I know." Jose kissed her cheek. "Let's go get you married. I've never seen a more handsome groom in all my life."

"He is handsome, isn't he?"

"Very. Though, his mother is not a fan of the beard."

"Only because it hides the face of her little boy. But, damn, the face of the man turns my insides into goo."

CHAPTER FIFTY-FOUR

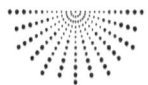

THERE WAS A GREAT APPRECIATION FOR BEAUTY, JASON thought as he stood in the gazebo with Ken by his side, and one of Ruby's cousins, who was a minister of all things. Lisa's back yard was decorated with lights and white chairs. It was reminiscent of when Lisa got married in that same space, back when Mindy lived in the house her grandmother had lived in, and her mother had been raised in.

His mother smiled up at him from her seat. His father's arm was draped over her shoulders. Their marriage was enviable. Jason wanted what they had, and he knew with Ruby, he'd have that. And, even if they had to go through the losses his parents had gone through, he knew they'd still have that same kind of love.

As the harpist began to play, Ken put his hand on Jason's shoulder. "I'm really happy that I get to be here," he whispered.

"I am too," Jason said, his attention directed toward his sister-in-law who sat with two boys on her lap, grinning up at him.

Tina was the first down the aisle, followed by Lisa who

looked absolutely miserable even though she smiled. Jason found it humorous that his mother had been smiling until Lisa passed her, and then the tears fell. Yeah, he thought, he and his brother knew their place.

Mindy followed Lisa, and Jason noticed Vic's eyes widen, as did his smile, when she passed him.

Then, on the arm of her aunt, Ruby appeared from the door to the house. A simple white dress, her hair pulled up with red ringlets framing her face, and a small bouquet in her hands—she was radiant.

Suddenly, everyone who had joined them for this moment disappeared. Jason saw nothing but Ruby and her glorious smile. His Ruby—His love.

As soon as Jose and Ruby made it up to him, Jose moved in and kissed him gently on the cheek. "You're a very lucky man," she said. "This girl is my whole world, and now she's yours too."

"She sure is," he replied, returning the kiss to Jose's cheek before she sat down.

Jason took Ruby's hands in his and stared down at her. "You're beautiful."

"And you're handsome," she said.

"Wanna get married?" he teased as he smiled down at her.

"I've never wanted anything more."

* * *

Vows had been said, and cheeks had been kissed over and over as each member of each family congratulated the newlyweds.

Ruby and Jason were married.

In their small venue, of the back yard, they did all the traditional things. Her cousin Ellie caught the bouquet, but at fifteen, she promised Ruby she'd wait to get married until after she graduated college. The garter had landed at the feet of one of the doctors Jason worked with, and he picked it up quickly, tucking it into his pocket. But by the end of the night, Jason had made him put it on his arm and wear it with pride.

Champagne had been drunk.

Cake had been eaten.

And Ruby and Jason had danced many dances as man and wife.

It was after midnight when the last cars pulled out of the cul-de-sac with family members who had flown in for the wedding.

Ruby had promised that she, Jason, and Jose would visit Kansas City when they had time off in the summer. They were as excited to have her in their lives as Ruby was to have them in hers.

Ken and Julie had gone back to the hotel with the boys, but Rose and John sat with everyone around the fire pit in the back yard in the wee hours of the morning.

Lisa had her feet up and bags of frozen peas rested on her ankles.

"Sweetheart," Mama Rose had reached a hand out for Lisa. "Why don't you go to bed? We can clean up and everyone will go home," she said, as if to get everyone to move.

Lisa held up her hands. "No one goes anywhere. And we can clean all of this up later. We are celebrating my brother and my new sister."

"And you look miserable."

"I'm fine," she said taking Rose's hand and giving it a squeeze. But when Rose's eyes went wide, Ruby noticed that Lisa's face contorted.

"You're not fine," Ruby stood, pulling Jason to his feet.

Jason moved to his sister. "Contractions?"

Lisa winced again. "I think so."

"You've been having these all day, haven't you?" he asked and Lisa nodded.

"But I have weeks."

"You have hours." Jason moved the bags of peas and helped his sister to her feet. "We're going to take Ruby's car," he said to Ryan whose eyes had gone wide. "She can't get into your Bronco."

Ryan nodded.

"Bag. I have a bag," Lisa said.

Rose, brushing away tears, moved to her. "I'll get it. We'll get a ride and meet you there."

"You have to be there."

"Sweetheart, we wouldn't miss this. Go with your brother and we'll be right there."

Lisa lifted her eyes to Ruby. "I'm sorry. I'm so sorry."

"Why?"

"This was your day."

Ruby laughed. "Okay, now you sound as dumb as I did. We get to share this day. I'll be right behind you. I can't wait to meet my niece or nephew."

"Call Ken," Lisa called back to Rose and John who both agreed to do so.

As Ryan helped Lisa out the front door, Jason turned back to Ruby. "Get some towels out of the closet and bring them."

"Why?"

He smiled wide. "In case her water breaks or, well, if she has the baby in the car."

"She might have the baby in Joellen?" Ruby referenced her car by name and felt faint at the thought.

"Yes. Are you going to be okay?" There was humor in his voice now.

"I'm fine. I'll hurry."

"I love you," he said in his calm doctor tone.

Ruby stared up at him. This man who had come into her life, embraced all of her movies, her quirks, and her drama.

And now she carried his last name.

He was hers.

She was his.

And now his sister, her best friend—her sister—was about to have a baby, in her car.

Ruby swallowed hard realizing that they were going to share the day after all. It never mattered when she got married, the world revolved around her three friends, her aunt, her new family, and her new husband.

"Ruby? Towels?" Jason said again.

"I love you, too."

With a chuckle, he leaned in and kissed her gently. "I love you too, now we need to hurry."

5 YEARS LATER

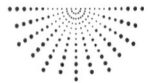

GREEN GRASS, LAWN CHAIRS, AND A BLOWUP POOL FILLED THE back yard at Mindy and Vic's house. The Fourth of July celebration had become tradition.

Vic stood at the grill with Aaron, each with a beer in their hand.

Ryan sat next to the swimming pool holding his youngest daughter in the water as she giggled. At only a year old, she'd already shown she loved the water more than her sister who sat at a table with Tina's two girls watching a movie on an iPad.

Mindy, rubbing the back of her two-year-old son, who had fallen asleep in her arms, leaned in toward Ruby who nursed her own son. "Who is starring in that movie that the girls are watching?"

"I think it's Barbie."

Mindy nodded. "Which trope?"

Ruby looked at her friend over the top of her sunglasses. "Trope?"

"Yeah, I mean the girls have all been to Rom Com Movie Club, don't you suppose they're forming their own club?"

"With Barbie and Ken at the helm?"

"Of course."

Lisa sat down in the chair next to Mindy and her daughter darted toward her, away from Tina's girls. "Are you discussing the movie?" she asked with a smile as she lifted her daughter onto her lap and planted a noisy kiss to the top of her head.

"We figured the movie bug has already hit them," Ruby confirmed.

"For sure," Lisa laughed.

When the door to the patio opened, Ruby's heart swelled in her chest. Her husband walked out of the house with his parents. He carried their two-year-old son, and his mother held the hand of their four-year-old son, each wearing the soft face of a good nap.

Ruby's older son let go of his grandmother's hand and ran to her, resting his head against her arm, his red curls wild just as hers had been at that age.

"Do you want to swim?" she asked, but he didn't answer. His attention was on the girls at the table watching the movie. "Do you want to watch the movie?"

After a moment he nodded and went to join Tina's girls.

Rose sat down next to Ruby, and when she was finished nursing, she handed the baby to her mother-in-law, who burped him, then accepted Lisa's daughter on her lap when she too felt as if she needed the attention of her grandmother.

Jason moved in behind Ruby and handed her his beer. "Would you like a drink?"

"I would," she agreed, taking a sip from his beer.

"We got the living room set up for the slumber party," he told them all. "Grandpa John even made a great fort."

"I did," John said as he picked up Lisa's daughter from

Rose's lap and nuzzled her neck with his nose, causing the girl to giggle.

"Did we vet the movie?" Tina asked.

"I brought *Psycho*," Ruby teased and Tina shook her head as she rolled her eyes.

"In time, I'm sure the boys will love that," Tina groaned.

"Who says it'll only be the boys? All of the girls may be the blood and gore type, no matter what we raise them on."

Lisa waved at her husband and daughter in the pool, then pulled her glasses down to peer over them. "I guess we can keep the rom coms to ourselves, right? I mean, if the kids start to like them, when they get older, they'll take over Rom Com Movie Club." There was a collective laugh at that.

Ruby looked around the yard, and reached for her husband's hand. She'd spent years with the girls discussing movies and the silly romances that gave them all hope. They'd all vied for a happily ever after. Now, she sat among her friends, and their husbands, and children, and in-laws, and she realized that happily ever after couldn't be summed up in two hours. The proposal and a ring didn't mean it would all work out.

In the five years since she'd said, "I do," to Jason, they'd had a lot of ups and downs. Kids weren't easy. Moving was a bitch. Doctors don't really make a lot of money, and they worked stupid hours. And careers, when you're a mom, sometimes they just don't fulfill anymore.

No, Ruby now realized the sheer entertainment value in her beloved rom coms. Real happily ever afters took a lot of work, and she was in it for the long haul. After every fight, there was the makeup. Sometimes that makeup had sex. Sometimes it had flowers. Sometimes it had hours of silence, but it melted away because they loved one another.

Happily ever after meant laughing at the most inopportune times, sharing inside jokes without saying a word, and just watching someone for the sheer joy of seeing them in your space.

Ruby looked down at the faded Oxford Rowing Team T-shirt she wore, now covered in ketchup and applesauce, a small wet spot forming from her breast when she'd nursed, and she knew that she was living her happily ever after to its fullest.

Jason leaned in close to her ear. "My mom told me that my brother is having another baby," he said.

"You don't say?" She smiled up at him.

"Christmastime. I'm going to ask for the time off. Do you think Jose would like to join us in England for Christmas?"

Ruby stood, moved the lawn chair, and wrapped her arms around her husband. As she did so, their two-year-old wrapped both of his arms around their legs.

She smiled down at their son.

"I think she would love that."

"Good. Then an English Christmas it is." He kissed her gently. "Nothing like holiday travel with three little kids across the pond."

Ruby swallowed hard and winced. "We could film our own rom com, couldn't we?"

"It'll always end with a happily ever after. I promised you that."

"You sure did."

PLEASE REVIEW

We hope you enjoyed *The Rom Com Movie Club - Book Three* by Bernadette Marie. If you did, we would ask that you please rate and review this title. Every review helps our authors.

Rate and Review: The Rom Com Movie Club - Book Three

MEET THE AUTHOR

Bestselling author Bernadette Marie began writing in the eighth grade. She sent off her epic family saga at the age of sixteen, but it was years before she would publish and eventually find her home in contemporary romance, and at the top of the charts.

The married mother of five promises romances with a Happily Ever After always...and says she can write it because she lives it. She also claims that her books are the antidote to anything heavy you might read.

Obsessed with the art of writing and the business of publishing, a chronic entrepreneur, Bernadette Marie established her own publishing house, 5 Prince Publishing, in 2011 to bring her own work to market as well as offer an opportunity for fresh voices in fiction to find a home as well. To date she has published the works of over sixty other authors.

When not immersed in the writing/publishing world, Bernadette Marie can be found spending time with her family, traveling (mostly to Disney parks), and running multiple businesses. An avid martial artist, Bernadette Marie is a second degree black belt and certified instructor in Tang Soo Do, and loves Tai Chi. She's a lover of a good stout craft beer, she might also have an unhealthy addiction to chocolate.

OTHER TITLES FROM

5 PRINCE PUBLISHING

www.5princebooks.com

www.ingramcontent.com/pod-product-compliance
Lightning Source LLC
Chambersburg PA
CBHW030643020726
47493CB00006B/1852